GRAVE EXAMPLE

GRAVE EXAMPLE

by

BARNABY DOGBOLT

WILDSIDE PRESS

FIRST PUBLISHED 1953

GRAVE EXAMPLE

by

BARNABY DOGBOLT

WILDSIDE PRESS

FIRST PUBLISHED 1953

To
BYRD STUART LEAVELL

A fortune-teller told a gentleman
His son should be a man-killer, and hanged for't;
Who, after prov'd a great and rich physician,
And with great fame ith' University
Hang'd up in picture for a grave example.

RICHARD BROME, *The Jovial Crew* (1652).

Chapter One

FIFTEEN CADAVERS LAY on fifteen soapstone slabs, where Wilfred, a fat and outwardly phlegmatic negro, had just stretched them out in three rows of five. Shortly the medical students would begin to cover them with grease, then wrap them in bandages like Egyptian mummies to prevent them from drying out. Wilfred had no imagination, which was fortunate for a department of anatomy in a southern medical school, but in the course of many years of performing his annual task on the day the freshmen medical students proceeded from dry bones to embalmed flesh, he had come to cultivate an inborn æsthetic sense in a somewhat surprising direction. No one but Wilfred ever knew that each year, using the coloured and white bodies furnished by the State, he would place each in such a position on one of the dissecting slabs that the fifteen cadavers made an over-all pattern in chocolate and corpse-white. One year, when he had had seven whites and eight negroes, he had made a light cross on a dark ground. Now, having similar raw material to work with, the artist in him had scorned to repeat the same pattern, and he had set out a pale double diamond on a field of brown. If Wilfred's designs were simple, that did not mean his taste was primitive: with only fifteen spaces available, and tiles of only two colours to manipulate, the most skilful of Byzantine masters of mosaic might have found his own genius a bit cramped. Nor was it strictly true to say that he had no imagination, for he often sighed as he looked into the anatomical laboratory, and visualised five rows of seven slabs each, on which were laid cadavers in such intricate designs that his soul was transported with

1

ecstasy. When one of the other coloured janitors or order-lies came across Wilfred at these times, he gave him a wide berth.

While Wilfred was bestowing a final glance of critical admiration on his current design, Rufus Crotey, the instructor of anatomy, entered the dissecting-room. This was Rufus's first year of teaching in the medical school of Zebulon University; he was of an age to match his position, and he had crisp dark red hair.

"Good-mawnin', Doctah Crotey," said Wilfred.

"Good-morning, Wilfred." Rufus cast a critical eye on the cadavers, for he was not so much anxious as deter-mined to succeed in his first job. "I like your double diamond design," he said. "Very pretty."

"Thank yo', suh." Wilfred spoke phlegmatically, but inside he felt bubbly as a bottle of warm beer at this first recognition of his work since his third wife had left him in horror.

"Pity they didn't send us a couple of Chinamen," said Rufus, gesturing towards the brown bodies occupying the centres of the double diamond. Wilfrid's mouth dropped open as he encompassed in a flash of revelation the possibilities inherent in mosaics of three colours. He glanced at Crotey with eyes opaque with admiration, but all he said was yessuh.

"How are they this year," Rufus asked; "pretty good?" His tone was that of a second-lieutenant asking advice of a veteran top sergeant. Crotey's predecessor had always acted as though he knew as much as Professor Nimble-wit, and as though Wilfred had known less.

"Yessuh, prett' good," said Wilfred. Tactfully he left the room in order that Doctor Crotey might confirm his judgment in private.

Rufus was examining the cadavers when a very pretty girl entered the anatomical laboratory. She wasn't one of the few women medical students, who dressed either in utilitarian-looking clothes or starched white jackets, depending on their progress in Medicine. "Hi," she said

2

to Rufus, and came over to the slab by which he was standing. Her perfume fought a brave but losing battle against the pungent smell of embalming fluid. Rufus would surely have remembered seeing so good-looking a girl before, but she didn't seem to act like a stranger. She looked down on the cadaver, a stringy old woman who in life might have served as the third hag in *Ecclesiazusae*. She poked it with her finger like a housewife testing a chicken, then proceeded to the next stone-topped table, Rufus trailing along as though he were magnetised. "Too fat," she said critically. She passed to the next slab, flexed the cadaver's left leg, looked judicial for a moment, and finally nodded; moved to the next body, and said: "Pretty!" in professional approval of a villainous type who had been executed for murder. Then she turned towards the adjacent table on which lay a peaceful-looking old white man. Her eyes widened. She shrieked once, and cut the sound off short by clapping a hand over her mouth.

Rufus thought she was going to faint, and caught her around the body to ease her to the floor. The girl gasped, blushed, and slapped him indignantly. "You maniac!" she exclaimed.

"M-m-m-m-m," he stuttered, gingerly feeling his smarting cheek. The sound was no effective demonstration of his sanity; there were occasions when Rufus still stammered, and this was one of them. "M-m-m-maniac?"

"Why didn't you tell me he was here?" She pointed at the inoffensive cadaver, and gave the innocent Rufus an angry look.

He drew a long breath, held it, let it out slowly; pulled a packet of cigarettes from his pocket, offered the girl one, took one himself, and lighted both. He drew in a lungful of smoke, and exhaled it and his words together. "I didn't know it."

Suddenly she laughed. "Of course you wouldn't," she said in a friendly voice; "he retired long before you came here."

"Who?"

She gestured with her cigarette towards the old man. "Doctor Ruddock. He was once professor of anatomy here. I've known him ever since I was a little girl, and it was a shock to come across him so unexpectedly."

"I thought you were going to faint," he said. "Who snatched his body?"

"I don't know, but I'm going to tell Daddy——"

"Daddy?"

The girl's eyes widened again, this time with a more pleased surprise. "I'll bet you don't know who I am!"

He shook his head.

"Susan Nimblewit," she said.

"N-n-n-n——"

"Nimblewit. Dean Nimblewit's daughter."

"D-d-d-d——"

"Professor Nimblewit's daughter."

"P-p-p-p——"

"Your boss's daughter."

"I—I—I——"

"Well, he has."

Rufus held his breath until his ears rang. "You don't look it," he said. "Thank God."

Susan frowned. She loved her father, even if he did resemble a hound. "Thank God you're his daughter," Rufus re-phrased it. In the six weeks since he had entered upon his new job, Crotey had developed a hero-worship for Horace Nimblewit, who was dean of the medical school as well as its professor of antomy; but until he met his daughter it had never occurred to him that his chief wasn't as handsome as Hippocrates. He now wanted to tell Susan how much he admired her father, but was forestalled by the entrance of Wilfred.

"Good-mawnin', Miss Susan," said Wilfred in a tone which was almost enthusiastic. Though his physical build made it next to impossible, he gave the impression of bowing from the waist. "Whut yo' think a them this year, Miss Susan?" he asked as one expert to another.

4

"Pretty good, Wilfred," she said judiciously, "all except —Wilfred! Doctor Ruddock's here!"

"Yessum."

"Does my father——"

"Yessum, Miss Susan. Doctah Ruddock always say, he comin' back when he die. Well, he heah. I done fo'get," he said apologetically, "yo' goin' inspect these cadavahs this year like always, othahwise I leave old Doctuh down in the vat until latah."

"I've heard of professors of anatomy leaving orders their body was to be dissected in their old laboratory," said Rufus. "I'll give him to the best group in the class."

"Don't tell them who he is, mind," Susan warned.

Rufus promised not to. She turned to go. He added: "You'll come back from time to time to see how he's getting along, won't you?"

Wilfred slid his great bulk tactfully out of the laboratory. "Yes," she said. Rufus spread a brown cloth over the ex-anatomist. Then a young man who looked like an Irish tenor entered the room.

"Hi, Suze," he said.

"Hi, Wish."

"Wilfred told me where you were," he said. "Phew, it stinks in here! Let's get the hell out of it." As he spoke he reached familiarly for her arm, but swiftly she grasped the arm of the cadaver by which she was standing; and Wish found he had seized a cold, damp, embalmed arm instead of her own. "Holy Mother of God!" he cried out in horror, flinging the arm away from him and jumping back.

Rufus decided not to catch this fellow when he fainted; let him muss his hair against the concrete floor; it would serve a layman right for poking his nose into an anatomical laboratory. Susan, however, seemed quite astonished by the effect she had produced. "I should think by the time a boy got to his senior year of medicine," she said, "he'd be used to dead bodies."

"Ugh," Wish shivered, "I never could stand them. I

5

never touched a stiff in my life before," he said in mingled pride and distaste.

Rufus couldn't help but ask how he got through first-year anatomy. "This is P. A. O'Hoe, Jr.," said Susan.

This was the answer to Rufus's question; he took it for an introduction. "How do you do," he said.

"Hi, kid," said P. A. O'Hoe, Jr.

Rufus felt the red from his hair creep over his ears. He began to count to himself, but before he got to five, Susan said in a severe tone: "This is Doctor Crotey, the new instructor in anatomy;" and Rufus was so pleased to discover she knew his name, he forgot his anger.

"Hi, doc," said O'Hoe graciously. "What you got under this sheet, some hot little number, huh?" He whipped the cover from the remains of old Professor Ruddock. Susan put her hand on Rufus's sleeve, and when he looked at her, she shook her head: apparently she wanted him to swallow the insult rather than focus attention on the dead anatomist. O'Hoe dropped the sheet over the disappointing cadaver, and said: "Look, Suze, I'll drive you out to Pinehurst for dinner, and then we'll——"

"Thanks very much," she interrupted in an ironical tone, "but I've already got a date with Rufus."

Rufus started.

"Who the hell is Rufus?" O'Hoe demanded.

"Twothreesevnten," Rufus muttered swiftly, and took a step forward. O'Hoe whipped a dog-whistle from his pocket, and blew a single long blast. Rufus stopped short in astonishment, his fists relaxing in surprise. The door to the laboratory opened, and in lumbered a giant in a pork-pie hat. Without his hat he would have been six feet four inches tall.

"Da hullo, Wish," he said. "Hullo, Suze. Hullo, doc."

"Hi, Fido," said Susan.

"What's up, Wish?" Fido rumbled.

"I just wanted to introduce you to Rufus—beg pardon, to Doctor Crotey," said O'Hoe.

6

"Hullo, doc," said the giant in a gruff, slurred, but amiable voice.

Rufus looked from one of the men to the other, getting the idea. Wish watched him get it, then ostentatiously dropped his dog-whistle back into his pocket. Ignoring Rufus, he said: "I'll be seeing you, Suze," and left the room.

Fido said: "So long, Suze; da so long, doc," and followed him.

Rufus fumbled for a cigarette, and, mimicking Wish, said: "Holy Mother of God, what sort of a medical school is this?"

"Well, it's the only one in the country with Patrick Aloysius O'Hoe, Junior, in its senior class," said Susan.

"Patrick Aloysius O'Hoe!" he exclaimed, memories of the last presidential campaign suddenly fitting themselves to the name. "The Boss of Mercia? Big Pat O'Hoe?"

She nodded. "And Little Wish is Junior."

"Fido is his bodyguard, I presume?"

"Yes; but he also stands first in the senior class——"

"You don't mean to say that gorilla's a medical student too!"

"Uh-huh; and the most remarkable one we've ever had," she assured him. "Doctor Slipstream—he's our professor of psychiatry—says Fido's an idiot savant. You know: like Blind Tom, who could play any composition on the piano, however difficult, if he'd only heard it once before; and Rube Fields, who was an illiterate dope with a genius for mathematics. Well, Fido's a dope with a genius for medicine."

"You mean, one of those guys who memorise textbooks?"

"He can do that too," she said. "In Fido's freshman year, Doctor Slipstream tried to find out what made him tick. He took Fido into his office, and closed the door. Six hours later he came out, mopping his face, and told Daddy: "Da, Fido's a genius, da that's all." She moved

7

towards the door, saying: "I'm glad you're with us, Doctor Crotey. Daddy's last instructor was a drip."

"Hey, Miss Nimblewit," he called, "what about that dinner date?"

"What dinner date?"

"The one you told Patrick Aloysius O'Hoe, Jr., we had."

"Oh. I'm sorry about that. But he's so unbearably conceited I wanted to do more than simply turn him down; and I knew you'd understand."

"I wonder if you understand," said Rufus. "If I don't take you out to dinner this evening, Little Wish will think his acromegalic Osler has scared me off. And I don't scare."

"I should think not, with hair like that. Well, if you want to put it on that basis, call for me at seven. Good-bye, Doctor Crotey."

He watched her leave, ruffling his crisp red hair with a hand smelling of embalming fluid. Damn it, he didn't want to put it on that basis at all.

Chapter Two

HORACE NIMBLEWIT SAT in the dean's office, whose door was wide open on the corridor which connected the lobby and library of the medical school, and whose windows overlooked the busy High Street outside. On his face, which really did bear a striking resemblance to a worried hound, the dean wore horn-rimmed reading glasses. These he removed with his left hand as he swung his swivel-chair around to face the windows, and gazed with insatiable curiosity at the street scene spread before him. Then he replaced his spectacles, swivelled back to his desk, and shuffled through some papers, only to remove the glasses once more and pivot his chair towards his open door as he heard footsteps approaching

8

down the corridor. A medical student on his way to the library passed the doorway, darting a frightened glance sideways as though it were the entrance to a kennel in which some Cerberus were insecurely chained. As soon as he had identified the passer-by, Nimblewit returned to his desk; but at the squeal of brakes in High Street outside, he immediately unshipped his glasses again and swung around to peer out of the window, rubbing the bridge of his nose with his right hand. A taxi had apparently cut sharply in front of some student's jaloppy, or else the latter had suddenly pulled out from the kerb into the path of the former: the dean couldn't decide which, and his expression grew more worried. Then once more came the sound of footsteps in the corridor. The dean whirled around quickly in time to see Dr. Slipstream pass the door coming from the direction of the library. Nimblewit looked still more worried, for the medical library had only the one entrance and exit, and he could not recollect having seen Slipstream pass his door on his way to the library. The dean sighed and again rubbed the bridge of his nose; his was a difficult life.

Occupied as he was with his official duties, his mind was independently active with a pressing personal problem. Both were interrupted by his secretary entering his office from her adjacent own. "Long distance, Dr. Nimblewit," she said. "Mr. O'Hoe."

The dean nodded, and removed his horn-rimmed glasses with one hand while he picked the phone from its cradle with the other. The receiver uttered a tinny blast against his ear. "Still very satisfactory, Commissioner," he replied; "his instructors are very satisfied with Wish's progress." The receiver rattled again. "Yes; I realise that, Commissioner," said Nimblewit, gazing out into High Street. The receiver murmured confidentially before it fell silent with a click. The dean thoughtfully replaced his phone in its cradle, then called over his shoulder: "Dorothy!"

"Yes, Dr. Nimblewit," said his secretary, hurrying in.
"My broker."
"Yes, Dr. Nimblewit."
When a buzzer sounded, the dean picked up his phone again. "Roger?" he said. He lowered his voice. "Buy me two hundred Amalgamated Tanks at the market. I'll call you later. Good-bye." He replaced the phone and his reading glasses, and began to make pencilled calculations on his desk pad; but as his personal problem insistently intruded itself into this pleasant task, his pencil gradually slowed to a halt.

Nimblewit's problem was this: One of his own professors, a Willoughby Chouse, had just had a large portrait painted of himself, and had held the unveiling in his home the evening before. Those of his colleagues who remained unimpressed by Art were overcome by the glittering rococo frame in which the painting had been housed; and all were overwhelmed by the size of the cancelled cheque to the artist which Chouse displayed. Now, the cancelled cheque, though admissable evidence in a court of law, did not really convince those of his friends who knew Willoughby Chouse the best. They suspected something fishy; while his enemies (and alas, what conspicuously successful man in any field has no enemies!)— his enemies knew there was. But if the cheque for $1,500 cashed by Rembrandt Bigginson himself, as the artist's endorsement on the back proved, was somehow suspect, there was no getting around the twenty-odd square feet of genuine oil-painting in its ornate genuine gold-leaf frame—the cost of which was extra, as Chouse informed his guests. Chouse was so unaffectedly modest in the face of a self-bestowed honour unprecedented in the annals of the medical school that more than one of his colleagues enviously wished he had thought of it first. Now that he had set the fashion, however, his colleagues would have resigned before following his lead. It was a truly impossible situation; and nothing remained but to admire Chouse's inspiration, and to remark that, so far as the portrait itself was concerned, there seemed to be something the matter with the mouth.

And so Dean Nimblewit, gazing out over High Street without his glasses, or doodling on his desk pad through them, was getting nowhere at all in his search for a reply to what he considered a studied impertinence, for Chouse was the leader of the anti-administration faction in the dean's own medical school. For one mad moment Nimblewit played with the idea of having an even larger portrait painted of himself, at a cost of two thousand dollars; and it wasn't altogether the money which made him reluctantly discard it. For if he could put Chouse in his place by the expenditure of this immense sum, any one of the surgeons attached to the medical school might start an inflationary spiral by deciding to spend five thousand dollars, or even ten, on a portrait of himself. What is money to a surgeon? the professor of anatomy thought gloomily: simply staying home from the movies for a couple of evenings to perform a few extra operations. No; it must be on some other basis than money, the dean realised, that Willoughby Chouse must be humbled. . . .

Inspiration came to him so suddenly he felt as dizzy as the time a students' fight in the corridor, and a simultaneous wreck out on High Street, had kept him revolving in his swivel-chair like a drunk on a piano-stool. His vision cleared to discover that two of his Faculty had just entered his office.

"Good-morning, Mr. Dean," they chorused.

"Good-morning, Byron," said Nimblewit to the elder of the two. If the dean physically, or at any rate facially, resembled a hound, Byron Drumslager, head of the department of clinical medicine, was spiritually akin to one of those smaller breeds, cocky and yappy, which make up in activity and noise for want of presence and dignity. "And Doctor Wanion," the dean said to the other man, his voice not so much colder as less warm than when he had greeted Drumslager, who was his chief henchman.

"Mr. Dean," said Drumslager, "I've been thinking——"

"*We've* been thinking, Mr. Dean," Wanion corrected. As a matter of fact, the idea had originally been his alone, and he had counted upon it to gain him his promotion. But realising that a mere associate professor didn't carry enough weight to swing the scheme, he had rashly invited Drumslager into partnership. Like a cuckoo hatched out in a hedge-sparrow's nest, Drumslager had promptly shoved the original tenant overboard, and he now listened unfeelingly to Wanion's cheep of dismay.

A slight frown clouded Drumslager's face, and he abandoned first-person personal pronouns altogether—a difficult task, bravely executed. "Mr. Dean," he said, "do you remember what happened to you twenty-five years ago?"

"Why?" Nimblewit asked in astonishment, yet cautiously too.

"Because——" Wanion was eager to explain his great idea.

"Albert," said Drumslager petulantly, "if you don't stop interrupting, we'll never get anywhere."

"Well, I bought ten shares of G.M.," said the dean, who had had time to recollect his brightest memory of that far-off day, and to decide there was nothing incriminating in the admission, since the stock had afterwards risen spectacularly.

"You did!" Drumslager exclaimed. "Mind if I use your phone, Mr. Dean?"

"No, no, Byron; that was twenty-five years ago."

"Oh. I thought you'd just heard something."

"Oh no," said the dean. Another thought occurred to him. "I was married then too."

"That's no good," said Drumslager, still cross that he'd been unable to get in early enough on General Motors. Wanion poked him in the ribs to remind him to get off the subject of the dean's wife. The dean, who knew very well that whatever had been in Drumslager's mind, it had not really been Mrs. Nimblewit, caught Wanion's tact-less exhibition of tact, and flushed.

"It doesn't have to be an even number, Byron," said Wanion.

"No, of course not," said Drumslager sarcastically. "I suppose we can have a testimonial portrait of the dean painted on the occasion of the twenty-third anniversary of his professorship, or on his sixty-first birthday."

Nimblewit started. A testimonial portrait had been the very inspiration which had come to him ten minutes before. He removed his glasses, swivelled to face the windows, and, gazing out into High Street, said over his shoulder to the delegation: "As a matter of fact, though it has been twenty-three years since I became a full pro-fessor, it is exactly thirty since I first joined the Faculty of this medical school."

"Mr. Dean," said Drumslager, addressing the back of Nimblewit's head (looking out into High Street was the dean's favourite listening position; it was as though he could then honestly deny later, as his high position only too often makes it necessary for a dean to do, that certain things were ever said to his face), "Mr. Dean, I have been thinking——"

"*We* have been thinking," said Wanion doggedly.

"That in view of your long and distinguished service to the medical school of Zebulon University, all your fellow Faculty members and students would welcome the opportunity to show their esteem. And I thought——"

"*We* thought——"

"That to have a testimonial portrait painted of you on your thirtieth anniversary would meet with universal approval."

"Hok, hok," said the dean. Under his thinning hair, combed across his head from ear to ear, his scalp, normally the colour of one of his Caucasian cadavers, turned a rusty colour. "Very flattering of you, Byron."

Wanion coughed for his share.

"Of course," Drumslager went on, "as a dean, your

portrait would be painted eventually anyway, but——"

"There's no use waiting until you're dead," said Wanion. Nimblewit passed one hand nervously over his face.

"But," Drumslager scowled at his tactless colleague, "this would seem to be a particularly suitable time." He spoke with peculiar emphasis, and the back of the dean's head vibrated in sympathy with the intimation that only a free and unsolicited testimonial portrait of another man could reveal in its proper light Willoughby Chouse's vainglorious conceit in paying for his own testimonial. "With your permission, Mr. Dean," Drumslager continued after a pause, "we'll have your portrait painted, and present it to the medical school——"

"To hang in the medical library beside all the other dead dea—ow!" Drumslager had repaid Wanion his jolt in the ribs with interest.

"Well," said the dean, his careful words still coming from over his shoulder, "I don't know that I can stop you, gentlemen."

"Ha, ha!" said Drumslager. He consulted his watch, then said briskly: "Got a lot of patients waiting, Mr. Dean. 'M busy man, busy man; but I'll be happy to serve on any committee you may appoint."

"It would be most improper for me to appoint such a committee; most improper."

"Who else is empowered to appoint a Faculty committee?" Drumslager asked somewhat impatiently; he suspected any profession of modesty but his own.

Nimblewit swung round in his chair, donned his glasses, picked up a pencil, and printed on a sheet of paper: "THE HORACE NIMBLEWIT PORTRAIT FUND." He said: "You'll be chairman, of course, Byron."

Drumslager shook his head, his garrulity become suddenly laconic. "Haven't time; do all I can; give what c'n afford; but 'm busy man, busy man. Great respons'bilities; no help."

"Yes, yes," said the dean hurriedly; "somehow we must enlarge your department." With obvious reluctance, he turned towards Wanion. "Then Doctor Wanion——"

Wanion grinned happily, but as Drumslager's head began to shake more and more vigorously, Wanion's smile and the dean's voice both faded away. "Best man you could have," said Drumslager, injecting an anæsthetic before wielding his hatchet, "but it won't do, Mr. Dean; it won't do. It's bad policy. Albert's only an associate professor. That means, no full professor would serve under him; and he hasn't the prestige to beard heads of departments and put the bite on 'em."

Nimblewit thanked Drumslager with a glance. Wanion blurted out: "Well, the dean could promote me, couldn't he?"

"Ha, ha!" Drumslager gave a shout of laughter, and clapped Wanion on the back. Understanding that it had been a joke, the dean condescended to smile faintly; then immediately grew serious, and said:

"I'll ask Ashby Tippett to serve as chairman."

This was, after all, an inevitable choice. Tippett was a natural-born committee-man, and was kept so busy by the duties of his manifold committees that he had no time left for the less important duties of teaching and medical practice. "Then you two will serve on the body of the committee," the dean went on, "and we'll need two more." He began audibly to canvass the names of his most faithful supporters.

Once more Drumslager shook his head. As a politician he was almost in the class of Patrick Aloysius O'Hoe himself, arriving at answers by instantaneous intuition which Dean Nimblewit reached only after tortuous thought. "Old Carnifex must be the fourth member," Drumslager said, and it was immediately apparent to the dean that he was right; for Carnifex, however laughable he might otherwise be, was a monument of integrity, and his name was necessary to lend respectability to this transparent academic blackmail. "And for the fifth——" Since the committee was now packed with three administration stalwarts, Drumslager felt it only politic to include a member of that opposing faction which must be appeased before being bled. "C.O.D.," he said at last.

The dean nodded approval of this final choice, and underneath his printed heading he wrote in descending order: "Dr. A. Tippett, Chairman; Dr. B. Drumslager; Dr. L. Q. Carnifex; Dr. C. O. Dee; Dr. A. Wanion." When he looked up again, the now obsolete Committee of Two was just leaving his office.

"Byron," he said with a beckoning gesture. Wanion reluctantly continued on his way alone as Drumslager returned to the dean's side. Nimblewit lowered his voice to a confidential and grateful whisper:

"Amalgamated Tanks."

Chapter Three

YOU COULDN'T SAY that a marriage was no good that had produced so delectable a fruit as Susan Nimblewit, which was perhaps why Wanion had punched Drumslager in the ribs. Like many other good things, Susan had not been produced without a great deal of trouble on the part of her creators; and promptly after recovering from her daughter's birth, Gloriana Nimblewit had firmly retired to a bedroom of her own, and, like some latter-day Gulliver disillusioned with Man, had taken refuge among Horses. It was known that the salubrious climate of the seat of Zebulon University did not agree with Mrs. Nimblewit's delicate constitution, for which she took the air at various seasons of the year in the more healthful surroundings of Hialeah Park, Churchill Downs, Saratoga, Belmont, Pimlico, Jamaica, and Bowie. Since his wife had her own income, Nimblewit could not object, however much he might deplore the inhumanity with which she wasted her substance. He himself had turned to a nobler form of sublimation: he had then begun to work for the reversion of the deanship of the medical school; and like most great men, he could say with truth that he owed his ultimate success in the world to his wife.

What Nimblewit minded more than anything else—more than his long deprivation of his wife's services; more even than her heretical idea that money was made in order to be gambled away—was the calm indifference with which she accepted his success. She seemed unable to realise that a dean was a veritable god in his little pantheon, and she unkindly refused to make any concessions at all to the lesser deities. What, stay home and jeopardise her precious health to entertain medical professors and their wives, not one of whom knew that Asafetida had won the Smellie Stakes in the mud on April 13, 1939!

Nevertheless, at the moment Mrs. Nimblewit was at home, seated with her husband in their living-room, digesting dinner. One must blame this unusual domestic scene on the happy geographical accident which had placed Zebulon University on the direct route between Belmont and Hialeah; though Mrs. Nimblewit was always glad to see Susan, whom she dearly loved in spite of her disappointment that her daughter, from the time she had been able to toddle into the dissecting-room, had shown much more interest in cadavers than horses.

The dean cleared his throat and said: "Pussy."

"Yes, Poochie," Mrs. Nimblewit murmured without looking up from the *Racing Form*.

"You might refrain from your reading on the rare occasions that you visit your family," he said irritably.

"Indeed, Poochie."

The dean jerked off his glasses, and seemed about to trample them into the carpet. But restraining himself, he said in a whisper: "Thimblerig in the fifth at Pimlico."

Mrs. Nimblewit snapped her eyes from her paper to her husband, and said eagerly: "Yes, Poochie?"

17

"I said, I learned today there was a movement on foot to have my portrait painted. As a testimonial." Here the dean turned that rusty colour which served him as a blush.

Chagrined at having her attention mouse-trapped, Mrs. Nimblewit said: "Yes, Poochie" in a tone which meant: Well, let's get it over with.

"And I've been wondering—— In fact, Pussy, I'd like your advice."

"Thimblerig in the fifth at Pimlico," she said nastily.

"On what to wear."

Mrs. Nimblewit gave her husband's figure the once-over. "Clothes," she said.

Resolutely choking down a *tu quoque*, "Of course," he said, "deans are invariably painted in their academic robes, but it is discretionary whether I wear my cap or not." As his wife's attention began to wander back to her *Racing Form*, he added, cunningly: "It has a gold tail."

"Tail?" This was close enough to a horse to recapture her interest.

"Gold tassel," said the dean smoothly. "Had it only the professorial black tassel, I should be inclined to leave my head bare. But a gold tassel, repeating, as it were, the accent of the gilt of the frame——"

"Why, Poochie!" his wife exclaimed, impressed in spite of herself. "I didn't know you had such a feeling for art."

"Perhaps you'd spare a moment to look at me both ways," he said, taking swift advantage of her astonishment. "My gown is hanging in the hall closet; I'll be right back." And indeed, before she could recover her senses, he was back in the room carrying his academic regalia. "Help me into my gown, Pussy, please."

Mrs. Nimblewit laid aside her paper, and helped the dean into his black doctor's gown with its facing and sleeve bars of green velvet, then aided him to slip his doctor's hood over his head, and arrange its orange and purple lining to perfection. "Now stand away from me

18

and look, Pussy," he said; and, jutting out his jaw, struck a pose.

"Oh, stop looking like a hound!" Mrs. Nimblewit exclaimed. The dean suddenly deflated. "Put your cap on," she commanded. The dean donned his mortar-board, and hung its gold tassel over his left eye. "Now take it off." He obeyed. "Put it back on." He did so. "Off again. . . . On again. . . . Off."

"Can't you tell which way is best?" he anxiously inquired.

"I can't decide which way is worst."

Since no one else ever dared to speak to Dean Nimblewit in this fashion, it was perhaps good for his soul that occasionally his wife did visit her family; but if it was good for his soul, it was bad for his blood pressure. "Ha, ha, ha," he said hollowly. He jammed his cap back on his head so that its gold tassel hung down behind like a tail. "One thing more before you return to your studies, my love," he said between his teeth. "All previous deans have been painted holding a book in one hand. Now, Pussy, I trust I am not too unconventional in holding the view that, instead of a book, a man of my background might hold——"

"The *Racing Form?*"

The dean picked up from a table that common orna-ment of anatomists' homes, generally used as a tobacco jar. "A skull," he concluded. He cradled the grinning fleshless head of some long-dead visitor to his laboratory in his arm, and struck a pose like a canine St. Francis musing on human mortality.

"Growl," said Mrs. Nimblewit.

The dean growled, gripped the cranium, and drew back his arm. "Why, Daddy!" Susan exclaimed from the doorway. "What are you doing?"

Nimblewit drew a deep breath, and began to dandle the skull on the palm of his hand. He looked at Susan, who was dressed to go out for the evening, with a fond smile, and wondered again how a woman like his wife had ever managed to produce such a sweet and lovely offspring. Mrs. Nimblewit too was smiling at her daughter, and shaking her head as though she would rather doubt her own virtue than believe such a lovely, sweet girl could have been fathered by her husband.

"What are you doing, Daddy?" Susan repeated.

"Why, I am going to have my portrait painted, free, as a testimonial from my colleagues and students," he said. "Your mother has been helping me decide on a costume and accessories."'

"Don't you do it, Daddy!"

"Eh!" said the dean, staring incredulously at his daughter.

"It's bad luck," she explained; "it's horribly bad luck. Don't you remember, Dean Chincough had his portrait painted for the medical library, and a month later he had a stroke, and died. And Mr. Grudgins, the dean of the engineering school. He had his testimonial portrait painted, and a few weeks later he stumbled into a cement mixer." The dean dropped his skull. "Don't you let them do it to you, Daddy. Mother, you tell him."

"Well," said Mrs. Nimblewit with a glint in her eye her husband didn't relish, " he can hardly refuse the honour. Can you, Poochie?"

"What good is honour to a cadaver?" said Susan.

The dean shivered. He raised his mortar-board to swab off his brow. He was not superstitious; no anatomist can afford to be; but he had no desire to be cited as another coincidence. "Ha, ha, ha," he said hoarsely. "Chincough had been on the verge of a stroke ever since psychiatry had been introduced into the medical curriculum; and Grudgins's legs were unsteady ever since Repeal. There's nothing the matter with my health."

"Knock on wood," said his wife callously.

The dean rapped on the table top, and went on querulously: "I should think my own family would be pleased I was going to have my portrait painted."

"It's *how* you're going to have it painted we don't

20

like," said Susan. "Having a testimonial portrait done is like erecting a tombstone to you in the university cemetery while you're still alive; it might give Someone ideas. It would be entirely different if you were to commission your own portrait, and pay for it yourself." Here the dean gave a convulsive start. "Lots of people do that, and the only thing that ever happens to them is, their friends say it looks so much worse than they do, and think it looks so much better."

"I'm afraid I'm a little too modest to commission my own portrait, as Willoughby Chouse has done."

"Well, let Mother commission it then; that will spare your life and modesty both, Daddy. Isn't that a good idea?" she asked her parents.

The dean and Mrs. Nimblewit stared at one another. "Phoo!" they said. Susan was about to renew her familiar efforts to bring her father and mother to terms when the door-bell sounded.

"Who is that?" Nimblewit's ever-present curiosity immediately diverted him from thoughts of his portrait.

"My date," said Susan, leaving, and closing the living-room door behind her.

'Who is Susan's current boy-friend, Poochie?" Mrs. Nimblewit asked, her voice waving flags of truce.

"Young Wish O'Hoe," said the dean. "Patrick Aloysius O'Hoe, Junior. That boy has a brilliant future ahead of him in Medicine, Pussy. Positively brilliant."

Mrs. Nimblewit was regarding her husband almost with respect. "He hasn't such a bad future out of it, either," she said. "Bring him in and introduce him to me."

The dean raised his voice and called through the door at the murmur of voices in the entrance hall: "Bring your young man in here for a moment, Susan."

The door to the living-room opened, and Rufus Crotey came through, the look of reluctance on his face in striking contrast to the spasmodic forward leap of his body, which had just been vigorously shoved from behind by

Susan. "G-g-good-evening, D-d-d-doctor N-n-n-n-n-n——"
Rufus stopped, took a deep breath, and exploded:
"NIMBLEWIT."

When little Rufus first began to speak with a stammer,
his parents obstinately refused to take him to a child
psychologist or a speech clinic, professing to believe he
would grow out of it. Rufus himself had been infected
with this foolish belief, and (as he was unlucky enough
never to meet a psychologist to convince him of its falsity)
he was not at all surprised when in fact he did outgrow
his childish defect. He stammered now only in the grip
of some powerful emotion—an overbearing anger, a
sudden astonishment, awe. And to him the dean of the
medical school was a truly awful figure, an Olympian
beyond mortal passions, above human failings; holding
the fate of his faculty and students in his god-like hand.
Rufus had never once been permitted to speak to the
dean of the great medical school in which he had done
his graduate work. Indeed there, where only powerful
heads of departments ever spoke directly to the dean,
and then in hushed voices, the very thought of that
mighty cloud-wrapped Thunderer had been sufficient to
constrict Rufus's throat. No wonder then that this
unprecedented situation at Zebulon University, where
the dean of medicine was also his own chief, was more
than Crotey's nerves could support. Between the wor-
shipper and his god there should stand a priest; between
the instructor and his dean there should have been a
professor of anatomy. That the latter was also the dean
himself was enough to throw the whole theogony out of
joint along with Rufus's tongue.

During his instructor's struggles with his greeting, the
smile of welcome the dean had arranged for P. A. O'Hoe,
Jr., had dissolved into an expression of patient fortitude.
The laudatory letters of recommendation with which
Rufus's former professors had supported his application
for the instructorship of anatomy had not so much as
mentioned Crotey's serious speech defect, and the dean

considered he had been taken in. It was almost as painful for him to listen to, as for Rufus to stammer out: "Doctor Nimblewit", and once through this difficult beginning, professor and instructor alike generally found themselves in a sweat.

"Mother," said Susan, "this is Rufus Crotey, Daddy's new instructor."

Rufus contented himself with a silent bow; with the dean glaring at him in the full majesty of his robes, he could not trust himself to speak.

"How do you do, Mr. Crotey," said Mrs. Nimblewit graciously.

"Rufus is a doctor, Mother."

"Indeed?" Mrs. Nimblewit opened her *Racing Form*, and to ensure herself the peace in which to study it, she said: "Poochie, why don't you ask Doctor Crotey's advice about your tail?"

Rufus turned round and stared incredulously at the dean. Here was no Jupiter Fulminator: if Rufus could have believed his own eyes, he might have seen a pleading look in Nimblewit's, for it was Poochie's fond delusion that no one outside his family knew of his hated pet name. They were relieved from mutual embarrassment by the sound of a tremendous clash and clang of metal in the street outside.

Rufus shut his eyes in prayer. His car, a second-hand Ford convertible, was parked by the kerb outside, and he thought he had recognised its cry of agony. Fortunately the dean, consumed by curiosity, immediately dashed out to the street, the skull tucked under his arm like a football, his gold tassel bouncing, robes billowing behind him. Rufus and Susan were right on his heels.

The little Ford was crushed between the front and rear bumpers of two great black Buick sedans. One of the Buicks must have parked close behind the Ford, while the other, attempting to back into the space in front of it, had crashed into it heavily, catching Rufus's car, as it were, between hammer and anvil. The Ford was down

B

on one wheel forward, and in the silence, before Rufus groaned, there arose the sound of water trickling from its ruptured radiator.

Then P. A. O'Hoe, Jr., lazily climbed out of the Buick in front. He surveyed the remains of the Ford, then turned to the people on the pavement and said: "Good-evening, Dean Nimblewit; hi, Suze. I wonder whose heap is that?"

"M-m-m-mine."

"Oh, I didn't see you at first, Doctor Crotey," said Wish. "Was it really y-y-y-yours?"

Rufus took a step towards O'Hoe, who glanced quickly at the dean, then at the Buick behind, and held his ground. "Da hello, Dean," Fido rumbled, emerging from the second Buick, and tipping his pork-pie hat politely. "Hullo, Suze. Hullo, Doc. What's up, Wish?"

"Guess I must have miscalculated, backing," he said. "Have it hauled off and repaired, Doctor Crotey. Tell 'em to send me the bill; I'm insured. Oh, and frightfully sorry," Wish added.

"You're sure you're not shaken up, Wish my boy?" the dean asked solicitously. "That must have given you a terrific jolt." O'Hoe put his hand to his forehead and staggered slightly. Nimblewit took him by the arm, saying: "Come into the house and rest until you've recovered from the shock."

Supported by the dean, Wish entered the house. Fido leaned against a tree in the Nimblewits' front garden, crossed one leg over the other, and stared at a street light. Rufus said to Susan in a low bitter voice: "As long as he did for mine, I've got a good mind to borrow that son's car for our date."

Vigorously she shook her head. "Nothing doing," she whispered. "Fido's a deputy sheriff, and Wish would sic him on you for car-theft. Come on!" she cried suddenly, and ran towards the driver's door of Wish's Buick. Rufus sprang into the other side. Fido pushed himself away from the tree and said plaintively:

"Hey, you can't do that! Da that ain't right, Suze."

Susan stepped on the starter, shifted into gear, and roared off down the street. Fido pulled his revolver from its shoulder holster, waved it uncertainly in the direction of the fleeing car, then scratched behind his ear with its muzzle, and bawled:

"Hey, Wish! Hey, Wish, commere quick!"

He sounded as though he were about to burst into tears.

Chapter Four

"I GUESS WHEN you steal P. A. O'Hoe, Jr.'s car, it's just borrowing," said Rufus to Susan's profile tantalisingly revealed in the dashlight of the swiftly moving Buick.

"That's what I'm counting on," she said.

"Is he in love with you?"

"You flatter me."

"I guess I'll have to beat hell out of him some day."

"If you do, Fido will beat hell out of you."

"Well, it might be worth it,"

"You just say that because you've never seen anyone Fido has hit."

"Have you?"

She nodded. "There was a boy in the freshman class with Wish and Fido. He didn't like Wish's manners, which aren't exactly ingratiating to his inferiors—and who isn't?—so one day he took a sock at Wish right in the corridor outside Daddy's office."

"Did he connect?"

"And how! Well, Wish complained to Fido that he'd been assaulted; I told you Fido was deputy sheriff. Afterwards, Fido claimed this boy was resisting arrest, and they didn't do a thing to him."

"To the boy?"

"To Fido. The boy is in law school now; you can hardly tell he has a glass eye."

"Susan," said Rufus.

"Yes?"

"I'm a liar."

"Are you?"

He nodded, then realised she was too preoccupied with her driving to see him. "Yes," he said. "I told you I didn't scare."

"Well, tougher men than you make a wide detour around Patrick Aloysius O'Hoe."

"Junior?"

"Senior. Fido works for him."

"What the hell is this, anyway?" he asked in perplexity. "What's the son of a big-shot political boss doing in a medical school?"

"Wish is a nasty little reptile," she said. "If he were on his own, he'd be a race-track tout or something. But he happens to be the only son of the most powerful political boss in the east, and that's why he rides around in an armour-plated bullet-proof Buick with a bodyguard. Some of Big Pat's friends play rough. Well, political bosses can't will their empire to their sons——"

"They can will the spoils."

"The odd thing is, in Mr. O'Hoe's case there really seem to be no tangible spoils. Big Pat doesn't need money, any more than the Pope or Stalin needs money. Whatever he wants he has only to ask for, not pay for. According to those sanctimonious interviews he gives the newspapers—and Wish confirms it—he contents himself with his salary as Commissioner of Taxes."

"Out of which he buys his son two Buick Specials?"

"Don't be dense. These cars belong to Mercia; Fido's salary is paid by Mercia. Mr. O'Hoe makes use of Mercia as though it belonged to him personally, but he really doesn't own it; he can't bequeath it. That's why he has been so careful to arrange his son's future in such a way that Wish would be adequately provided for later, and

26

at the same time beyond the vengeance of Big Pat's successor or the reach of some future troublesome district attorney."

"What did he do?"

"Well, first he entered his son in medical school; then he built the Mary Margaret MacSweeny O'Hoe Memorial Hospital and Medical Centre; and the day Wish gets his M.D. degree, he is to be appointed Medical Director for life with an annual salary of twenty-five thousand dollars."

"My God," said Rufus in an awed voice.

"The only way he could be removed would be for malfeasance or by bill of attainder. The latter is unconstitutional and as for the former—well, our medical school hasn't been able to teach him much, but he's learned he can hire a competent deputy medical director for ten thousand to keep him out of all official trouble."

"Now I know just how my poor little Ford felt, up against those two armoured cars. By the way, where are we going in this one, Susan?" he asked as she swung the Buick round a corner.

"I'm going to park it in front of the fraternity house where Wish and Fido live. I hope they spend the rest of the night driving around looking for us, too."

"If I were a little boy again, and had never heard of Fido," said Rufus wistfully, "I'd let all the air out of Wish's tyres. Hey!"

Just as she had been about to draw up before O'Hoe's fraternity house, Susan had suddenly twisted the steering-wheel hard left, then right, while kicking the accelerator to the floorboard; and Rufus barely had time to notice the menacing black Buick already parked by the kerb, waiting for them. Before Susan shot away, Rufus heard O'Hoe's falsetto: "Hi, you, stop!" and Fido's rumbling: "That's them, Wish!" Then the second engine roared, and the second black Buick's tyres screeched on the pavement in a racing start.

"Keep looking out of the rear window, and tell me

27

when I've shaken them off," Susan commanded, and began to weave in and out of the Zebulon streets like a rabbit trying to confuse its tracks. But the armoured Buick was too big and heavy to manœuvre long in this fashion: along the short stretches of street between turns, it accelerated too slowly; and when it had gained sufficient speed, she had to brake sharply to take the next corner.

"They're still behind," he reported.

"We'll see if we can't outrun them, then. Who's driving?"

"I can't tell. Why?"

"If it's Wish, he's too yellow to push the accelerator all the way down and hold it there. If it's Fido, it all depends on which car runs out of petrol first."

Rufus gave a startled glance at the petrol gauge. "Don't think I'm curious, but what happens if we run out first?"

"You get beat up by the side of the highway instead of in front of Wish's fraternity house."

"Look, Susan," said Rufus: "it's sweet of you to play Pocahontas, but if it's all the same to you, just let me out beside the next rock about the size of a baseball we come to."

"But it isn't all the same to me," she said. "Do you think I want Little Wish to get the idea he can scare off all my dates?"

"Well, if you put it like that, give her the gas."

Susan swung the Buick into a highway, flicked the headlight beams to driving position, and pressed on the accelerator. "You handle this thing like you used to drive for Murder, Inc.," he said.

"I dated Wish for a while just to hear about his father," she said; "Mr. O'Hoe is fascinating. Now listen, Rufus: here's what I'm going to do. This road runs north for about ten miles before it crosses U.S. 70. If I can get to the junction far enough ahead of them, I can disappear; and by the time they've explored the three directions I might have gone, we'll be back in town and unload this hot buggy. Look out of the rear window, and hang on!"

A joyous excitement filled her voice. Rufus wished he could see her face, but she had switched off the dashlight for better vision on the road ahead. Without the dashlight he could no longer watch the speedometer needle, either; and he didn't know whether it was better to be sure, or only to suspect they were now hurtling down the ribbon of highway at eighty miles an hour.

"It's all the way down," she remarked.

"What is?"

"The accelerator. There's nothing else we can do but hold it there."

Briefly illuminated trees, fences, culverts, and bridges rushed towards them with sickening speed. "How fast do you suppose we're going?" he asked in a very casual voice.

"Well, I don't know which of the two Buicks we have. The last time I had one's accelerator all the way to the floorboard, we were doing ninety-five on the level. See anything behind you now?"

"My heart," said Rufus. "It jumped right out of my mouth, and is lying half a mile back on the road."

"No cars?"

"Not a headlight in sight."

"Wish must be driving, then. All right; hold on now." She braked the car as swiftly as she could without leaving tell-tale tyre-marks on the concrete surface, then turned sharply to the left into an opening in slash pines that only a native familiarity with the country could have found in the darkness. "Old logging road," she explained briefly. She proceeded slowly about a hundred yards up the dirt road, then switched off the lights and motor, and sighed happily.

"Holy Mother of God," he breathed. "What did Wish say when you used to chauffeur him?"

"The same."

"There they go," she remarked, as a lance of light and a crescendo and diminuendo of sound marked the rush

29

of a car past the entrance to the logging road. The autumn leaves rustled in the wind of its passing. "Well, I guess we can light a cigarette now, before we head back to town."

Rufus lighted their cigarettes. He inhaled deeply, then said: "I could even do with a drink."

She switched on the dome light of the Buick, then climbed into its rear seat, and motioned him to follow. When he had joined her, she pressed a button, and the back of the front seat sprang open to reveal a miniature bar lavishly stocked with bottles and glasses.

"D-d-d-d—they do themselves well up in Mercia, don't they?" he said. He poured a jigger of Scotch into each of two glasses, split a small bottle of soda between them, and handed her one of the drinks. "Sorry there's no ice, madame," he said. She opened an insulated compartment at the bottom of the bar. It was full of ice-cubes.

The Buick loitered back to Zebulon at a mere fifty miles an hour. Half-way home, the headlights picked up a gesticulating figure standing in the centre of the road. For a moment Rufus's throat constricted, until he perceived that the man was only half as tall as Fido and twice as fat as Wish. Susan braked the car to a gentle stop, and an elderly man stood blinking in the powerful light: a short plump figure, his lower chins hidden by a Windsor tie, his spats gleaming whiter than his face. He raised a wide-brimmed black felt hat with a flourish.

"Good-evening, madam or sir," he said. "Would you be kind enough to lend me a jack, a tyre-pump, and a match?" He motioned towards the far shoulder of the road, where they saw an ancient touring-car whose prow-like nickel radiator shell shone in the reflected light. "I have a flat."

He was so obviously amiable, so transparently confident that the occupants of the Buick were as ready to extend aid as he to receive it, that Susan could not bring herself to admit they hadn't a pump, nor Rufus to explain they had no time. They said, together, reluctantly: "I'm sorry. . . ."

He broke into a beaming smile. "I am very glad. Patching a tyre on an old Mercedes is a major operation; that's why I don't carry the tools myself. Would you be kind enough, madam and sir, to give me a lift back to town?"

"We'll be glad to," they said. Rufus unlatched the rear door on his side, and threw it open. The man trotted to his Mercedes, puffed and pulled two battered and be-labelled travelling-bags from its tonneau, and transferred them to the back seat of the Buick. On his second trip he brought a large wooden sketch-box and an enormous polished wood palette. On his third, he staggered back under a heavy folding easel, and panted: "But one thing more, madam and sir." This was a covered woven-willow basket from which came a querulous meow. He then settled himself on the back seat of the Buick, cradled the basket on his lap, and said: "There is really no way to lock my car. Besides, one is unhappy without one's few chattels around one." The basket now began to emit loud purrs. "May I trouble you for a match, sir?"

Rufus passed a book of matches over his shoulder. The man lighted an Old Virginia Cheroot taken from a blue packet. "A lovely car, madam and sir—thank you, sir," he said, returning the matches. "I dare say you get twenty miles to the tyre?"

Susan tried not to laugh, but finally did so; it would have been a shame to have bottled up so delightful a sound. "It's no joke, I assure you, madam," he said sadly. "I was hoping to shake the dust of Zebulon forever from my feet, and here I am, thanks to your kindness, being carried back there with the speed of—— But I beg your pardon, madam and sir: you yourselves may be residents of that charming town?"

"Yes," said Susan; "we are." The lights of Zebulon were in sight, and she asked: "Where can we drop you, sir?"

"Now that is precisely the question. I cannot return to the hotel," he mused aloud; "and I will not return to the Chouse. I do not suppose," he said hopefully, "there is a Harvard club in town?"

"No; I'm afraid not." She whispered to Rufus: "Suppose I drop you and this gentleman at your apartment, and then leave the car by the fraternity house? If we wait for him to make up his mind, Wish and Fido will have had time to scour the country for us and return."

"Well, all right," he said doubtfully. He couldn't quite decide whether she was giving him an out, or leaving him with the baby. He said in a louder voice to the man on the back seat: "Will you come home with me, sir——"

"Thank you, sir; thank you," he said immediately, as though this invitation were exactly what he had been waiting for. "It is very kind of you to take a homeless artist in. Permit me to introduce myself. I am Rembrandt Bigginson."

"M-m-m-m——," said Rufus, overwhelmed by the misconstruction which seemed to have been put upon his innocent words, "my name is Rufus Crotey, and this is Susan N-n-n-n——"

"Here we are," said Susan, stopping in front of the house in which Rufus had his apartment. "Help Mr. Bigginson out with his luggage, quickly now."

Rufus piled Mr. Bigginson's two bags, sketch-box, and easel on the ground while the artist helped by gathering up his palette and willow basket. As soon as the Buick was empty, Susan waved her hand, and roared away. Rufus loaded himself like a pack-horse and started up the cement path leading to the house. A narrower offshoot of the cement walk curved around to the left of the house and ended at a half-flight of concrete steps leading downward; for Rufus's apartment was half underhalf above-ground.

He unlocked his door, switched on the light, and dumped Mr. Bigginson's luggage in a pile in the centre of a fibre rug covering most of the red-painted cement floor. Where the rug did not cover, the floor showed a damp, greasy-looking film. The walls were unadorned buff-coloured plaster; they looked uncommonly clean, for Rufus, after losing an argument with his upstairs landlord, had just finished painting them himself. The room possessed two worn and sprung over-stuffed chairs, a bookcase, a student's wooden table and hard chair, and a day bed masquerading as a sofa.

"This is my living-room," he said proudly.

Mr. Bigginson, who had had a depressing vision of squeezing his plump body into half of a narrow bed, brightened. He placed his palette flat on the table, then stooped with a grunt to uncover the willow basket. "I am happy that Vigée-Lebrun will not be forced to sleep in the open tonight," he said. "She is in a very delicate condition." As he spoke, a red tabby Persian cat emerged from the basket, mewed at Mr. Bigginson, then stared at Rufus. She had slanting green eyes, ear-tufts like a lynx, and a white-tipped plume of a tail like the disdain of a fairy-tale princess. Her coat was so long, thick, and glossy it concealed her condition. She began to explore her new home, sniffing daintily at its strange smells, and cataloguing them in her curious brain.

"That's a beautiful animal, sir," said Rufus.

"She may look like an animal, but, young sir"—Mr. Bigginson was sixty—"she is a cat. Come here, Vigée!" he called. The cat gave her white-tipped tail a flirt, and became even more engrossed in the smell of a chair leg. "You see? A dog would have come immediately."

"Is that bad?"

"Well, yes," said Mr. Bigginson. "I don't like dogs." He took off his overcoat and laid it on the day bed. Then he began to remove his jacket. "Delightful place you have here, Mr.——"

"Crotey." Rufus was alarmed at what was going on, but unable to cope with it.

"It reminds me of a little flat I had in Paris before the

33

Great War." Mr. Bigginson glanced up at the room's radiators, which, in order to get any circulation at all from the boiler, were flat against the ceiling. "Ah, young sir, that place was cold in winter too. But when one is young, when one's blood is hot, one doesn't know when one's feet are cold. Fortunately, I have a hot-water bottle." He opened one of his bags, pulled out a crimson velvet smoking-jacket covered with red-gold cat hairs, and struggled into it. He fastened the existing buttons through embroidered frogs, smoothed down the black silk lapels, and looked at Rufus expectantly.

"What about your car, sir?" he asked.

Mr. Bigginson shuddered at the memory. "Sufficient to the day, young sir, are the punctures thereof. I'd like to see any mere amateur fix that tyre."

"Good Lord!" Rufus had suddenly thought of his own car lying wounded and bleeding outside Dean Nimblewit's house.

"Think nothing of your omission, young sir," said Mr. Bigginson, extracting an almost full bottle of cognac from his opened bag. "Will you join me?"

"Thank you; I'll just get some glasses and water."

"And if you possess one, a saucer for Vigée-Lebrun," said the artist. "If not, a clean ash-tray will serve admirably."

"Surely she doesn't——"

"Bless me, not in her condition! No; at present she drinks milk." Mr. Bigginson pulled a large silver flask from his hip pocket, upon which the cat trotted over to him, and put her forepaws on his knees.

Rufus brought a saucer and one glass from that corner of the bedroom which doubled as the kitchen to prepare his breakfasts in. The second glass, filled with water, came from the bathroom. Mr. Bigginson poured milk into the saucer from his silver flask, and placed the dish on the floor. Vigée-Lebrun began to lap with her rough pink tongue, splashing minute droplets of white milk, which hung on the ends of her whiskers like tiny pearls. Then he handed the bottle of cognac to his host, who poured a modest amount into the empty glass, and added half the water from the other one. Rufus passed the bottle and glass of water to Mr. Bigginson.

The artist drank off the water, and filled the glass to its original level with cognac. "Your good health, sir," he said. This reminded Rufus of Fido, and, mumbling a reply, he took a quick pull at his drink.

"Young sir," said Mr. Bigginson, "by some happy chance our paths have crossed. Destiny wills that in the morning we shall part, never to meet again—unless you should remove from Zebulon," he put in parenthetically. "Yes; after tonight we shall never see one another again, for it is my inflexible habit never to rise before ten; and alas! long before that time you will have left for your place of employment, wherever that may be." He drank some cognac, and presently went on: "I can only repay you with advice, which you may accept from a man old enough to be your father, or even grandfather, had I and my hypothetical son been child brides: Young sir, never attempt to play out of your league."

"Thank you," said Rufus.

"For many years I have travelled over this country, painting portraits. The tools of my trade," Mr. Bigginson said, waving a hand at the palette, easel, and sketch-box. "In boom and depression alike, my prices were always the same: $250 for a bust, $500 for a half-length. My wants are few and simple: my Persian cat, my Mercedes, my—may I trouble you for the bottle? Thank you. My wants are few, and I had all the work I cared to do at these prices with which to supply them. One satisfied client would put me on to another likely prospect, and so it went." The artist emitted a long and aromatic sigh.

"Young sir," he resumed, "destiny gives us unhappy meetings as well as happy ones." Here he bowed to Rufus. "A physician in Richmond, whose wife I had just painted, referred me to one Willoughby Chouse of the medical school of Zebulon University. I came to

North Carolina; I gave this Chouse my sales talk; I found him all too eager to have his likeness delineated in the largest possible, to wit the $500 size.

"But this Chouse put a counter-proposition to me, and in my innocence, young sir—in the innocence of these grey hairs, I agreed. He proposed that he pay me the sum of $1,500 for his portrait, of which I was to return him in cash the sum of one grand. In this way, he said, I would gain the reputation of being a high-class fashionable artist, and he would own a fabulously expensive portrait—at no extra expense. He told me, when he himself had asked merely $10 for a consultation, no one employed him, whereas as soon as he raised his fee to $50 he had to book his appointments six weeks ahead. I could see what he meant. Whenever I have an attack of asthma, I always go to the most expensive physician wherever I may happen to be; he is also less likely to sue." Mr. Bigginson drained off the last of his cognac, and seemed to forget what he had been talking about.

"What happened then?" Rufus prodded him.

The artist flung out his hands. "The Chouse had a great reception for me when his portrait was unveiled. He boasted to all the doctors there what it had cost him. Fifteen hundred dollars! Pooey, they could buy a second car for that; who wanted a portrait?"

"Couldn't you go back to $500?"

"A $1,500 painter is willing to do a portrait for one-third that price: what's the matter with it?" Mr. Bigginson said bitterly. "No, young sir; it only remains for Rembrandt Bigginson to go to some part of the country where the machinations of the Chouse are still unknown. Let my fate be a warning to you, young sir. Do not attempt to play out of your league. And now, if you will show Vigée-Lebrun and me the bathroom," he concluded, taking a red rubber hot-water bottle from his travelling-bag, "we shall retire for the night."

Chapter Five

FROM THE TIME Rufus had parked his car before the dean's house, until that five hours later when he bade Rembrandt Bigginson and his cat good-night, young Doctor Crotey had led a full life; and that night he slept the sleep of exhaustion. He arose at his usual hour of seven-thirty, tiptoed into the bathroom to brush his teeth and fill the electric percolator with water. Back in the kitchen corner of his bedroom, he filled the percolator basket with coffee, and plugged in the electric cord: there would be three cups of coffee awaiting Mr. Bigginson when he awoke at ten.

For some odd reason Rufus discovered that he didn't mind ministering to his uninvited guest. He felt sorry for the battered artist with the debonair manner and grandiloquent style. In spite of Mr. Bigginson's reminiscences of pre-war Paris, and his somehow touching use of "young sir", Rufus felt himself the older in everything but years. This absurd feeling would have amused the artist even as he capitalised on it; for as a matter of fact, it was Crotey who, in a worldly sense, was young for his age.

Inspired in his early youth by that first of since infinite popularisations of medical science, *Body Snatchers: The Romance of Anatomy*, Rufus had determined then and there to add himself to the illustrious line of Vesalius and William Hunter. But the great age of Anatomy is over; his was an anachronistic ambition; and his training for a long-dead if still necessary science prepared him to work but not to live. His graduate studies leading to a Ph.D. in anatomy taught him more medical science than the M.D.s knew, but he lacked that clinical training, that contact with human beings at their best and worst, which makes a young doctor of medicine cynical and sometimes wise beyond his years.

The percolator was beginning to puff out fragrant

37

steam when Mr. Bigginson appeared in the doorway of Rufus's bedroom, a well-worn Paisley silk dressing-gown tied tightly around his protruding belly. His soft hair was tossed, as if by anxious hands, into a grey halo; there were bluish pouches under his eyes; but he was beaming with happiness and pride. He beckoned to Rufus, led him into the living-room, and pointed a pudgy finger at his opened suitcase on the floor. There, in a nest of the artist's velvet smoking-jacket, lay Vigée-Lebrun and four new-born kittens, three dark red ones and one a tawny cream, like tea with milk. The cat looked up, slowly blinked her wide-pupilled green eyes, and began to purr.

"But for you," said Mr. Bigginson, his voice trembling, "they might have been born under a park bench." He and Vigée-Lebrun looked confidingly up at Rufus. The tiny kittens squirmed their way into his heart.

"You surely won't move them now, will you?" he asked anxiously.

The artist sighed. "We cannot trespass on your hospitality."

"Well, I can't sleep in two beds at once," said Rufus.

Mr. Bigginson's chubby face wreathed itself in a smile, and Vigée-Lebrun, sensing that she had nothing further to worry about, fell to washing her kittens. Mr. Bigginson sniffed. "Is that coffee I smell?"

Rufus said in a worried voice: "Will she eat buttered toast? I haven't anything else to give her——"

"She will want only a little milk and water this morning. Perhaps, though, on your way home from your place of employment, you will bring her a quarter of a pound of hamburger, ten cents' worth of liver, and a small fish."

"I certainly will."

"There is no need to pay more than five cents for the fish."

Rufus Crotey's mind was not in the dissecting-room that morning, and it is to be feared that Vesalius would not have agreed with some of the answers he gave inquiring students; but, then, a freshman medical student swallows whatever his instructors tell him as confidingly as a nestling gulps down a pebble. For Rufus was wondering whether Susan had succeeded in ridding herself of the hot Buick, and when Wish O'Hoe was going to send Fido around to discuss his part in the affair; whether Mr. Bigginson's advice did not apply to his present case; whether, in competing against all the resources of Mercia, he were not in fact playing out of his league. He wondered when Vigée-Lebrun's kittens would be old enough to travel, and whether, as reward or memento, Mr. Bigginson might not leave him one to present to Susan.

So, before he knew it, the lunch-hour had arrived. The students vanished, to offend delicate noses at their various boarding-places; and Rufus, as usual, went across the street for a milk-shake and sandwich. Dinner, which he ate in one or the other of Zebulon's restaurants, was his main meal of the day. After lunch he visited a near-by butcher and bought hamburger and calves' liver, but he had to go all the way down-town to the fish-market for a ten-cent fish. He stopped by his garage on the way to inquire after his injured Ford, which had been hauled in for reconstruction and repair. "I don't want to know how much it will cost," he said; "just how long it will take." He was discovering how fiendish had been O'Hoe's ingenuity in depriving him of the services of his car.

Back in the department of anatomy, he placed the cat's food in a cold-room until he should leave for home at the end of the afternoon. Presently an idea struck him, and he left the dissecting-room and made his way to the office of Professor Dee.

Cedric Osbert Dee (known not without cause as C.O.D.) sat before a wide desk in his office. Facing him on the wall was a row of framed photographs of the great or famous of his profession: Louis Pasteur, Robert Koch, Edwin Klebs Friedrich Loeffler, Theobald Smith, Maurice Arthus, Alexander Besredka, and Karl Landsteiner, with an autographed likeness of Cedric Osbert

Dee himself occupying the central place of honour. Half a dozen telephones (one the conventional black, the others colour-coded red, yellow, blue, orange, and green for quick reference) rested on the top of his desk along with the plastic box of an inter-office communications system. The room also contained a large steel safe, a chair in which profitable callers were invited to sit, and a leatherette-covered couch on which Dee rested from time to time from his incessant labours.

For he was always busy. He lifted the yellow phone from its cradle, dialled a number, and said: "Zebulon Bee-hive Industries, C. O. Dee, president, speaking. I want five hundred-pound bags of sugar." While he was haggling over the terms, another of the phones began to ring. Each was adjusted to ring in a different frequency, and Dee's trained ear could instantly tell which was clamouring for his attention. "Just a moment," he said into the yellow phone, then lifted the blue one and said: "Zebulon Real Estate Associates, C. O. Dee, president, speaking." He listened to one of the tenants of his apartment house complain that the water closet made a banshee-like noise, then replied: "Call 2-2579." He replaced the blue phone, and spoke into the yellow one for a few moments until the red phone sounded, when he picked it up and said: "Zebulon Plumbing and Heating Company, C. O. Dee, president, speaking. . . . I'll send a man over right away to fix it, then, Mrs. Leverett." The yellow phone had gone silent on him, so he replaced it; then pushed a button on the intercom. and shouted into it: "Ulysses!"

"Yessah?" the voice came back immediately.

"Run over to my apartment house and fix Mrs. Leverett's flush-tank for her; it needs a new washer. Try reversing the old one first, though, mind!"

"Yessah," said Ulysses. "Whut I do 'bout this experiment I workin' on?"

"Let it go. You get right along now."

"Yessah."

Dee pushed another button on the intercom. and said: "Ethel!"

"Yes, dear?" The departmental secretary was the professor's wife.

"Debit Zebulon Real Estate Associates with a service charge of five dollars; bill Mrs. Leverett in Apartment 5 for $1.50 for repairs; credit Zebulon Plumbing and Heating with $3; put fifty cents into undistributed surplus."

"Yes, dear," said Mrs. Dee.

"Phone Zebulon Poultry and Dairy Farm to increase laboratory deliveries of skim milk to three gallons daily."

"Yes, dear."

Dee clicked off the intercom. and with the same motion picked up the orange phone just as it began to ring. "Zebulon Poultry and Dairy Farm," he said, "C. O. Dee, gentleman farmer, speaking. . . . Yes, that's right: three gallons daily. Debit the laboratory with——" Here the black phone buzzed, and Dee said: "Just a moment, Ethel." He lifted the black phone impatiently, knowing no good ever came from this official connection with the rest of the medical school. "Doctor Dee speaking. . . . Oh yes, Mr. Dean."

"I tried to get in touch with you yesterday," said Nimblewit.

"I was away at the convention," Dee said into the black phone, and into the orange one: "Credit the Farm with——"

"You didn't tell me how much to debit the laboratory, dear."

"What convention?" Nimblewit inquired at the same time.

"Fifty cents a gallon," said Dee into the wrong phone.

"What did you say?" the dean demanded.

"Fif—— I beg your pardon, Mr. Dean. The South-Eastern Bee-Keepers' Association." Dee clicked on the intercom., said: "Later, Ethel"; replaced the orange phone, and heard the dean say from the black one:

"I see. I am happy to learn that your farming, real

41

estate, and steam-fitting activities still permit you to keep up with the latest in bee culture."

"It's all in organisation, Mr. Dean. Just a moment; hold the wire, please."

In his office, Nimblewit removed his glasses, and stared out of the window into High Street, patiently waiting. He had to put up with Dee; it would have taken a bill of attainder to remove a full professor with tenure; and Dee knew as well as Patrick O'Hoe that the Supreme Court had more than once declared such a proceeding unconstitutional.

"Now, Mr. Dean? I'm sorry to have kept you waiting."

"Not at all," said Nimblewit ironically. "I want to ask you to serve on a committee——"

"I'm sorry, Mr. Dean," he cut in. "But my teaching schedule is so heavy this term, and I'm in the midst of critically important experiments; and what with the small staff you allow me——"

"Minor difficulties, I am sure, alongside your genius for organisation," said the dean smoothly; and before Dee could recover from this under-handed blow, Nimblewit had explained the purpose of the committee, after which not even a professor with tenure could refuse. "Ashby Tippett will inform you of the time of meeting," he concluded. "And by the way, Doctor, I hope your many interests will not prevent you from attending the Faculty meeting tonight. I particularly desire all Faculty members to be present at the first meeting of the academic year." He rang off quickly before Dee could protest.

Dee replaced the black phone in its cradle. If it weren't for his salary of $8,000—and his wife's salary—and Ulysses's extra-curricular services—and the perquisites of his position, like lunching off the milk the Zebulon Poultry and Dairy Farm sold the laboratory for the nourishment of its experimental animals—he thought he would resign his professorship, and devote himself to a less onerous way of making a living. Slaving, slaving, slaving; sacrificing his own welfare and his family's security for Science. . . .

Dee stretched himself out on his couch to relax and recover. The yellow phone rang. He leaped up, seized it. "Zebulon Beehive Industries, C. O. Dee, president, speaking." It was the wholesale grocer, seeking to close the deal on five hundred pounds of sugar. Dee beat him down half a cent per pound, slammed the yellow phone down in triumph, and turned to find Rufus Crotey knocking diffidently on his office door.

"Come in," he shouted. Rufus entered, and said goodafternoon. "Ah, doctor," said Dee, "I was just thinking of you."

"M-m-me?" he stammered in astonishment. He had met Dee but once before, and hadn't realised he had made such a powerful impression.

"Sit down, Doctor." Rufus sat gingerly on the edge of the profitable visitors' chair. Dee pointed a finger at him and said: "Do you want to go on paying rent for the rest of your life?"

"No, sir," said Rufus.

"You will unless you build. Now, Doctor," said Dee in confidential tones, "it so happens that I have a wonderful lot out in the Crusty Hill sub-division—50 foot frontage, 390 foot depth; a full half-acre—and all I'm asking for it is eighteen hundred."

Rufus could only reply: "But I haven't got eighteen hundred."

"Then I have just the thing for you, Doctor! A lot out at Pinehurst—a steal at five hundred and a half."

"But I don't have——"

"You don't?" A little less enthusiastically, Dee said: "Well, then, let me show you a beautiful little piece of property I happen to have over by the gas-works—a gift at two hundred and a quarter."

"I'm sorry, sir," said Rufus; "all I want is a white mouse."

"A white mouse?"

"Yes, sir. I came to see if you could spare me one from your colony."

By a miracle of mental reorganisation, the disappointed president of Zebulon Real Estate Associates instantly became the keen scientist whose likeness looked down from the wall from between Pasteur and Theobald Smith. "Male or female?" he asked.

"Well, it doesn't make any difference, sir."

Dee stared at so unscientific a statement. "No difference!"

"No, sir. I just want a mouse for a cat."

"You appreciate, Doctor, that my laboratory has to employ a man to care for these animals. My laboratory has to purchase their food. And I had to buy the breeding stock in the first place."

"Oh, I meant to pay for it," said Rufus hastily.

Dee clicked on the intercom. "Ethel," he asked, "what is the current quotation on a mouse?"

"Thirty-five cents, dear."

"Thirty-five cents," said Dee to Rufus, "C.O.D. your cage."

"I'll carry it in my hand." He laid a dime and a quarter on the professor's desk.

Dee said into his squawk-box: "Ethel, tell Ulysses to let Doctor Crotey have one mouse."

"He hasn't come back from the apartment yet, dear."

"I can come back for it later," Rufus offered.

"No, I'll get it for you myself." For it had just occurred to Dee that he might be able to choose a white mouse for Crotey which was, well, not exactly sick, but perhaps a little under the weather. He motioned Crotey out of his office, started to follow; then paused. With a furtive gesture he picked up the quarter and dime, and slipped them into his trouser pocket.

In the animal-room Dee came up against an unsuspected difficulty. The white mice, when he went to catch one, skittered about so wildly in their cages that it seemed at first he might give Crotey a healthy one by sheer chance. Finally, however, he spied a cage containing a single white mouse. This one didn't skitter at all

44

as he reached in to seize it, from which he deduced the animal was not feeling too well; and he gave it to Rufus, who thanked him and left.

"Organisation," Dee muttered to himself, jingling the coins in his pocket. "Organisation."

Back in the anatomical laboratory, Rufus put his mouse into a small glass jar with sides too high to jump. The little beast had not skittered at the approach of a human hand, not because it was sick, but because it was Ulysses's pet tame white mouse.

"How are the kittens, Mr. Bigginson?" Rufus asked as he stepped across his threshold. Then he stopped in amazement, for on the wall he had left bare in the morning now hung a gold-framed painting of Vigée-Lebrun lying on a turquoise cushion like a feline odalisque. Even an instructor of anatomy could tell it was skilfully painted; but it had been carelessly hung. The nail supporting the inverted vee of picture-wire had broken away some of the plaster as it had been driven into the wall; moreover, the top of the frame was not parallel with the floor. The scientist in Rufus (after he had put down his mouse, fish, liver, and hamburger) could not help going over to the wall to set the picture straight.

He raised his hands to the picture-frame. They encountered nothing but smooth flat wall. For a moment, the conflicting evidence of hand and eye was too much for his brain to grasp. "Wh-wh-wh-whuh," he stammered.

Rembrandt Bigginson, still enveloped in his paint-encrusted smock, chuckled with delight. "Tut-tut-tut, young sir," he chided, as Rufus's fingers scrabbled at the painted nail, "it's still wet; don't touch it. It's only a *trompe-l'oeil*."

"Sir?"

"*Trompe-l'oeil*. My hand, as it were, deceiving your eye."

"It's—I've—You—— Gosh, I've never seen anything like it before!"

45

Mr. Bigginson looked pleased at the effect he had achieved. "I wish my portraits were half as good as my *trompe-l'oeil*," he sighed. "You see in me, young sir, an unappreciated genius in a field of art which no longer exists, and a melancholy dauber of portraits where art demands a genius."

"Yes, sir." Rufus stared at the painter as though he were a magician who might at any moment turn his own three dimensions into two.

"Enough of art," said Mr. Bigginson, waving it away. "From the way she is sniffing at that butcher's paper, Vigée smells food. And what is this! Bless me, a white mouse in a jar!"

"I thought she might like some fresh meat."

Mr. Bigginson was so touched he could not trust himself to speak; he wrung Rufus's hand. At last he said: "Vigée-Lebrun is ordinarily very fond of the house or mouse-coloured or cheese-eating mouse. If she should devour this little fellow here, and thus develop a taste for white mice, I might find it difficult at times to satisfy her passion for such an exotic food. So perhaps——"

"I'll turn it loose," said Rufus, disappointed in spite of himself and the diplomatic way in which his gift was being refused. "Or return it for credit."

"My dear boy!" Mr. Bigginson cried in distress. "You must let me finish! So perhaps we had better impress on Vigée from the moment of introduction that this little fellow is to be a member of the family, not an article of diet. Perhaps it might be wiser to introduce them," he added on reflection, "after she has eaten a quarter of a pound of hamburger or liver." He unwrapped the butcher's package while the cat wound herself around his ankles, mewing commandingly. Mr. Bigginson licked his lips. "One might manage to grill half of it *en brochette* on the electric toaster," he said wistfully.

"Haven't you had anything to eat all day, sir?"

"I was too busy painting to notice. Besides, as a matter of melancholy fact, young sir——"

Rufus was embarrassed; he thought he knew what was coming, and wanted to assure the artist that it was a host's duty to feed his guests, but he didn't know how to say it without having it sound like a work of charity. "If I'm young enough to be called 'young sir'," he said, "I'm young enough for you to call me Rufus."

"I should prefer to be called Rembrandt myself."

"Well, I've got a faculty meeting tonight at seven-thirty," said Rufus as casually as though he were not bursting with pride at his impending initiation into the confraternity, "so we'll have to leave for dinner early. Where I generally eat is just a couple of minutes' ride from here, but it's ten minutes' walk."

Mr. Bigginson uttered an exclamation. "I'm afraid I neglected to inform the garage about my car."

"I'll attend to it myself tomorrow." Then he had an idea. "Rembrandt," he said hesitantly, "would you lend me your car until mine is repaired?"

"Between you and me," said the artist, "there is no longer any question of *meum et tuum*."

Chapter Six

AFTER DINNER RUFUS and Mr. Bigginson separated, the artist to return to Vigée-Lebrun, Rufus to attend his first Faculty meeting. He walked to the grey stone medical school building where he and his colleagues were to assemble in a third-floor class-room at seven-thirty. This odd but traditional time prevented dining at a fashionable hour, and disturbed the calm digestion of an earlier bolted dinner; perhaps it had been chosen to release several important Faculty members in time for the second, nine o'clock, showing of the movies. There were about two score professors of various grades, apart from lowly instructors, to attend the Medical Faculty meetings, although some of these showed up only for the dramatic

47

meeting in June when the Faculty voted on the candidates for the M.D. degree. When he was a student, Rufus had always imagined these mysterious meetings of his own professors as conclaves of the gods, wherein with religious gravity and after weighty reflection expressed in winged words they solemnly settled the affairs of the microcosmos over which they ruled supreme. He had never read Lucian (indeed, while he knew the names and achievements of the most obscure second-century anatomists, Rufus had never so much as heard of Lucian), and so he could not know how true his imaginings really were.

The meeting-room contained two wedge-shaped sections, twelve semi-circular rows deep, of tip-up wooden seats facing a soapstone-topped demonstration table. The entrance door was in the front of the room, to one side of the table, so that anyone passing through it was framed for an instant in full view of the occupants of the seats, like an actor emerging through a door in the back-drop instead of stealing on-stage from the wings. When Rufus entered, quite early as became a mere instructor, only a handful of men were present to observe him come through the door. The dean was standing behind the demonstration table, gazing off into the distance with far-seeing eyes as though eighteen inches of plaster, structural steel, and stone were not cutting off his favourite view of High Street. Rufus had to pass in front of the table to enter the centre aisle and make his way to an obscure seat in the back of the room. As he slid past the dean, he stammered out: "Good-evening, Doctor Nimblewit."

The dean started at being so cacophonously summoned from his thoughts. Rufus tiptoed up the aisle and sank down in the right-hand seat of the last row, trying to blend into his surroundings; but, like a rabbit crouching in his form, whose fearful staring eyes still betray his presence to the hunter, so he could not help goggling at the dean. Nimblewit frowned, and adding his new instructor's protruding eyes to his stammer, began to think that Crotey's letters of recommendation had been deliberately flowery in order to palm off a psychopath on another school. As he was about to light a cigarette, Rufus caught the dean's fishy eye upon him, as though in presuming to smoke he was committing a crime. He had a book of matches in one hand, a lighted match in the other; he got rid of the offending cigarette by rapidly drawing it into his mouth by ape-like contortions of his lips. The dean passed his hand over his eyes.

Rufus was brought to himself by the smell of tobacco smoke and the sound of someone sliding into the seat next to him. The newcomer was a tall, thin man a few years older than Rufus, wearing glasses on a thin high-bridged nose, and smoking a cigarette in a black holder. "Hi," said the thin man in a friendly voice.

Rufus glanced towards the dean, who was once more staring out into space; then removed the cigarette from inside his mouth. "Hi," he said.

"Light?" The thin man spoke in the most nonchalant of tones, and by his utter lack of surprise at the emergence of a cigarette from this unusual storage place showed himself to be a young clinician, whom nothing ever astonishes. Of course a psychiatrist would not have been surprised, either; but he would have looked at Rufus as though he were saying "Aha!" to himself: it is with this expression on his face and trembling on his lips that a psychiatrist picks his way through a mad world.

"Thanks," said Rufus, happy that smoking was after all permitted on Olympus.

The nonchalant clinician pressed the glowing tip of his cigarette to the slightly damp end of Rufus's. "I'm Johnnie Mazzard," he said; "internal medicine."

"Rufus Crotey, anatomy." He added: "This is my first year here."

"How do you like it?"

"Well——"

"You get numbed," said Mazzard kindly. "The important thing to remember is——"

Here Nimblewit tapped on the stone table top before

him, and said: "The Faculty will please come to order."

The Faculty stopped chattering, and listened to Ashby Tippett, the secretary, drone out the minutes of the preceding meeting like a bluebottle trapped against a window-pane. "Move minutes be 'ccepted as read," mumbled Doctor Nudge on the front row.

"Second," said Furbelow.

"Allthoseinfavoursignifysayingaye," muttered the dean.

"Aye," murmured the Faculty; and Rufus had cast his first vote on Olympus.

Then the dean began to read from a sheaf of cards on which he had inscribed a diversity of statistics about the entering freshman class. He had no passion for such things, but he had an obscure feeling that he and his Faculty should know them. The first card contained an analysis of the students' ages; Nimblewit finished reading this, transferred the card to the bottom of his pack, then began on the next, a summary of their academic backgrounds. The third card epitomised the distribution by States, and so on. The Faculty drowsed gently, and the dean so hypnotised himself by the sound of his own voice that after he had slipped the final card to the bottom of the pack, he began again without seeming to realise he was repeating himself: age, minimum, 19 years; maximum 28; median, 23.5; average, 22.4. Then he went through academic backgrounds, distribution by States, and all the rest of it.

Eventually, by a mighty effort, someone roused, and hearing Nimblewit still reading facts and figures, plaintively remarked: "Mr. Dean, there seem to be more statistics than usual this year."

"I read them purely for the Faculty's benefit," he said stiffly; "I am perfectly familiar with them myself." He turned the top card under, and proceeded: "Age, minimum, 19 years; maximum——

"I believe I have read that once before," he said sheepishly.

Apparently Rufus was the only member of the Faculty

to grasp that Nimblewit had read completely through his statistics twice, and was beginning on a third round; but when he looked around at the distinguished company, he shook his head and concluded that his understanding must have played him falser than their ears.

Having passed the torpid stage of digestion, the Faculty now began to wake up. They listened carefully to the chairman of the committee on scholastic deficiencies report on those students who, having failed some course during the preceding academic year, had been required to make up their deficiencies during the summer vacation. To Rufus the names of such upper-classmen were completely unfamiliar, with the exception of that of P. A. O'Hoe, Jr. Wish's practical work in third-year obstetrics and surgery and been unsatisfactory (the dean glanced reproachfully at Professors Wimbledon and Carnifex), but the chairman went on to explain that he had a letter from the acting medical director of the Mary Margaret MacSweeny O'Hoe Memorial Hospital certifying that P. A. O'Hoe, Jr., had served brilliantly as a summer extern on obstetrics and surgery.

"I'm sure that will be perfectly satisfactory to Doctor Wimbledon and Doctor Carnifex," said the dean.

Timothy Wimbledon—a big slow man, and cynical, as who would not be if half his practice consisted of women who couldn't have children demanding them, and the other half of woman about to have babies who wanted to get rid of them—Wimbledon shrugged his shoulders and said: "Perfectly" in an ironical voice; it was obvious that O'Hoe would never practise obstetrics, anyway.

"Who is chief of surgery up there, Mr. Dean?" Carnifex inquired.

Nimblewit frowned; as usual, the old man was being difficult. Then he smiled, and said: "This is not a matter for the Faculty as a whole, Doctor Carnifex; perhaps we had better not take up their time with it."

"Move the report of the committee be adopted as read," said Nudge.

Furbelow seconded.

"Discussion?" said the dean with an apprehensive glance at Carnifex, who promptly arose.

"As I understand the report, Mr. Dean, the committee has seen fit to remove Mr. O'Hoe's deficiency in surgery on the basis of some letter——"

"Question, question!" cried Drumslager and the more quick-witted of the dean's party.

Carnifex waited until the clamour had died down, then resumed: "The department of surgery alone can remove the deficiency it imposed in the first place."

Johnnie Mazzard said in a low voice: "Sic 'em, doc!"

"I beg to disagree, doctor," Drumslager said. "A vote of the Faculty is always over-riding."

Carnifex said he appreciated that, but desired to go on record against such a high-handed if technically legal procedure. When he had finished his remarks, the dean said: "Further discussion? All those in favour of adopting the committee's report as read, signify by saying aye."

"Aye." It was almost a growl, in which Rufus's bleat was lost.

"Contrary, no."

"No," said Carnifex.

"Now, gentlemen," Nimblewit began to introduce the next item of business, when the door opened and Dee entered the room. The Faculty swivelled their eyes to him. He smirked, then ostentatiously tiptoed to a seat. As he passed in front of the dean, he said in a loud whisper: "Sorry I'm a bit late, Mr. Dean; I was unavoidably detained."

The price of admission to the movie theatres was only thirty cents until six o'clock, but thereafter forty. "How was the show?" Nimblewit asked.

"Rather good," said Dee. "Rather g—— What show?" Indignantly he sat down alongside Carnifex, who moved slightly away from him.

"Now," the dean resumed to his Faculty, "I have a

petition, in fact two petitions, from the students to lay before you, gentlemen."

This statement raised a laugh which was incomprehensible to Rufus. The fact was that, fostered by the dean himself, it was the custom of the students, individually and *en masse,* to present petitions to the medical faculty on the most frivolous as well as serious occasions. A student dropped from medical school would petition the Faculty for reinstatement, citing unique extenuating circumstances. Or a whole medical class might petition the Faculty to revise a course or schedule; and once, indeed, the entire school brought the dean a petition begging that Professor Dee be liquidated. Nimblewit's first impulse had been to sign this one himself; his more cautious action was to refuse it on the grounds that it did not lie within the jurisdiction of the Medical Faculty.

This had been one of the few decisions Nimblewit had ever brought himself to make. He hated making decisions. Every categorical pronouncement inevitably offends someone or other; and a dean who makes a long enough string of decisions succeeds in course of time in offending every member of his Faculty: this is why the passing of an old dean is always a joyful occasion. Nimblewit had developed several skilful techniques to avoid these unpleasantnesses. So far as the students were concerned, his invariable procedure was to inform them with regret that the dean personally had no jurisdiction over a matter which only the vote of the full Faculty could decide; and his swivel-chairside manner was so sympathetic that the students would leave his office to sweat great drops in putting their petitions into the most pathetic terms an unfamiliar dictionary of the English language could suggest. The dean would then gravely read every word to an attentive Faculty, and at the end they would all smile, or occasionally burst into unquenchable laughter, and invariably, if not always unanimously, turn the petition down.

The Faculty were not stony-hearted. They laughed because they realised what the students never caught on to, that Nimblewit had once more succeeded in dodging a personal decision. Yet when the dean passed the buck in matters affecting the Faculty itself, only he smiled. These he would pass on with a wink to the chancellor of the university, who said no. Nimblewit would then pat his disappointed colleague sympathetically on the back with an "I did my best for you, but the chancellor . . ." And the bamboozled Faculty member, who could not help laughing at the students' simplicity in believing in the efficacy of petitions, would leave the dean's office thinking that old Nimblewit was okay.

"This first petition, I understand," the dean said preparatory to reading it, "has been signed by the entire student body of the medical school."

"I suppose they want to change the date of Thanksgiving," said Drumslager.

"When is Thanksgiving this year?"

"The last Thursday in November."

"The next-to-last Thursday."

A wrangle began over the date of Thanksgiving, with which Mr. Roosevelt had once experimented like a Roman emperor engaged in calendar reform. Rufus heard his colleagues in amazement. Johnnie Mazzard fitted another cigarette into his holder, and listened with a beatific expression on his face.

"Gentlemen! Gentlemen!" The dean finally made himself heard, and the argument, which had spread throughout the room and gone far afield, died down. "Gentlemen, this petition has nothing to do with the Thanksgiving holiday, which falls on——" He coughed. "I shall find out from the chancellor's office, and inform you later."

"I should just like to remark, Mr. Dean," said Dee, rising, "that my classes are held on Monday, Tuesday, and Wednesday. Since the Thanksgiving holiday, whatever date it may be, falls on Thursday, Friday, and

54

Saturday, it seems a little unfair to me that I should have no vacation at all. May I respectfully request that during the week of Thanksgiving, I exchange class days with Doctor Flitch——"

Immediately Flitch jumped to his feet and vehemently protested.

"I meant to say, with Doctor Geason," said Dee having had the opportunity during Flitch's remarks to make sure that Professor Geason was safely absent.

"You are out of order, doctor," said the dean coldly. "We are considering this petition, which I beg you will now permit me to read." Dee gave Nimblewit a dirty look, and too late the dean remembered that he was a member of the portrait-fund committee, and hence to be handled gently until the money was all in. While he read the petition aloud, the dean's mind was on this latter problem.

In the petition, the student body pointed out that they had no place to rest or relax, and they asked that some space in the great medical building be set aside for a student lounge and snack-bar, which they could equip and care for themselves.

The dean finished reading, removed his horn-rimmed glasses, stared out over the heads of his Faculty, and said: "Well, gentlemen?"

The gentlemen of the Faculty exchanged puzzled looks; so strange a petition had never before been presented to them. (But Rufus did not think it strange: his old school had a very comfortable lounge and snack-bar.) Finally Drumslager arose and said: "Mr. Dean, I do not believe in pampering students. When we want them on the wards, they'll be in the lounge, listening to the radio and drinking dopes." He looked challengingly about him, and sat down.

A hulking shock-haired man now stood up, and began: "Mr. Dean, I often listen to the radio myself, and drink——"

A great shout of laughter stopped him, and he stood

waiting for it to die down, a patient expression on his face. Rufus felt very sorry to have missed the point of so excruciatingly funny a remark, and leaned towards Mazzard to ask in a whisper, "Who is that?"

Johnnie Mazzard stopped laughing long enough to say: "George Slipstream, the professor of psychiatry. Those are his boys, O'Shawnessey and Drubetskoy, on either side of him."

Meanwhile Slipstream waited out the familiar phenomenon. No matter how serious his remarks in Faculty meeting, they were always greeted by bursts of laughter; for in the modern medical school all psychiatrists are cast as comic characters. So, while surgeons, internists, and pre-clinical scientists all roared, Slipstream reminded himself that once Christ had been mocked and Pinel jeered, and that the kingdom of Freud was at hand. Finally the laughter ceased; several members of the Faculty replaced their handkerchiefs; and the psychiatrist continued as though there had been no interruption at all:

"Dopes."

He sat down amid a perfect gale of laughter, in which Rufus, now he knew what was what, heartily joined. But Slipstream, Drubetskoy, and O'Shawnessey sat with calm patient faces awaiting the second coming of Christ.

Then Carnifex said: "May I ask what you think of the matter yourself, Mr. Dean?"

Nimblewit visibly suffered. He passed his hand over his face, then looked at his palm before wiping it on the leg of his trousers. "Well," he said at last, "like Doctor Drumslager, I should like to see the students on the wards, and like Doctor Slipstream I sometimes listen to the radio myself."

"Thank you, Mr. Dean. I too am thoroughly in accord with the petition."

"The kiss of death," Mazzard whispered to Rufus. "Now Byron will murder it."

In one corner of the room an argument had broken

out as to where a student lounge might be put. Someone thought of a certain room in the basement which might be cleared out and utilised; immediately half a dozen department heads claimed it for their own. As the argument rolled on towards the back of room, Rufus thought it spelled the doom of an admirable plan. But Mazzard looked surprisingly hopeful, and remarked to Rufus that with so many departments struggling over a single basement room, each would rather award it to the students than to a rival. The dean stood gazing off into the distance; he was too experienced not to realise that anyone mixing in a dog-fight is liable to be bitten. Finally the argument stopped as suddenly as it began, and Drumslager's voice rose high and clear in the silence:

"If the students put in their own snack-bar," he was saying in an attempt to gain a vote for his side, "what will happen to that self-service Coca Cola box you installed in your laboratory, C.O.D.?"

If the hot, tired students wanted a cold drink, Dee saw no ethical reason why he should not get their nickels instead of the drug-store across the street. But he felt reluctant to advance his arguments before his eagerly listening colleagues; and he made a virtue of necessity by proclaiming in a loud virtuous voice: "For years I have felt the desirability of a student lounge and snack-bar, Byron; and I have been endeavouring to fulfil the need on a departmental level. I'd like nothing better than to have the medical school take over a burden which I alone have been supporting. Mr. Dean," he now spoke directly to Nimblewit, "I move that the medical school itself equip and run a students' lounge and snack-bar, and that you appoint a Faculty committee to take up the matter immediately."

"Second the motion," said Furbelow.

"Discussion?" The dean's voice was abstracted; he could see the thoughts swimming in Dee's mind like goldfish. If the motion were carried, he would be bound by convention to appoint Dee chairman of the Faculty committee, which meant that the Zebulon Plumbing and Heating Company would install the fixtures and the Zebulon Poultry and Dairy Farm Supply most of the snacks. His only hope was that this awkward position, like every preceding one, would be beaten down.

"Question, question!" Drumslager cried with shrill confidence. The dean took heart, and asked all those in favour to signify by saying aye.

"Aye," said half the Faculty, Rufus among them.

"Opposed, no."

"No," said the other half.

The volume of sound had been approximately equal. Tippett, the lanky secretary of the Faculty, whose business it was to record the vote, said something to the dean in his inaudible voice. "All those in favour, please stand," said Nimblewit.

Rufus and fourteen others arose. Together Tippett and the dean counted them. When he came to Rufus, Nimblewit said: "Instructors are permitted to attend the meetings of the Faculty and take part in the discussions, Doctor Crotey, but only those of professorial rank are entitled to a vote."

Rufus blushed a fiery red, stammered out: "I'm s-s-s-sorry, D-d-doctor N-n-n-nimblewit," and sat down in the most acute embarrassment he had ever known. Slipstream, O'Shawnessey, and Drubetskoy all turned with a single movement to stare at him, their lips moving in unison as they murmured: "Aha!"

"All opposed, now please rise," said the dean.

Fourteen professors stood up, and Nimblewit was repaid for his courteous treatment of his instructor, for the vote was thus a tie; and the dean, in the face of his grinning Faculty, was forced to make a public decision. For a good two minutes he stared out over the heads of his colleagues, unconsciously picking his nose, trying to make up his mind to say . . . anything. His mouth opened; he snapped it shut before either aye or no could emerge.

The Faculty began to laugh: the dean turned the rusty colour which served him as a blush. He cleared his throat; whispered to Tippett, who shook his head. (He had pleaded for a recount.) Finally, rolling his eyes in desperation, Nimblewit's gaze met Dee's glittering stare, and therein he read a message: Dee was promising that unless he were given the students' snack-bar (Zebulon Poultry and Dairy Products Served Exclusively), he would damn well sabotage the Horace Nimblewit Portrait Fund. The dean threw a bitter look at Drumslager, whose political genius had got him into this predicament; moistened his lips; said hoarsely: "Aye."

There were anxious eyes on the big clock on the side wall as the dean, after recovering himself somewhat, began to read the second petition. This one was from the senior medical class. It appeared that these students, looking back over three years of medicine and forward to their early graduation, were distressed to discover how little they had been taught about Sex. (The Faculty roared with laughter.) There had been a dab of sex in anatomy, in embryology, physiology, obstetrics and gynecology, urology, and psychiatry; but no single integrated course in What a Young Doctor Ought to Know.

"Great God," said Mazzard in disgust, "you'd think they'd have been ashamed to confess it."

"Yeah," said Rufus.

Up in front, the accused members of the Faculty, after squabbling among themselves, had suddenly decided to dump the guilt on the broad shoulders of the head of the department of obstetrics and gynecology. "Oh hell," said Wimbledon, "Mr. Dean, I move the petition be granted."

"Second the motion," said Furbelow.

"Discussion?"

There was a good deal of discussion, but as it all went on at once, Rufus, to his great regret, could make nothing of it except that everyone thought someone else should

59

be responsible for giving the course. At last Drumslager called out: "Mr. Dean, I offer a substitute motion that the petition be denied."

Furbelow seconded.

"Mr. Dean! Mr. Dean! What are we voting on?" a number of voices cried. Nimblewit consulted with Tippett, and finally announced:

"The vote is to be on whether Doctor Drumslager's motion is to be substituted for Doctor Wimbledon's motion. All those in favour, signify by saying aye."

"Aye!"

"Contrary?"

"No!"

"The motion is carried."

"Move we adjourn," Nudge called.

"Second," said Furbelow.

"Your motion is out of order, Doctor," said the dean. "We have yet to vote on the petition."

"Oh, I thought we just did that, Mr. Dean."

"No; that was a motion to substitute a motion."

"I'm sorry, Mr. Dean; I didn't understand that," Nudge apologised. "In that case, I'd like to withdraw my motion for adjournment, and make a motion for reconsideration of Byron's motion to substitute his for Doctor Wimbledon's motion. Will that be in order, Mr. Dean?"

"Oh, brother!" Johnnie Mazzard murmured rhapsodically.

"It seems to me, Mr. Dean, we need only one motion before the Faculty," said Slipstream. "Those who vote in favour of Doctor Wimbledon's motion are *ipso facto* voting against Doctor Drumslager's, and those who are voting for Byron's are automatically voting against Tim's. Any fool can see that."

And once more the Faculty burst into unquenchable laughter. When the tears were wiped away, everyone had forgotten the parliamentary status of the petition, and it was decided to begin all over again from scratch.

"Mr. Dean!" said a dozen voices at once.

Nimblewit recognised Carnifex, who said: "I move the matter be referred to the dean to be settled at his discretion."

"Second the motion," said Furbelow.

The dean put his forefinger under his collar and tugged. "Discussion?" he said feebly.

Dee arose and inquired if the emolument of whoever gave the new course on Sex would be correspondingly increased. This question threw a new light on the matter. The dean removed his glasses and again passed his hand over his face. He stared out into space, thinking thoughts which would have horrified Professor Dee; for Nimblewit was about to decide to give the course himself. His soaring imagination saw not so much Dee's "increased emolument" as a celebrated new textbook on sex for medical students by Horace Nimblewit, B.A., M.D.: a compulsory textbook bringing in kudos and a nice little annual income as well. In his mind, royalty figures multiplied themselves like guinea-pigs. Unknown to himself, he began to smile happily.

"Mr. Dean!" Dee prodded him.

Nimblewit started. "Allthoseinfavoursignifysayingaye," he said rapidly. A thunderous chorus of ayes drowned out Dee's protest that he hadn't been answered.

"Move we adjourn!"

"Second," said Furbelow, breaking for the door and the nine o'clock show.

"The important thing to remember," Johnnie Mazzard resumed his interrupted advice to Rufus as they left the deserted Faculty meeting-room together, "is that, taken individually, all these docs are fairly sensible and—except for C.O.D.—reasonably competent. But when you gather them all together in a Faculty meeting, you've got the Congress of the United States."

Chapter Seven

RUFUS WALKED BACK to his apartment in a ruminative mood. The suspicion that most of his new colleagues had just been acting like fools, and a few of them like rogues, lay heavy on his mind; and his only digestive powder was Johnnie Mazzard's parting reflection that wise men singly might prove fools in Congress. Well, for that matter Rufus looked upon himself as a wise young man, yet he had surely made a complete fool of himself in company. He felt hot all over again at the memory of the dean's reminder that an instructor had no vote. And the way the three psychiatrists had stared at him when he stammered! After his quasi-medical training, he now knew enough to realise how wrong his parents had been to believe one could grow out of stammering as though it were acne. He knew now that such a speech defect was the outward sign of a cesspool of psychologic aberration, and he often felt what Slipstream and his boys would have called a guilt-complex because he stammered so rarely. But what awkward times his cesspool took to erupt!

He gloomily descended the four concrete steps to his apartment and entered. Rembrandt Bigginson, clad in his shabby red velvet smoking-jacket, was seated in one of the easy chairs, a beaming smile of greeting on his chubby face, a pair of reading-glasses perched low on his nose, a copy of *Gray's Anatomy* open in his hands, and Vigée-Lebrun and the white mouse lying in sisterly amity on his lap.

"Rufus my boy," he said, "why didn't you inform me that Angelika Kauffmann was tame?"

"Who?"

Rembrandt prodded the mouse, which ran up his arm to his shoulder, where it sat on its haunches, its forepaws curled against its chest, its whiskers vibrating. "Angelika Kauffmann."

"Oh, he's a she?"

"That is my opinion. I have been consulting one of your authorities to confirm it."

"But Gray is a human anatomy."

"Rufus my boy," said Mr. Bigginson with the air of one imparting a secret of Nature, "Angelika Kauffmann is almost human."

"Oh. How do she and Vigée get along together?"

"Well, in public they act like ladies, but——" Here he shrugged his shoulders, at which the white mouse lost its balance, took fright, and scampered down his arm to the stability of his lap, "who would trust two women artists alone together in private?"

"Oh," said Rufus, enlightened. "Vigée-Lebrun and Angelika Kauffmann are the names of women artists?"

"Yes: and by the way, Rufus, you had a caller while you were away."

"Who was it?"

"A very large young man in a bizarre hat."

Rufus swallowed hard. "Did he leave a message?"

"He said," Rembrandt deepened and slurred his voice, " 'Tell doc Fido called, da that's all.' "

"That's enough," he muttered.

"A delightful young man."

"Well——"

"A dope," said Mr. Bigginson, as though this were the highest possible praise.

"Well, take good care of my apartment for me while I'm in the hospital, Rembrandt."

"My dear boy!" he cried, in his distress bouncing up and spilling his cat and white mouse upon the floor. Vigée-Lebrun stalked angrily off to her kittens, and Angelika Kauffmann fled under the bookcase. "My dear boy, are you in trouble?"

"And how!" said Rufus; and told him about it.

"Bless me," said Mr. Bigginson thoughtfully. "You

63   c*

could resign your pretensions to the young lady."

"*Sir!*"

"Give up the dame," he interpreted. "However, if you will take the advice of one who is old enough to be your father—and I wish my own father, God rest him, had fulfilled his own paternal duties so conscientiously the first time I got into trouble over a dame—my considered advice to you is: 'Slug it out!'"

"Thank you," said Rufus, shuddering at the thought of Fido's physique.

"Figuratively. Metaphorically speaking. The power of mind over matter. No, no; that will never do! That large young man has a great deal too much matter; we had better try the power of matter over mind. Yes; surely it will not require much matter to triumph over Mr. Fido's mind."

"Fido is a medical genius," Rufus protested.

"If I understood you correctly, he is a dope with a genius for medicine. In that distinction with a difference," said Mr. Bigginson, "I see the glimmering of salvation."

The next day Rufus sent a man from his garage to repair the tyre on the Mercedes, and drive the car back to town. After work he went to collect the Mercedes, which was surrounded by wide-eyed little coloured boys. It was the first time Rufus had seen the car in a revealing light, and its antique battered elegance seemed to him to match its owner. When the artist had acquired the Mercedes a generation before, its long body (*a torpédo* it was then called) had rivalled in colour a van Gogh sunflower; its interior trim of Circassian walnut had the lustrous polish of a Louis XVI commode; its canvas top was taut; its six red wire wheels (two spares in fender wells) were brave and unbent. With Mr. Bigginson, then with only two chins, behind the wheel with a handsome woman beside him, even grown-up white men had turned to watch him roll by. A lesser man than Mr. Bigginson, in

64

view of the superb craftsmanship with which European workers had built the splendid car, might still have displayed the Mercedes in almost its original condition. But the artist, with a sound sense of the fitness of things, had chosen to allow his car's fortune to decline with his own. The yellow enamel of the Mercedes was now faded and scratched; many spokes of its wire wheels were red with rust instead of paint; its stained canvas top was sagging and patched (in one place with the head of a rejected portrait); yet the little coloured boys, staring at the wreckage, told one another in admiring voices: "Man, theah is a cah!" It was the same unconscious tribute to personality which Rufus paid to Mr. Bigginson himself.

Rufus drove back to his apartment to pick up the artist and take him to dinner. On the way to the restaurant, Rufus said in an off-hand voice: "Say, Rembrandt, when the fellow at the garage was brushing out your car, he found a few things behind the front seat that must have slipped out of your trouser pockets from time to time."

"Indeed?"

"Here they are."

"Bless me!" exclaimed Mr. Bigginson, for Rufus had given him a crumpled five-dollar note, a half-dollar, three quarters, two dimes, a nickel, four pennies, and (Rufus considered this a stroke of genius) a button. "Bless me! I should like to shake that garage attendant by the hand."

"I thanked him for you. I also tipped him." He added shrewdly: "With your money."

"Rufus, this is manna from heaven. Positively I feel like Elijah—or is it Elisha? Perhaps you have been wondering why I, who only recently received the sum of $500 —and had I known at the time the Chouse was a colleague of yours, I would not have told you my story—why I, in a word, was reduced to asking you to purchase a five-cent fish for Vigée-Lebrun?"

"Not at all," said Rufus, who had been wondering just that.

"The fact is," said Mr. Bigginson, without a shade of

regret in his voice, "at the hotel I fell among thieves."

"Why didn't you complain to the police?"

"Metaphorically speaking; I was cleaned shooting craps. Actually," he went on, "I have no reason at all—none whatsoever—to suspect that the implements of sport were not kosher. The dice were, in fact, my own."

He insisted on paying for their dinner. Back in the apartment afterwards, Rufus said: "Rembrandt, if you're not going to use the car tonight, would you mind . . .? I have a date."

"Use both with my blessing," said the artist; "and do not forget to park heading down-grade, for the battery is weak. I myself shall endeavour to teach Angelika some new trick while you are gone."

By the time Rufus returned, the white mouse had learned to roll over and play dead. Mr. Bigginson had Angelika perform for him, then said: "By the way, the large young man with the irremovable hat called to see you again."

"What did he want this time?"

"Apparently he wanted to see if you were under the beds, for after he had looked and found you were not, he scratched his head and went away. I think," he added thoughtfully, "your possession of my Mercedes has them temporarily crossed up."

"Susan loved it."

"Ah, a young lady of taste!"

"Would you mind if I brought her to see Vigée's kittens?"

"Vigée would be proud, and I should be delighted."

"I'll bring her over tomorrow evening, then."

But the next night, as he was about to leave for the Nimblewits' house, there was a knock on the apartment door, and Fido entered. In the low-ceilinged room he loomed gigantesque; the top of his pork-pie hat almost scraped the lower surface of the radiators. "Hullo, doc," he said in his gruff, amiable voice.

"Good-evening, Mr.—er—Fido." Rufus was every inch

66

the instructor greeting a student, his dignity marred only by the fact that he didn't know Fido's real name.

"Aw gee, doc, not mister."

Senior medical students often do not like to be called mister, so Rufus said: "I think you and Mr. Bigginson are already acquainted, Doctor Fido?"

"Aw, not doctor, doc."

"If you'll excuse me, then, I'll leave you to entertain Mr. Bigginson."

"You ain't thinking of going out, are you, doc?" Fido asked anxiously, grasping Rufus by the arm with a hand like a bear-trap. "Da I wanted to ask you somethin' about anatomy."

"Come to my office tomorrow. I'll be glad to help you then."

"Aw, doc, I got classes and ward-rounds all day. The only time I got for you to help me is in the evening."

"Nothing doing; the union would have my card for working overtime."

"I brought my book," said Fido, showing a great red medical textbook which looked small as a primer in his hand. Rufus tried to shrug off the bear-trap; then tried to pluck its steel fingers loose from his arm. Fido appeared all unconscious of his efforts.

"Young sir," said Mr. Bigginson suddenly, "a gentleman removes his head-gear within the precincts of a private home."

"What's he sayin', doc?" Fido whispered hoarsely to Rufus.

"Young sir," the artist thundered, "take off your hat in the house!"

Fido snatched off his pork-pie hat, releasing Rufus's arm to do so. "Hang it on the rack," Mr. Bigginson commanded, pointing to a rather dimly-lighted space behind the entrance door which had been blank the last time Rufus had happened to notice it, but which now seemed to be occupied by a small oak hat-rack with brass hooks. On one of these hung the artist's black felt hat. Rufus should have been sliding out of the door to freedom; instead he goggled at what could not have been, but must be, another of Rembrandt's *trompe-l'oeil*.

Fido obediently lumbered over to hang his hat on the bare wall. It fell to the floor. He stooped, picked it up, once more attempted to hang it on a two-dimensional hook. It fell down. This time he re-hung it with extreme accuracy and care; it fell down. He tried once again before it came to him that the hitherto dependable laws of physics were letting him down no less than his hat. His brow furrowed.

"Young sir," said Mr. Bigginson, plucking Fido's hat from his nerveless fingers, and pushing him away from the wall, "permit me." He placed the pork-pie on the rack beside his own, where it remained as though the laws of physics, having nodded, suddenly started wide awake again. Then Rembrandt led Fido to a chair, and guided him into it: the dope with a genius for medicine was in a daze.

And so was Rufus. It took Mr. Bigginson half a minute to catch his eye and make a gesture towards the door. Rufus started; blinked; escaped.

A quarter of an hour later, Fido, who hadn't said a word or removed his eyes from his hat, arose and re-marked: "Well, I guess I got to be going." He seemed to have forgotten what he had come for. Mr. Bigginson skipped over to the wall-rack before him, whipped off the pork-pie hat, and after a second's delay turned round and offered it to its owner. Fido accepted the hat, stared at it, stared at the brass hook softly gleaming on the wall; then tried to hang the one upon the other. His hat fell to the floor. He tried once more, and was reaching out to feel for the brass hook when Mr. Bigginson took him by the arm and guided him out of the apartment. Fido was a very large young man, but at the moment he was putty in the hands of a great artist.

After he was gone, Mr. Bigginson plucked his own hat from the wall, clapped it on his head, and went out for a stroll in the bracing night air. He had no doubt that Rufus had decided to postpone introducing his young lady to the new kittens until a more propitious time. This was a sound deduction; Rufus returned alone about eleven o'clock. As soon as he came in, he silently took up Mr. Bigginson's hat, which was once more lying in its usual place on the bookcase, and tried to hang it on the *trompe-l'oeil* rack. He was no more successful than Fido, but whereas the premier medical student had seemed perplexed at the result, Rufus now felt exceedingly foolish. He ran his hand over the flat wall, replaced the artist's hat on the bookcase, then sat down and brooded.

"Thumb-tack?" he said at last to Mr. Bigginson, who was in the other easy chair, smoking a cheroot, and looking highly pleased with himself.

Rembrandt shook his head. "Chewing-gum."

The next evening there came a small hesitant knock on the door. Rufus opened it, expecting from the sound to find five feet of inferiority-complex. It was Fido. "Hullo, doc," he rumbled. He gave Mr. Bigginson an apprehensive look, snatched off his hat, and tried twice to hang it on the wall-rack. After he had picked it up the second time from the floor, he touched the wall with an enormous forefinger, then jerked it away as though the wall were red-hot. He replaced his hat on his head, said "So long, doc" with eyes carefully averted from Mr. Bigginson. He went away.

Thus was the pattern set for succeeding evenings. Fido would knock on the apartment door, rumble a greeting to Rufus, hang his hat on the painted hook, pick it up from the floor, feel the wall with unbelieving fingers, and depart with a "So long, doc." As the days passed, he began to venture longer and longer glances at Mr. Bigginson, sitting plumply in his easy chair, smoking his Old Virginia Cheroots; and gradually the expression on Fido's mobile face changed from one of apprehension to awe.

·   ·   ·   ·   ·

Then Rufus would take the Mercedes and drive off for Susan Nimblewit. By now Susan was neglecting to date anyone else, and two people observed this state of affairs with mounting concern. The dean began to see a double danger in his daughter's unfortunate predilection for his instructor. On the one hand, he stood in peril of losing the precious Patrick Aloysius O'Hoe, Jr., as a son-in-law; on the other, he saw an even more frightening prospect of eventually acquiring Rufus Crotey in the same relationship. Nimblewit winced at the thought of Susan marrying a paraphrenic Ph.D., and he sat in his office gazing out into High Street, almost missing in his preoccupation with this new problem the sight of a trailer-truck 11 feet 8 inches high wedging itself under the railway bridge over High Street whose clearance was only eleven feet and a half.

The other person who chafed in helpless rage under Susan's monomania was Wish O'Hoe. Moreover, his bodyguard had let him down. Hitherto it had been sufficient to order the loyal Fido to do something, and Fido would do his duty—with but a single exception: he flatly refused to beat anyone up unless Wish were in imminent danger or had actually been damaged first. (This knowledge, which P. A. O'Hoe, Jr., was careful to keep to himself, would once have been a great comfort to Rufus and Susan.) But this time Wish's ingenious scheme had had nothing to do with wrecking Crotey physically; he had merely ordered Fido to show up at Rufus's apartment every evening, and ask him questions about anatomy from seven-thirty to half-past ten, keeping if need be a friendly grip on the instructor's arm. But something had happened to upset this Machiavellian plan, and Fido either could not or would not tell him what it was. It was true that he called on Rufus every evening at seven-thirty, but he only stayed a few minutes; and all Wish could learn of what went on there then was that doc had a guy staying with him.

"What kind of a guy?" Wish inquired, but Rembrandt

Bigginson was beyond Fido's experience and vocabulary both, and he merely shook a puzzled head. "Well, what's to keep you from asking Crotey questions in front of the guy? Is he bigger than you?"

"Aw, he's only a little old fat guy, Wish."

"Afraid of a little fat guy!" he taunted.

"It ain't that, Wish. He got a mouse named Kaufman and a cat named V. J. Lebrun."

"Well, you aren't afraid of them, are you?"

"The cat is a mother," said Fido. "She got kittens, Wish."

Then Wish tried another tack. He attempted to get Fido to help him wreck the Mercedes as they had smashed the Ford, but Fido stubbornly shook his head. "That ain't right, Wish," he said. Mr. Bigginson himself was innocent of any wrong-doing and, moreover, Fido obscurely felt that it might not be wise to offend so powerful a magician. Nor had Wish the courage to undertake such dirty work without his bodyguard's support.

Chapter Eight

THE DEAN HORACE NIMBLEWIT Portrait Fund Committee was meeting in one of the seminar rooms off the medical library, Ashby Tippett in the chair. Around the corner of the long table to his right sat Byron Drumslager; to his left, Albert Wanion. A good way down the table, facing one another, were Lucius Quintus Carnifex and Cedric Osbert Dee. Tippett opened the meeting in a low-pitched voice which with his air of chronic fatigue and manner of resting his chin on his chest made his words inaudible two feet away. At frequent intervals he cleared his throat with a batrachian croak; his conversation sounded like a despondent frog trapped in a hive of bees.

Evidently the chairman proceeded beyond the mere

71

formality of a parliamentary opening, for after a longish drone, Drumslager interpreted for the benefit of the rest of the committee: "Ashby says, he thinks the first thing we should deal with is finances. Correct, Ash?"

"Bsmbsm—ER—bzmbzmbzm."

"Ash says he's open to suggestions."

"There is a fellow who advertises in the Personals column of the *New York Times* that he'll paint a portrait for fifty dollars," said Dee. "Less ten and ten that would be——"

"Please, doctor," said Carnifex. "A dean's portrait is an official document. Let us not confuse what may be due Horace Nimblewit with what we owe to the university."

"Furthermore," Drumslager gave Dee a look of disgust, "Willoughby's portrait cost fifteen hundred."

"Bzmbzmbzm—ER—bzm bzmbzm—ER—bzm."

"Plus the cost of the frame, as Ashby says."

"I move," said Wanion, "this committee plan to raise the sum of $2,000 for the dean's portrait."

"Bzmbzm—ER—bzm."

"Together with whatever sum is necessary to purchase a suitable frame, as Ashby suggested," Drumslager amended. "I second the motion."

"Two thousand dollars!" Dee cried aloud in anguish. "You could have him stuffed for less than that!"

Wanion snickered until he saw that Drumslager was not amused. He turned the sound into a cough. "I suggest, gentlemen," said Carnifex, "our primary concern be to choose a competent painter, and leave the question of price——"

"Question," Drumslager sang out, "question, question!"

"Bzmbzmbzmbzm—ER—bzm aye; bzmbam—ER—no."

"Aye," said Drumslager and Wanion.

"No," said Carnifex and Dee.

"Aye," said Tippett to break the tie.

"Three to two," Drumslager triumphed; "the motion carries."

Dee began to argue the advisability of advertising for bids, and then asking for a cash discount off the lowest. "By the way, Ashby," said Drumslager to the chairman, ignoring Dee's clamour, "I made a hundred and a quarter out of A.T. How did you do?"

"I haven't sold yet," said Tippett, too distinctly for Drumslager's comfort.

"You heard something else, Ash?"

Wanion listened with envy. If he had his rights, he too would be sharing in the loot; but a jealous conspiracy thwarted him. Dee licked his lips and asked in a casual voice: "What's A.T., Byron?"

Drumslager turned his clear candid gaze on his colleague. "Associated Television," he said.

"Gentlemen," said Carnifex, "*revenons à nos moutons.*"

"I beg your pardon, doctor?" said Drumslager. Old Carnifex was a relic of that bygone day when a physician often prided himself on being a man of culture, and he sometimes disconcerted his younger and more scientific colleagues by his habit of quotation. When he spoke in a foreign language, it was evident enough that he was quoting; it was when Carnifex quoted in English that they failed to comprehend.

"*Cabricias arci thuram catalamus singulariter nominative haec Musa.*"

"Exactly," said Dee. "As Doctor Carnifex says, the mazuma. Let me ask where you're going to raise this $2,000, Ashby."

"Byron?"

"I've already talked to the president of the senior class," said Drumslager. "He eventually agreed with me that they would be happy to contribute towards the dean's portrait as their graduation gift to the medical school."

"How much?" Dee asked.

"Well, there are fifty-eight students, and the class president thought they would stand for five apiece."

"That's $290," Dee quickly calculated. "Less ten and t—— er that still leaves a nice piece of change."

"A couple of good operations," said Wanion, "that's all it would take."

"One on Byron's pocket-book," said Dee, who like all pre-clinical medical scientists was on a salary, which did not vary no matter how much or little work they did; whereas the clinicians, being permitted to have private patients, were able to run their incomes to astronomical levels by the simple expedient of borrowing time from their medical school duties.

"Hour for hour," said Drumslager to Dee, "you pre-clinical men get more money for less work than anyone on the Faculty. No night calls; every evening and week-end free; Thanksgiving, Christmas, and Easter vacations; three months off in the summer—hell, I don't see how you have the gall to cash your salary cheques."

Tippett pounded his fist on the table, and said: "Order, order!" so audibly the disputants fell into an astonished silence.

"Speaking of artists," Wanion tactfully attempted to change the subject, "my wife's aunt——"

"What about the alumni, Ashby?" Dee said abruptly. "Why shouldn't they contribute towards the dean's portrait? There must be a couple of thousand of them still living, and," he soared off on the wings of inspiration, "if only half of them contributed two dollars, we wouldn't have to chip in at all!"

"And the Faculty could pay for the frame," said Carnifex; but his irony was lost on his colleagues, three of whom were gazing on the fourth with reluctant respect.

"Mr. Chairman," said Drumslager, "I move a sub-committee be appointed to draw up a letter to be circulated to all the living medical alumni, inviting contributions to the Dean Horace Nimblewit Portrait Fund."

"Second," said Dee.

"Bzmbzmbzm." Tippett announced passage of the motion without delay, then: "Bzmbzm—ER—bzm—ER—bzmbzmbzm?"

"Sorry, Ash," said Drumslager, "haven't time. Do all I

74

can, but 'm busy man; great respons'bilities; no help."

"Dee?"

"Not me! And I don't know what Byron means, *he's* busy. He's got a hospital full of interns and residents to do his scut work—evenings, week-ends, holidays, and vacations in Florida," Dee interjected nastily; "and who've I got? Kahlkopf and Ulysses!"

"Isn't Mrs. Dee working in your department any more?" Drumslager innocently inquired.

"Doctor Carnifex?" the chairman said hastily in a loud voice. Carnifex shook his head without other reply. "Bzmbzm—ER—Wanion," said Tippett.

"Fine, Ash!" said Drumslager enthusiastically. "Couldn't have picked a better man for the job. Albert, you let me see your letter before you get it mimeographed," he said to the sub-committee.

"Printed would be more fitting, I think," said Carnifex. "Bzmbzmbzm—ER—bzmbzm—ER—bzm."

"I agree with Ashby; printing costs too much."

Dee gave Drumslager a dirty look. "Make a motion the letter should be printed."

"I second Doctor Dee's motion," said Carnifex.

On a vote, the motion was defeated, three to two. "Now that we have the finances all settled, gentlemen," said Drumslager, rubbing his hands together, "it so happens that I know just the right artist——"

"Relative of yours?" Dee inquired as innocently as Drumslager had asked after Mrs. Dee.

"What does it matter who the man is? It isn't the artist; it's his work. Look at——" Drumslager tripped over an example.

"Van Gogh is a good one, said Carnifex.

"Well, anyway, just look at my man's work, that's all I ask. If the committee doesn't like it on a fair and open vote——"

"That's all I ask too," Wanion put in. "Let the committee look at my artist's work, fair and square. And she'll do it for $2,000 too."

"So will my cous——, my man," said Drumslager. "He asks five thousand, but for me he'll take two."

"No doubt," said Dee.

"Order!" Tippett pounded the table just in time to save the amenities. This is a—ER—most unparliamentary —ER—discussion."

"Personally," said Carnifex, "I think the ideal painter for Dean Nimblewit would be Sir Edwin Landseer."

"Nothing doing!" cried Dee. "Those English lords come high, and we're spending entirely too much as it is."

"We'll spend whatever's necessary," said Drumslager grandly. Old Carnifex's suggestion was right down his alley, for once Drumslager had spent a few months in London working under Sir Henry Pepercul, and had never lost his enthusiasm for boasting of this distinction. In course of time his anecdotes had progressed from "When I studied under Sir Henry Pepercul . . ." to "When Sir Henry and I . . ." So he was only too happy to sacrifice his cousin to Carnifex's noble proposal. "I think I may say I know the British better than you do, C.O.D.," he went on; "and I can assure you that in a situation like this, Sir Edwin would be perfectly willing——"

"ER—bzmbzm bzm," Tippett murmured, "ER—dead." Drumslager shot a malignant glance at benign Doctor Carnifex. "Now I," said Tippett very distinctly, "happen to know an artist——" He stopped short, for Slipstream had just entered the committee-room.

"Evening," the psychiatrist greeted the committee: "Doctor Carnifex, Ash, Byron, C.O.D.—gentlemen."

The five committee-men saluted the professor of psychiatry. "Byron told me your committee was meeting this afternoon," he said to Tippett, "and since I'm a little early for my clinic in the amphitheatre, I just thought I'd stop by and see if you had come to any decision regarding an artist?"

Had Slipstream been a full professor of any other subject, Associate Professor Wanion might never have made so bold, but in view of the equivocal position psy-chiatrists occupy in medical schools, he said: "Doctor Carnifex has just suggested we get Sir Edwin Landseer;" and the committee sat back maliciously to await the reply.

"What do you want with a foreigner?" Slipstream asked.

The committee began to laugh, and Drumslager's glee sounded above all the rest. Slipstream waited patiently for the outburst to cease, then he went on as though it had never been: "It just happens that I know a very fine artist——"

"Relative by blood or marriage?" Dee inquired.

"A patient of mine."

"A nut!"

"A paraphrenic," Slipstream corrected.

"What is a paraphrenic, George?" Carnifex asked.

"A person who is slightly nuts," said the psychiatrist. "But you gentlemen realise most artists are paraphrenics. .Just look at——"

"Van Gogh," said Drumslager.

"My man's work; that's all I ask. Of course I realise you will not be influenced by this, but he'll work cheap—just for the cost of materials, hospitalisation, and——"

"George's fee," Dee said in a stage whisper to Carnifex.

"Honi soit qui mal y pense," replied the latter. Dee nodded.

"The salary of a guard to protect the dean while he is posing," Slipstream patiently proceeded. "I should like very much to have you examine this artist's work, gentle-men. He has just completed what my staff agree is a very fine portrait of me. For some reason, all my patients desire to do portraits of me; I have quite a collection."

"Well, gentlemen," said Carnifex, "I don't see why we shouldn't be willing to consider the work of any artist suggested to us in good faith. I am sure the committee will be pleased to view your portrait, George," he said to Slipstream.

The psychiatrist fingered his bulbous nose in some

embarrassment. "It's a mural," he said; "its painted on the lavatory wall."

At this point a stout middle-aged man stuck his head through the open doorway, and called out breezily: "Any secrets, gentlemen? I'm coming in."

The committee greeted the professor of orthopædics with cordiality. He advanced into the room saying: "Ash told me his committee was meeting this afternoon, and I just happened to be passing by, so I thought I'd look in. Very much interested in the dean's portrait; fine fellow; gentleman of the old school. By the way, have you decided on an artist yet?"

Slipstream glanced at the wall clock. "Four o'clock!" he said. "I must be off or I'll be late for my clinic. Remember, gentlemen, come over to Quackenbush and view my portrait."

As the psychiatrist left, Wanion said to Nudge, the orthopod: "Billy, Doctor Carnifex has just suggested we get Sir Edwin Landseer."

"Never heard of him," said Nudge airily. "But if you want a man with a real reputation, I just happen to know an artist myself. He's painted all kinds of famous people, even Big Pat O'Hoe, but he's willing to work cheap. Fact is, the old fellow needs money bad."

"We'll be happy to interview him, Billy," said Carnifex. Though he wasn't chairman of the committee, he was its only disinterested member; and it was by a sort of tacit consent that he was taking charge of the special pleaders.

"I'll tell you, gentlemen," said Nudge. "Operated on him last week, and he won't be able to work for a while yet." He breezed out of the room, adding over his shoulder: "I wish you'd let me know in a day or two whether you'll consider my man, Ash. If you won't I'll have to move him out on the wards."

By virtue of this postscript Nudge collided with Willoughby Chouse, who was just entering the room. "Ah, gentlemen," said the latter to the committee as soon as he had regained his balance, "C.O.D. told me you were meeting here this afternoon, and I thought I might stop by and see if you've decided on an artist yet?"

Wanion trotted out the old joke. "Doctor Carnifex did suggest getting Sir Edwin Landseer."

"A very good man," said Chouse. "However, I have a better one: Rembrandt Bigginson, the chap who painted my own portrait. Of course he isn't cheap, but I can use my personal influence with him——"

"Make a motion," Drumslager said between his teeth; "make a motion this committee choose its own artist——"

"Amend the motion to read 'with the exception of relatives by blood or marriage,'" said Dee, who despaired of finding either of his own who could paint or give him a discount.

"Amend the amendment to add, 'and all patients,'" said Wanion.

"And all men dead over fifty years," said Carnifex. He could well afford to make his own amendment so impersonal. Thirty years before, a grateful patient had advised him to buy a tract of worn-out farmland to the west of Zebulon. In time the city had expanded in that direction, as the perspicacious patient had foreseen, and Carnifex had ultimately realised over a hundred thousand dollars on an investment of one-hundredth of that amount. Money is said to corrupt; it purified Lucius Quintus Carnifex. From the day he came into possession of it, he never performed an unnecessary operation; never put private profit above his duty to his students, profession, and school. He admitted his own good fortune, and often said there was nothing the matter with any of his colleagues, except their love of money, which another $100,000 wouldn't cure.

Chapter Nine

THE HOSPITAL ATTACHED to the medical school of Zebulon University had no psychiatric wards. There was, however, a private N & P wing known as the Quackenbush Pavilion after the local planter who had first discovered there was a living in the intensive cultivation of nuts. Of course the psychiatric staff could not ethically demonstrate their private patients to classes of curious medical students, and so Slipstream had effected an arrangement whereby the State Hospital for the Insane lent him an assortment of bedlamites as the teaching need arose.

The students enormously enjoyed these psychiatric demonstrations. When the staff borrowed a patient who thought he was God (a never-failing annual laugh), the students thought of Byron Drumslager, who shared the same delusion but derived a princely income from the confidence his belief inspired in his patients. A lunatic who believed his direct gaze was fatal as a basilisk's stare, so that he never looked at any living thing save in a mirror, reminded the students of Cedric Osbert Dee, whose glares were more truly said to have a lethal effect on a budding medical career. A case of persecution mania put them in mind of Albert Wanion, whose lectures were devoted one-fourth to D & S and three-quarters to the conspiracy which kept him from his full professorship. A trio illustrating the several grades of mental deficiency irreverently reminded the students of Slipstream, O'Shawnessey, and Drubetskoy themselves. Indeed, until this day of the portrait-committee meeting, when Slipstream provided Lute Becco to illuminate still another chapter of the textbook, the students wondered why the department of psychiatry went to so much trouble to import their cases when the medical Faculty was so accessible. But Lute Becco, who had one day quietly strangled his wife, bore no outward analogy to any of their teachers, and the senior class of the medical school sat on the edge of their seats, tense with interest, as Slipstream put Lute through his paces.

Lute himself sat stiffly on the edge of his chair in the well of the amphitheatre, pale blue eyes staring blankly ahead at the tiers of medical students rising in front of him, one six-fingered hand resting on each knee. O'Shawnessey and Drubetskoy lounged watchfully behind him; Slipstream crouched in front, endeavouring to make him talk. But to all Slipstream's questions, regardless of cunning phraseology or wheedling accent, Lute made only the one toneless reply, the only words ever to pass his lips since the sheriff had slugged him on the day of his arrest:

"They tole me to do it," said Lute of those voices which made of one hearkener a saint, of another a murderer, "an' I done it."

The powerful amphitheatre floodlight, pouring down on the tableau beneath, reflected off the oily bulbous nose of the professor of psychiatry directly into the blank eyes of his patient. Lute suddenly blinked. Under the hypnotic spell induced by the gleam of Slipstream's schnozzola, the voices inside Lute's head began to whisper another suggestion. With rising excitement, Lute stared cross-eyed at his tormentor's nose. "They's a-tellin' me to do it," he muttered, his twelve digits beginning to twitch uncontrollably on his knees, "an' I'm a-goin' to."

Ha!" cried Slipstream in triumph. He had induced his patient to change the fixed pattern of his words, and how great a victory for his Science this was, only his fellow psychiatrists could appreciate. Behind Lute, O'Shawnessey and Drubetskoy, forgetting that the first principle of a lion-tamer or asylum-guard is to keep his eye on the animals, were shaking hands with one another. Slipstream thrust his face even closer to his patient's. "Say that again!"

81

With one vicious snap of his long yellow teeth, Lute bit the bulb off Professor Slipstream's nose.

Slipstream gave a piercing scream, and fell over backwards. For one timeless instant the students saw Lute Becco, still upright on his seat, his polydactylic hands resting quietly once more on his knee-caps, an expression of ineffable contentment on his face, the raw end of Slipstream's nose protruding from his lips. Then, echoing their chief's cry, Drubetskoy and O'Shawnessey threw themselves on their patient; his chair crashed backward to the floor; and the entire senior medical class joyously flooded down into the well of the amphitheatre and joined the mêlée. It was Bedlam at its seventeenth-century best. In a moment the science of psychiatry had shucked off three hundred years, and returned to its most satisfactory form of beating somebody up.

Above the tumult could be heard Slipstream bawling for his nose, and Fido's rumbles of reassurance. For Fido, in a flash of his strange intuitive genius, had realised even before Slipstream himself that if they could recover the severed portion and promptly suture it back in place, the vascularity of the organ would cause it readily to reunite. So while Slipstream bellowed impotently for his nose, Fido flailed his way through the rioting students towards it. In an incredibly short time he had reached the centre of disturbance and plucked out Lute Becco by the collar of his coat. Lute was calm as the centre of a cyclone, and from between his lips still protruded the morsel of flesh.

"Come on, Lute," said Fido, holding an enormous cupped palm beneath Becco's mouth, "give doc his nose like a good guy."

Perhaps Fido spoke in the tongue of one of Lute's inner voices, for the madman's jaw began to relax just as Wish O'Hoe, following in the wake of his bodyguard, courageously kicked Lute hard in the tail. Lute gave a convulsive start; Slipstream's nose disappeared from sight; Lute's Adam's apple rose and fell.

"That ain't right, Wish," said Fido in a reproving rumble. Then he turned to the stricken psychiatrist. "I'm awful sorry, doc. I thought I had it for you."

A bloody handkerchief pressed to the centre of his face, Slipstream staggered from the amphitheatre. O'Shawnessey and Drubetskoy, battered by students who had nothing much against them personally, but who could not resist turning the tables on the Faculty, crawled out from under the human pile and painfully followed their chief. After paying off a few old scores among themselves (this is why clever Wish O'Hoe stuck so close to his bodyguard), the senior medical class untangled, stood up, and stared at Fido, who was still supporting Lute Becco by the collar of his coat.

"They tole me to do it," said Lute, back once more in the groove, "an' I done it;" and Fido, looking at his classmates with deep disgust, said:

"Da you dopes!"

Meanwhile, Dean Nimblewit was sitting in his office, reconstructing (like a paleontologist hypothecating a prehistoric monster from a jaw-bone and a few ribs) what had taken place in the committee-room off the library from the procession of professors down and back along the corridor outside his door. At three o'clock Drumslager had passed by, his arm thrown familiarly over the high shoulders of Ashby Tippett, Wanion treading anxiously on their heels. A few minutes later old Carnifex ambled by alone, and lastly Dee hurried down the corridor, late as usual, and obviously worried whether his wife would be able to cope with five coloured phones in his absence.

Then, at a quarter to four, George Slipstream had gone towards the medical library. Five minutes later, Nudge followed him; then Slipstream returned; Chouse passed libraryward; Nudge retraced his path with less buoyant steps; then Chouse. From all this Nimblewit deduced that none of them had been able to sell the committee on their friends and relatives.

Funny, the dean mused, gazing out over High Street, he had thought Art as foreign to his medical school as Chinese therapeutics, yet here were his colleagues swooping down on his portrait like turkey buzzards, each with a pet artist gripped in his talons.

At four-fifteen the committee repassed the dean's door. First Dee, hurrying back to his telephones, face set and angry. Then Drumslager alone, radiating petulance. Tippett stalking by in high dudgeon; Wanion looking persecuted and sullen; and finally Carnifex with an air of disgust. None so much as glanced through the dean's open door.

Skilfully Nimblewit reconstructed the committee meeting. Obviously it had deadlocked, and the impasse could only be over the choice of an artist. The dean smiled gently; his conclusion pleased him; he had a candidate of his own.

Yet the curious dean, to whom any unsolved mystery was a perpetual torment, could not help speculating on whom his various colleagues were supporting. Chouse was easy: he would be seeking the commission for (and from?) that rotund Rembrandt Bigginson, who was still hanging around town, buttering up to his daughter Susan before enlisting her support. But Byron's man? Ashby's? Billy's? Old Carnifex's? Wanion's? Dee's? Slipstream's?

As he thought of the psychiatrist, Nimblewit began to toy with the idea which had come to him during a family discussion the evening before. The dean and Mrs. Nimblewit, the latter surprisingly still at home, and threatening to stay there until after the Christmas holidays, and have a private wire installed direct to her bookmaker in Baltimore—the dean and his wife, pitching on the one subject that really united them, had cornered Susan and attempted to persuade her to take Patrick Aloysius O'Hoe, Jr., back into favour.

"Wish O'Hoe is a nasty little reptile," said Susan. "He deliberately wrecked Rufus's car right outside my house, and he tried to get Fido to pinch him for car-theft, only

I happened to be the one who stole his car, and Fido knew it."

"Susan!" both parents exclaimed together.

"And I told him, I never wanted to see him again." She heard a toot outside as Rufus squeezed the rubber bulb on the brass trumpet of the Mercedes, and grabbed up her camel's-hair coat and left the room. Behind her, Doctor and Mrs. Nimblewit exchanged sapient looks.

"Poochie," said Mrs. Nimblewit.

"Er——"

"Poochie, I'm afraid that imbecilic new instructor of yours has crowded O'Hoe to the rail." Her tone was so sweet, the dean found it bitter as gall.

"It's not my fault," he muttered.

"I knew no good would ever come of allowing Susan to hang around those stinking dissecting-rooms."

The delicate dean shuddered. Since she had taken to haunting race-tracks, his wife sometimes spoke the language of an alley cat. "I suppose stables don't stink," he retorted.

"Let's not quarrel, Poochie. You know very well, if you hadn't thrown Crotey in her way, Susan might be engaged to O'Hoe by this time. Now that you've made such a mess of things, it's up to you to straighten them out."

"If you had only stayed home," the dean said feebly, "instead of gallivanting——"

"It's lucky I came home when I did. And I'm going to sacrifice my health and stay right here until I have cleaned up the mess you have made of my daughter's life. Well," she said somewhat illogically, "what do you intend to do about it?"

With an unhappy air, the dean picked his nose. He had never before denied his daughter anything; but a paraphrenic Ph.D. . . .

It was at this point that the dean got his great inspiration. But first it is necessary to go back to the last presidential election but one. On Election Night, Zebulon

University once more wildly celebrated another Democratic victory. A troop of students conceived the idea of raising the Confederate Stars and Bars to the top of the university flagpole. In the drunken brawl to see who should have this honour, one of the celebrants—a medical student—was debagged, as English undergraduates term it; but seized the Stars and Bars and shinned up the flagpole. He fastened the flag triumphantly to the top, then slid down directly into the path of Doctor Slipstream. Now, every psychiatrist knows the meaning of a trouserless man embracing a phallic symbol; and Slipstream, recognising one of his own students, remembered the Hippocratic Oath and conducted the poor boy to a private room in Quackenbush Pavilion. The next day he instituted a free six months' course of psychiatric treatment, but, alas, to no avail. At the end of this period Slipstream had been forced to commit his patient to the State Hospital for the Insane as a confirmed and incurable phallomaniac. He had eventually reported the case in the *Transactions of the Tar-Heel Medical Society*.

If Susan really wanted young Crotey, the inspired Nimblewit had decided, it was his solemn duty as father and physician to see that Rufus was restored to a normal psychologic state. His stammering, his imbecilic stare, his habit of ingesting raw cigarettes; all these symptoms of mental unbalance would promptly disappear under skilled psychiatric handling. He would ask Slipstream to take young Crotey immediately in hand.

Chapter Ten

ON THE EVENING of the day Rufus became an unwitting candidate for psychotherapy, Mr. Bigginson remarked to him during dinner: "My boy, the kittens' eyes opened completely today."

Rufus felt a sudden qualm, as though the fried oysters

he was eating were disagreeing with him. "That doesn't mean you'll be leaving now, does it, Rembrandt?"

The artist blinked at the expression of consternation on Rufus's face; then he took out his handkerchief, and blew his nose like a trumpet. "No, my boy," he said; "I just meant, you might bring Susan to see the little lovelies now."

Rembrandt Bigginson had been rather guiltily enjoying his interlude in Zebulon. The feeling of guilt was there because he had never before sponged off anyone as young and tender as Rufus Crotey; and he was enjoying himself because he had grown very fond of Rufus; because he had leisure to delight in the ever-fresh, never-failing domestic comedy of a cat raising a new litter of kittens; and because for the time being he had abandoned the dismal art of portrait-painting for the labour of love of filling Rufus's apartment with *trompe-l'oeil*.

As he had told Rufus, Vigée-Lebrun was very fond of the common mouse. The basement apartment in which they were living, however, with its floor and outer walls of poured concrete, did not appear to harbour any of these small creatures; and so, to amuse his cat, Rembrandt had painted a mouse-hole on the baseboard of the living-room wall, with the head, shoulders, and whiskers of a mouse-coloured mouse peering out therefrom. In the intervals between caring for her kittens, eating, sleeping, and purring on Rembrandt's lap, Vigée-Lebrun would crouch motionless before the painted mouse-hole, waiting patiently for the painted mouse to emerge. Mr. Bigginson was highly pleased by the success of his artifice; and when Angelika Kauffmann began to stroll seductively back and forth before the mouse-hole, twitching her whiskers and undulating her pink tail at the grey charmer inside, the artist could hardly contain himself. He told Rufus it was a triumph worthy of being celebrated by Pliny, like that of Zeuxis, who painted a cluster of grapes on a table in so life-like a manner that the very birds of the air were deceived, and flew down to peck at the fruit.

But Mr. Bigginson had conceived an even more ambitious project, which was nothing less than a *trompe-l'oeil* of Fido himself. He planned to paint a false mirror on the living-room wall, with Fido displayed within its frame as though he were looking directly into the glass. Rembrandt burned to discover what Fido would do when he first gazed into the mirror and moved, and his reflection did not. Of course he could not paint Fido directly on the wall from life; he would have to make a preliminary sketch, and paint his *trompe-l'oeil* in private later.

That evening, Fido made his usual appearance in the apartment, hung up his hat, picked it off the floor, stared at the artist, then turned to leave.

"Sit down, young sir," said Mr. Bigginson.

(Rufus slipped out of the apartment to fetch Susan, and bring her back later to see the kittens.)

"Da me?" said Fido, pointing to himself.

"Yourself, young sir." Rembrandt pointed to the wooden chair beside the study table, and Fido sat down, holding his hat on his knees and looking very much like Lute Becco. Mr. Bigginson half closed his eyes and treated Fido to that impersonal artist's stare which turns his subject into an object. Fido blinked uncomfortably. "Put on your hat, young sir," Rembrandt ordered.

"Aw no," he demurred, shaking his head.

"Replace your headgear!"

"I couldn't do that, mister. I'm in a house."

"We shall consider it not as a hat, but as an article of costume."

"A gentleman don't wear his hat in the house."

"Merely as fancy dress——"

"It ain't right, mister," said Fido, shaking his head; and when Fido said something wasn't right, even strangers somehow knew he couldn't be budged.

So Mr. Bigginson said: "Young sir, have a cigar." He

motioned towards the half-opened blue packet of Old Virginia Cheroots on the table.

"Thanks, mister." Fido tried to pick a painted cigar from the flat surface of the table. "I'm gettin' outta here!" he yelled. He clapped his hat on his head and jumped to his feet in panic.

"Sit down!" Mr. Bigginson roared. Such is the power of personality that Fido sat down, his hat now on his head, his hands tightly grasping his knee-caps. The artist studied him intently. "How would you like to have your picture painted, Fido?" he asked at last in a gentle voice.

Now it happened that on the walls of certain public rooms in the university Wish O'Hoe and Fido had attended together, there had been a number of portraits. The medical library too contained half a dozen portraits of dead deans, so Fido knew people could be painted. But he had never seen a painting of anything non-human (or at least of an inanimate object), which was one reason why the possibility of a *trompe-l'oeil* had never occurred to him when confronted by an illusory hat-rack and packet of cheroots.

"I'm an artist," Rembrandt went on. "I painted those cigars on the table myself. They aren't real; that's why you can't pick them up."

Fido turned slowly towards the table, stared at the *trompe-l'oeil,* passed his hand over its smooth surface, looked at his fingers. Then he rose deliberately to his feet, and for an anxious moment the artist thought he was going to stalk out of the apartment. But he only went over to the painted hat-rack, rubbed his palm over the flat wall, sighed in explosive relief, broke into a broad smile; then returned to his chair and sat down. "Mister," he said, "you sure had me fooled for a minute."

"My name is Rembrandt."

"Yeah? They made a movie of you. I seen it."

"Indeed?" said Mr. Bigginson in an abstracted voice. He had seized a sketch-pad and was rapidly drawing Fido in his pork-pie hat. Like most artists, he liked to have his sitters talk; it destroyed their self-consciousness and enlivened their expression; and he began to question Fido to make him continue. "You are an educated young man. Where did you go to school?"

"Byrlady University."

"Indeed. Did you find it difficult?"

"Naw. I didn't have to learn all them signals. They just give me the ball and I run with it, da that's all."

"Indeed. What position did you play?"

"Full-back. I'd of been All-America the next year too," he said in a deep, aggrieved voice, "oney Wish hadda leave and come to medical school, and I hadda come along."

"Indeed. How do you find the study of medicine, Fido?"

"Easy."

"Indeed."

"Well, I like somethin' hard," said Fido apologetically. "Like—well, there was this Army guard, see, and he was always breakin' through the line and nailin' me before I could get goin' good. I liked that, see. I felt bad when they carried him offa the field."

"Indeed," murmured Mr. Bigginson. He might have been startled by Fido's implications, but he was so immersed in his work he did not even hear the entrance door opening behind him.

"Hello, Suze," Fido rumbled in greeting to the new-comers. "Hullo, doc."

Rufus and Susan were surprised to find him still there, and said together: "Hi, Fido." They added: "Hi, Rembrandt."

"Hang up your coat on the hook, Suze," said Fido, pointing at the *trompe-l'oeil* wall-rack, and giving Rufus an enormous cunning wink. Susan had heard all about the triumph of Rembrandt's matter over Fido's mind, and she slipped out of her camel's-hair coat and amiably hung it on the wall. When it crumpled limply on the floor, Fido said: "Psst! Psst!" to Rufus and Rembrandt.

She tried to hang up her coat again, and when it fell down Fido burst into a great roar of laughter. With an effort he calmed himself enough to say, pointing to the table: "Have a cigar, Suze."

"Whoever heard of a woman smoking cigars?" she said.

"My mamma does," said Fido.

"Indeed," said Rembrandt, putting up his sketch-pad and pencil. He arose, stretched his cramped limbs, and reached over to the table for a cheroot. "Bless me!" he exclaimed as his fingers picked vainly at his own painting. "Bless me!"

"Zeuxis deceived only birds," he said complacently; "Herman van der Mast deceived his master; but Rembrandt Bigginson deceives himself."

"Aw, never mind, Rembrandt," said Fido, "for a minute you even had me fooled. Honest, Suze!"

"No!" she said. She and Rufus exchanged puzzled looks. Evidently something had happened to Fido, as to Saul on the road to Damascus; and they had the strange feeling that he now considered himself one of the privy household.

"He's making my pitcher too," he said proudly. "Honest, Suze."

"What for?" she said unkindly. "For Wish to look at when he's scared?"

"Aw now, Suze."

"Susan," said Mr. Bigginson, "Vigée-Lebrun wants to show you her kittens."

The Persian cat was still living in half of Mr. Bigginson's suitcase, with the other half propped up vertically to make a shield and shelter against the disturbances of human life. Susan went over to the nest, sank to the floor beside it, clasped her hands, and said: "Oh!" Vigée-Lebrun began to purr loudly. "Oh, may I pick one up, Rembrandt?" she begged.

"Ask Vigée."

"May I, Vigée? They're such lovely babies, and I'll give it right back to you."

"Aw, cats don't understand people," said Fido scornfully, as Vigée-Lebrun allowed Susan to lift a squirming red kitten from its nest.

"Try picking up a kitten without asking her," said Rembrandt.

Fido obediently lumbered over to the suitcase, and thrust an enormous hand towards the kittens. Vigée-Lebrun struck like double-barrelled lightning. Fido jerked back his hand, and stared incredulously at ten long deep scratches in which blood was beginning to well. "I'm awful sorry, V.J.," he said contritely. "Honest. I didn't mean to scare you, honest. I just wanted to look at one of your babies, that's all. They're cute."

"Now pick one up," Mr. Bigginson said.

Fido cautiously reached down his good hand. The cat purred as the great fingers closed gently around a tiny kitten, and carried it off. "Gee, V.J.," he rumbled, "I didn' know you could understand people."

"Would you like a kitten after it has been weaned?" Rembrandt asked Susan.

"Oh, I'd love one!"

Rufus looked reproachfully at the artist. "I was going to beg one off you, and give it to Susan myself."

"Could I buy one off of you, Rembrandt?" Fido asked.

"I have never yet sold a kitten, Fido." The giant sadly laid his kitten beside its mother, who began carefully to lick it free of foreign scent. "But I shall be very happy to present you with one," he concluded.

"Aw gee, thanks, Rembrandt," said Fido happily. "It sure was lucky for me Wish made me come over here and keep doc from datin' Suze."

"Why, that nasty little rectus abominalis!"

"Rectus abdominis, Suze," Fido corrected.

"Say, Fido," Rufus asked, "what would you do if a guy told a guy to keep you from dating your girl?"

Fido thought it out slowly, his lips moving. "I ain't got a girl," he said.

"Well, supposing you had one." Rufus wanted to lead

Fido around to the admission that Wish deserved a sock on the jaw.

"You mean Suze, doc?" Fido gave Susan a fond, cunning look.

Rufus made an exasperated face at Susan, who was cuddling a kitten against her cheek. "Well, all right, Suze then," he said.

Fido sadly shook his head. "Suze is Wish's girl."

"Suze," she said distinctly, "is not Wish's girl. Will you please get that through your oxycephalic skull, Fido?"

"Aw now, Suze," he protested, "it ain't oxycephalic."

Rufus whispered to the delighted but uncomprehending artist: "She told him his head came to a point."

"Oh no?" she said. "Then why do you keep your hat on in the house?"

Fido reached up both hands, discovered his hat on his head, blushed vividly, and snatched it off. Mr. Bigginson decided to take over. "Fido was sitting to me with his hat on at my request, Susan," he said. "Rufus, while you brew a pot of coffee, I shall put the finishing touches to my sketch. Now, Fido, resume your pose, if you please."

Fido resumed his hieratic pose, rigid with self-consciousness before Susan. The artist sighed, put down his pencil and sketch-pad. "We shall continue tomorrow evening, Fido," he said.

"Rembrandt," said Susan suddenly, "why don't *you* paint Daddy's portrait?"

"Because, my dear young lady," he said sadly, "my reputation has been ruined by the unspeakable Chouse. Thanks to that monster, I am tagged irrevocably in Zebulon as a painter who gets $1,500 for a portrait. Fifteen hundred dollars! Bah!"

"Oh, but Rembrandt," she said, completely misunderstanding him, "Daddy told me at dinner they were going to pay $2,000 for his portrait, exclusive of frame."

"Bless me," said Mr. Bigginson weakly.

93

"Surely you'd be willing to paint it for that?"

"Hrrmph, hrrmph. Hrrmph."

"That guy Chouse," said Fido, who had just arrived at this point in the conversation. "Is that guy Unspeakable Chouse related to Willoughby Chouse?"

"They are identical."

"Wish give Doc Chouse two C's to pass him in his course last year," Fido amiably remarked.

"Fido!" Susan cried.

"Honest, Suze. Da course, Wish is too smart to give the guy the dough just like that. The guy might be dishonest and double-cross him. So about a week before the final exam., Wish goes to Doc Chouse and tells him his old man give him a hot tip on the market. Wish wants to know if Doc Chouse wants to take a little flyer. Wish tells him he'll phone his broker to buy a coupla hundred shares in doc's name, he don't even have to put up any dough, and when the market rises Wish'll collect his profits for him. Wish figures the guy will figure if Wish don't pass the course, there won't be no profits. Well, when the grades go up, Wish has a B, so he gives Doc Chouse two hundred smackers." Fido shook his head, puzzled rather than disapproving. "That seems like takin' an awful lot of trouble over nothin'. I don't see why Wish don't just learn the stuff."

Susan was biting her lip. Mr. Bigginson gave her a sympathetic glance, and said to Fido: "Perhaps Wish wouldn't like you to divulge his methods of passing courses in medical school."

"Aw, he don't mind." Having an audience hanging on his words seemed to have gone to Fido's head like scopolamine, and he went on: "Take the time we was taking anatomy——"

Susan squeezed her kitten until it mewed. For it was during Wish's and Fido's freshman year that Professor Nimblewit had bought his Cadillac.

"Wish don't like to touch stiffs," Fido was saying. "He says they give him the willies. Gee, Suze, you know there ain't any harm in a stiff. So I do all the dissectin', and they never catch on. I figure the instructor is just a dope, and gets me and Wish mixed up from the first day because when I demonstrate he marks down a A by Wish's name, but Wish claims it's because——"

"Coffee's ready," said Rufus, entering with the steaming percolator. When it became apparent that Mr. Bigginson was to be more than an overnight guest, Rufus had bought a small service of cheap china, and there were now cups and saucers for all. Susan gave the kitten back to Vigée-Lebrun and served coffee. She was no longer worried about the Cadillac; the dean was above taking demonstrations himself; that menial task he left to Pietro Spandone, his associate professor, and to his instructor—in this case that drip whom Rufus had recently succeeded.

Up till now it had been a noisy evening, or at least a white mouse might be excused for having thought so. As Mr. Bigginson and his three young friends sat quietly drinking coffee, Angelika Kauffmann ventured out from under the bookcase, minced to the centre of the room, raised herself on her hind-legs, and sniffed the air.

"Hullo, Kaufman," said Fido courteously. He put his pork-pie hat on his head, raised it politely, then returned it to his knees.

Chapter Eleven

BECAUSE OF THE unfortunate accident to Slipstream, Nimblewit had been forced to postpone the beginning of Rufus Crotey's cure, for the injured psychiatrist had gone into seclusion. Lute Becco had done either too little or too much: had he merely flayed the end of Slipstream's nose, Nature might have skinned it over without a thought; had he bitten deeper, a plastic surgeon might have reconstructed Slipstream a new organ of more classic beauty than his original model; but

D*

driven by his devils, Lute had chosen that exact amount of tissue too much for Nature to replace, too little for rhinoplasty to repair. The inescapable, the bitter fact was, George Slipstream was destined to have a permanently and peculiarly truncated nose.

It is a maxim in psychiatry that no deformity is bad, but thinking made it worse. Slipstream himself had helped many a luckless possessor of port-wine birthmarks and supernumerary mammae to rationalise their difference from the normal, and he had now to do this for himself. All through the Christmas holidays he lay on his leather couch, holding long conversations with himself like Sganarelle with his twin brother in *Le médecin volant.*

While Slipstream was psycho-therapising himself, the little world of the medical school continued to revolve. Enlisting the services of a professor of English literature, Wanion composed a letter to the medical alumni so full of eloquent persuasion he could hardly refrain from reaching for his cheque-book. Drumslager congratulated him, then read the letter, tore it apart, rewrote it, and returned it to its author to be mimeographed with the flattering remark that it was now the finest letter of the sort he had ever seen. Wanion had the letter mimeographed, advancing his own money to pay the printer. Then he went to the office of the Alumni Secretary to get a list of medical graduates. The secretary informed him that all requests to solicit money from university alumni must be cleared through his office. He very much regretted he couldn't give his approval to Doctor Wanion's letter; not, he added courteously, that he was out of sympathy with its object, but solely because the Alumni Association was on the point of launching an intensive drive for contributions towards a new fieldhouse and training-table for the Athletic Department. He observed, not without reason, that if a medical alumnus could square his conscience and show his College spirit by contributing two dollars towards a

96

portrait of Dean Nimblewit, he would be highly unlikely to respond to an appeal for $25 or $50 for the department of athletics. It was a question, the Alumni Secretary went on to say, of the greatest good for the greatest number; and if Doctor Wanion would return in two or three years' time, he would be happy to approve his letter. As an afterthought he said (for every other department of a university is convinced that its medical school is staffed by blood-sucking millionaires): "Why don't you just take up a collection among yourselves?"

When Wanion reported to the chairman of the dean's portrait fund, Tippett immediately called a meeting of his committee. Drumslager had left to spend the Christmas vacation in Florida; Dee was off attending the convention of the Master Plumbers of America; but Carnifex made up the quorum.

Wanion moved that he be reimbursed for expenses occurred in mimeographing his letter. The chairman was partially understood to say that since the letter was not to be used by the committee, he did not see why they should pay for it; and he ruled the motion out of order. Carnifex moved that the sum necessary to have the dean's portrait painted and framed be raised from among their colleagues on the medical Faculty, and that the other medical classes be also invited to make nominal contributions. He himself would open the fund with a cheque for $50. (He had a shrewd idea that his fifty-dollar contribution, while not spurring his colleagues on to emulation, would at least make them squirm as they wrote their own cheques for lesser amounts.) Wanion reluctantly seconded the motion; Tippett reluctantly acceded; and it was carried three to none. The chair appointed Doctor Wanion to call on members of the Faculty and solicit contributions. The committee then adjourned.

Mrs. Nimblewit did have a wire installed direct to her betting commissioner (it was her own money; the dean could wince, but not object), and for the first time since

97

she had followed the ponies, her bookie took a real beating. This was because Wish O'Hoe was passing on to her tips red-hot from Big Pat's outposts of empire, and her success, which meant more to her spiritually than financially, made her even more determined to incorporate this precious source of information into her family.

Her betting coups induced in her such an intolerable air of superiority that the poor dean could hardly stand it. Nimblewit's testimonial portrait she took as a joke, and even his triumphant announcement that it was to cost $2,000 exclusive of frame did not impress her. She told him Major Moon had paid more than that for his portrait of Busby's Pride of Kilsyth's Dick, who was only a Llewellin setter. The dean got so mad at this that each evening after dinner he shut himself up in his study and, for want of anything else to do there, began his textbook on sex for medical students. His first chapter, "The Anatomy of the Sex Organs", was masterful, brilliant. Like many another author, he took the result of the first flush of inspiration as a happy augury of the finished work, and he was so carried away by his beginning that he made the incredible mistake of boasting to his wife that he was writing a book.

Mrs. Nimblewit was impressed. A Llewellin setter might have his portrait painted, but writing a book was a supra-canine achievement. Respectfully she asked what it was about. The dean fatally replied that it was a textbook of sex for medical students. Mrs. Nimblewit laughed until her corsets creaked. Then she asked her husband in a very coarse manner what he thought he knew about sex. Plenty, said the dean with dignity. She said he must have learned it since her day. The dean stalked back to his study and slammed the door behind him. Mrs. Nimblewit followed, and spoke to the closed door for ten minutes.

The dean took his fingers from his ears and held his head between his hands. For he realised to the full now the enormity of his indiscretion. Some instinctive caution had kept him from announcing to any of his colleagues that he was writing a book on sex, and officially he had proceeded no farther in the matter of the students' petition; but telling the Faculty of his pretensions would have been far preferable to telling his wife. He could parry their awkward questions, and they would soon forget the matter in their preoccupation with their own affairs; but his wife would never forget, and her questions could not be parried, and only painfully endured.

His memory stimulated by his wife's commentary, the dean recollected having noticed several books on sex advertised at the back of the *Journal of the American Medical Association*. He picked up the current number from his desk and readily found an advertisement of a *Sex Manual for the Married,* by Philander Foilove, B.A., M.D., D.Sc., LL.D. Foilove's first chapter was entitled "The Organs of Sex", and Nimblewit assumed an air of confidence which the heading of Foilove's second chapter, "The Physiology of Sex", did not dissipate. But as he read down the list of succeeding chapters, the dean was aghast at what the author of a modern book on sex lets himself in for; he could not even read the list of subjects without a rusty blush. He found advertisements for two more books on sex which met the high standards of the A.M.A., and these too dealt with matters that, had he heard of them twenty-five years before, might have changed the course of his married life. Yes; had he had Philander Foilove's manual then . . . For the first time Nimblewit began to see the sense of the students' petition —at the very time he recognised with sinking heart the absolute certainty that he was not the man to reply to it. Nor, thought the dean, groaning aloud in his anguish, was he the man to admit his ignorance: he could see the look in his wife's eyes; hear her ribald laughter as he made his abject confession. . . .

Seizing a sheet of notepaper, Nimblewit wrote the *J.A.M.A.* to send him, c/o the medical school, Foilove's book and the two others on the same shocking subject. As he sealed the envelope, a final qualm shook him. If he, as authors of textbooks on other subjects did, stooped to paraphrase the textbooks of his predecessors, he might fool the medical students, but never his wife.

Mr. Bigginson had finished his preliminary sketches of Fido before the latter and Wish O'Hoe returned to Mercia for Christmas. During the holidays the artist planned to complete the *trompe-l'oeil,* though he felt a little reluctant to do this now, for Fido, before he left, had not only adopted Rembrandt but had been adopted by him. In the dim recesses of Fido's mind, strange thoughts were swimming around like tadpoles in muddy water. Ever since Wish had kicked the helpless nut in the tail, Fido had been inwardly disturbed. Not that Wish had never done nasty things before; merely that Fido, blind with dumb loyalty, had never seen them in that light. When Wish, for example, finagled some instructor into passing him, Fido obscurely felt this to be an unnecessarily clever piece of exhibitionism, much as though he were to skirt the ends and weave his way through the secondary rather than plunge straight through the centre of the line. And when he and Wish wrecked Rufus's car, Fido had placed that act in the same category with the fender-smashing parties wealthy students at Byrlady University indulged in; when the impulse took them, these students rammed their cars into one another's fenders for the innocent pleasure of hearing the crash, which Fido himself liked as much as they. But to kick Lute Becco in the tail was another matter. Fido could not tell why, but whenever he thought of it, he shook his head and rumbled to himself: "That ain't right!"

This heretical feeling was not only new to Fido, but novel to his whole family. Fido's father was one of Big Pat's oldest, most faithful, most unquestioning, and dumbest vassals; and Fido himself was raised to look upon an O'Hoe as a medieval serf upon the lord of the manor.

Thus, when the young lord went off to Byrlady, it was only natural—and prudent—that a loyal vassal's sturdy son of the same age be sent along to accompany him. It was the matter of a phone-call for Big Pat to secure Fido a diploma and certificate from a Mercia high school; and once technically admitted to the university, Fido's size, strength, and prowess in the game of football (which he had learned in Mercia sand-lots while his contemporaries wasted their time on book-learning) had served as the usual *quid pro quo for* intellectual exploits. Fido had been automatically enrolled in whatever courses Wish himself signed up for, and when O'Hoe left Byrlady at the end of three years with a pre-medical education he had obtained less through his own efforts than Big Pat's pious generosity, Fido had followed the young master into medical school with a similar training obtained more by his own battering-ram shoulders and pile-driving legs than Boss O'Hoe's regal charity which covered his son's bodyguard along with his son's sins.

The important thing in the master-slave relationship is not the slave's belief that his master can do no wrong, but rather his conviction that his master has no choice but to be right in whatever he does. Once the slave realises that his master is free to choose between good and evil, their old relationship is irreparably shattered, even though in actual practice the latter never performs a wrong action. When Wish O'Hoe kicked the nut in the tail, Fido at last got the idea which had earlier led to the French Revolution.

When Mr. Bigginson's sojourn with Rufus Crotey began to lengthen out even beyond that time when Vigée-Lebrun's kittens were of sufficient age to be tumbled into the covered basket with their mother and carried off in the Mercedes, the artist began seriously to consider, not deserting his young friend, but rather replenishing his own finances. With Rufus urging her on, Susan Nimble-wit had progressed from asking Rembrandt why he didn't paint her father to assuring him that she would see to it that he did. The artist was transparently touched by the sentiment which made them want him to enjoy this luscious $2,000 plum, but at the same time the man of experience refused to rest his fortunes on such a flimsy hope. Instead, he spent one Saturday morning while Rufus was at the laboratory making certain minute alterations in his pair of dice with a skill Pliny would certainly have celebrated in the 38th chapter of his seventh book. Then he dressed with unusual care, and that evening asked Rufus if he could borrow the Mercedes. Rufus, who had left his now fully-repaired Ford to languish in the garage, so attached had he and Susan become to the Mercedes, which he had surreptitiously caused to be rejuvenated here and there—Rufus looking at the plump, ageing little artist, flushed at his own selfishness and called himself a heel for taking advantage of such appealing innocence. Rembrandt then left him with a wicked wink and drove to the local hotel. There he represented himself to his old antagonists, the local sports, as having been off on a painting trip which had resulted in a bulging bank-roll and a large desire for action. Towards midnight he returned to the apartment with his wallet actually bulging with $730. Rufus had never seen so much money in all his life.

Having cultivated his taste for good food during his years in France, and a good many chins and a monk's paunch in not unsuccessful attempts to satisfy that taste in America, Mr. Bigginson had had enough of the restaurants of Zebulon. In a modest way he was a practitioner of the French cuisine, and he resolved to make his holiday from provincial portrait-painting complete by cooking for himself food fit for human consumption. So he drove down to the shopping district and filled the tonneau of the Mercedes with ingenious electrical appliances, an alcohol-burning chafing-dish, omelette-pan, cast-iron skillet, and assortment of saucepans and pottery casseroles. Then he called at a dry-goods store and bought a voluminous apron and some very large napkins; also some small table-cloths to fit Rufus's folding card-table. From there he went to Zebulon's one fancy grocery (which after Mr. Bigginson finally left town closed its doors, unnoticed and unwept, for want of support), where he bought a staggering amount of exotic tinned goods, imported cheeses, English biscuits, bottled sauces and condiments, and more familiar staples. At the liquor store he laid in a dozen straw-jacketed bottles of Chianti, another dozen of French sauternes, and several bottles of cognac.

When Rufus returned from work that evening, he was overwhelmed as soon as he opened the apartment door by the rich odour of fragrant steams. "Rufus my boy," Mr. Bigginson called from the bedroom, which seemed to be the source of steam and revolution, "go get Susan and bring her back for dinner at seven o'clock. Not a moment before, and not a minute later!"

The astonished Rufus said: "Yes, sir," and backed out of the apartment. He shared his bewilderment with Susan; it was all they could do to wait until the appointed hour. At five minutes to seven they stood together at the head of the underground stairs, gazing at the slow minute-hand of Rufus's watch. As it reached 12, they ran down the steps and burst into the apartment and a mist of tantalising aromas.

The linen-covered card-table was set with three places; the straight wooden chair was drawn up to one of these, and flanked by the two easy chairs; but the first thing they really noticed was the foreign-looking bottle of wine in its jacket of straw. Then Rembrandt Bigginson, enveloped in his apron, appeared from the bedroom with a tray of canapés. Followed wild duck soup with rice (tinned); veal cutlets in casserole in a sauce whose last drop the artist himself pursued with a crust of roll; broccoli; lettuce with oil and vinegar; French pancakes with black raspberry jelly; coffee and brandy. Followed also an inner content which Rufus and Susan had seldom experienced before, and Rembrandt not since he had arrived in Zebulon.

From this time on, Susan deserted her own family to dine nightly with Rembrandt and Rufus. After dinner, Mr. Bigginson settled himself in one of the easy chairs with a pot of coffee, a bottle of cognac, and a good 15-cent cigar, while Rufus and Susan together washed dishes and pots and pans in the bathroom. Rembrandt was an exuberant cook; in the preparation of each meal, no matter how simple or elaborate, he seemed to dirty every utensil in the bedroom wardrobe-cum-kitchen cabinet.

The dean and Mrs. Nimblewit were scandalised by Susan's desertion. Mrs. Nimblewit raised the question of a chaperone; the dean really missed his daughter's company, and looked at her with a face mournful as a hound's. "Cheer up, Daddy," she told him; "you have Mother with you now." And while her parents mixed it up from there, Susan escaped, unnoticed.

Chapter Twelve

NOT LONG AFTER school resumed following the Christmas holidays, Nimblewit summoned Rufus to his office. He went with a guilty conscience, which was not the result of any dereliction of duty. Indeed, for two reasons he knew he was being a good instructor of anatomy: Wilfred gave him his phlegmatic but unqualified approval; and Pietro Spandone, the associate professor, began to pile more and more of his own teaching load on Rufus's willing back. It was really Susan who made Rufus feel so guilty as he answered her father's summons. He had asked her once if the dean minded her having dinner all the time with Rembrandt and himself; she had tersely replied that he did. When the subsequent discussion began to distract them from Mr. Bigginson's Ris de Veau à la Napoli, the artist put an end to it by declaring that he refused to dine without a beautiful woman at the table, and that if Susan abandoned him, he would return to Greek restaurants regardless of the peril to his health and insult to his palate. She retorted that she might abandon him with a qualm, and Rufus without one; but she had no intention of forsaking his cooking. Rufus said he hoped she would prove to have profited by her experience when the time came. He was still smiling fatuously at the memory of her reply when he entered Nimblewit's office, where the dean's fishy eye upon him wiped the smile from his face like Mr. Bigginson removing gravy from his plate with a sop of bread.

"Sit down, my boy," said the dean in a voice like a dose of paregoric.

His eyes protruding at a greeting so unexpectedly kind and gentle, Rufus sat down gingerly on the edge of a chair, and stared at the dean with his mouth partly open, as though he had adenoids or a sudden shock. Nimblewit wondered anew at the incalculable reactions of women, especially those of his own family. He stifled a sigh. "My boy," he said, "I have been distressed to observe your slight difficulty in articulation which I fear, unless corrected, will ultimately interfere with your professional advancement. Fortunately, the psychologic disability under which you labour is one particularly amenable to proper treatment. The welfare of my young instructors has always been especially dear to me. Every Christmas I receive letters from those, many now in responsible positions, whose early footsteps I have been instrumental in guiding. One of these, only the other day, wrote——" Hopelessly off down the wrong turning, the dean stopped short, drew breath, and concluded: "In short, we must cure your stammer."

"B-b-b-but I d-d-d-don't st-st-st——" The expression on Nimblewit's face stopped him. "Ask the st-students," he exploded, "ASK SUSAN!"

The dean waggled his head. "We must do the best we can to clear up your trouble."

"My t-t-trouble?"

"I have already arranged with Doctor Spandone to release you from your duties at three each afternoon, so that Doctor Slipstream——"

"Dean Nimblewit," he interrupted, jumping to his feet and flushing, "I am not a n-n-n-nut."

"My dear boy!"

"And if I am not giving satisfaction in your department," said Rufus, blinking his eyes hard, "my p-p-place is not in a psychiatric w-w-w-ward, b-b-b-but elsewh-wh-where." He turned on his heel and left the office.

Behind him the dean, removing his horn-rimmed glasses, gazed out over High Street; it had not been as bad as he had expected. He had inserted the idea into young Crotey's mind; let it take root there and sprout. A judicious watering of the delicate plant every now and then. . . .

Rufus tried to stifle his feeling of outrage; then, out of respect to Mr. Bigginson's cooking, he did his best to keep it down until dinner was over. But during the Shrimp à la Newburg it burst uncontrollably forth, and he told Rembrandt and Susan of the dean's monstrous suggestion. His tone revealed how much he had been hurt.

"My dear boy!" In his concern, Rembrandt pushed his plate away from him. Susan said nothing; she knew that her father, in common with all his colleagues except Slipstream, O'Shawnessey, and Drubetskoy, either contemned the novel science of psychiatry or else looked upon it as a joke; and she saw as little sense as humour in his uncharacteristic suggestion.

"I couldn't tell him," said Rufus, "I only stammered when I was talking to him—or almost only then. He might have thought I was implying there was something funny about *him*." Susan and Rembrandt couldn't help laughing. "And I don't think that at all. I admire him tremendously, and I'm not just saying that because you're listening, Susan. It was his reputation as an anatomist that made me want to come here in the first place and work under him. It's something to be working under the dean of the medical school himself, too."

"Well, what did you tell Daddy then?" Susan inquired.

"I said to ask you or the students if I stammered." He grinned ruefully. "Only I guess it sounded like I said, 'Ask S-s-s-susan if I st-st-st-stammer.'"

"Bless me!" Rembrandt gasped, wiping his eyes with a napkin. Susan suddenly covered her face with hers.

"It isn't funny."

"It certainly is," she said. "If you can't see it, you'd better consult Doctor Slipstream."

"Oh, so you think I'm nuts too!"

Now Susan was almost as upset over her father's tactlessness as Rufus, and being on edge she took fire from his tone. "Daddy didn't say you were nuts," she retorted; "he said you stammered, and you do."

"I d-d-d-don't!"

"All right. If Daddy does ask me whether you do or not, I'll tell him you d-d-d-don't." She was horrified to hear herself mimic him. It really wasn't Susan doing this, but some inherited devil which should have been exorcised by George Slipstream. Contrite, frightened by his expression, she blundered on, pure nervousness adding a tremor to her voice: "I'm s-s-s-sorry."

Rufus shoved back his chair from the table and rushed out of the apartment. Susan put her head down on her arms and began to cry.

"Children," Rembrandt kept saying, helpless for once. Then as Rufus flung outside: "Susan! Susan, my dear." He patted her on the shoulder, his chins trembling in his distress.

The next afternoon, promptly at three o'clock, Spandone poked his head into the dissecting-room, and beckoned Rufus outside. He was a black-haired, beady-eyed little man, who considered himself the glory of the medical school, indeed of Zebulon University. Though no one else there subscribed to this eccentric notion,

Spandone had a score of well-thumbed press notices which served to prove his own opinion of himself was not unique. Several years before he had done a piece of research on the giant earthworm which had rocked the scientific world. Earthworms are hermaphrodites; that is to say, each worm is a male-female. By means of an incredibly delicate surgical operation, Spandone had succeeded in transposing the worm's gonads, so that a male-female became a female-male. He called this startling phenomenon "metakinesis of sex". He had himself photographed performing the Spandone Operation; then he himself took motion-pictures of the behaviour of his earthworm before and after sexual metakinesis. It was this movie that had made Spandone famous outside and somewhat envied within the walls of Zebulon University. For the first two years following his discovery, he had toured the country showing his movie before conclaves of psychiatrists, who seemed to find the worm's antics particularly significant. One of them told a reporter that Spandone had discovered "an invaluable tool, the fruit of pure fundamental research, with which psychiatry could attack the problems of sex in bewildered, confused and perplexed mankind." When any of his jealous colleagues asked Spandone what place research on fishing worms had in a department of human anatomy, Pietro smiled tolerantly, like Einstein being asked by Professor Dee just how his equation helped in calculating discounts for cash.

"It's three o'clock, Crotey," Spandone said. "The dean thought perhaps you would like to step around to Quackenbush."

"Thank you, sir." Rufus waited for Spandone to leave, so that he could return to the dissecting-room.

"Oh ah, if you see Doctor Slipstream, ask him for me if he wouldn't like to borrow my movie to illustrate his case report."

"I'm afraid——"

"Of course! You've never seen my movie, have you?"

Spandone seized Rufus by the arm, and led him towards his private laboratory, whose blinds were kept perpetually drawn and where a movie projector was kept in instant readiness. "And afterwards, you may read my press cuttings."

That evening Susan dined at home. Her mother asked her if she hadn't liked the *carte de jour* at her other boarding-house. Susan's eyes misted; she smiled tremulously. Mrs. Nimblewit had been saying cutting things to her husband for so many years that when she wanted, truly, to tell her daughter she was happy to have her at their table again, her tongue refused to obey her heart. The diplomatic dean said nothing, but secretly he congratulated himself that his scheme was bearing magnificent early fruit. At the first intimation that Rufus was about to become a psychiatrist's patient, Susan had retreated for a second thought: no girl likes to think her young man is officially labelled nuts.

Susan trimmed a bit off her pork chop, picked up the morsel of meat in her fingers, and held it down for Vigée-Lebrun. Two tears formed in her eyes, and rolled slowly down her cheeks. The dean's conscience smote him, and for a weak moment he almost hoped Crotey might become Slipstream's first successful case—successful, that is to say, in the vulgar rather than psychiatric sense of the word.

True to his threat, when Susan deserted him Rembrandt Bigginson exchanged his cook's apron for the paint-encrusted smock, abandoned his saucepans for his palette and brushes; and began the portrait of Fido gazing out from a painted mirror frame. He was hurt that Fido had not called on him immediately after the Christmas recess, and painting the *trompe-l'oeil* was his way of expressing his disappointment.

What had happened to Fido was this: on New Year's Eve Wish O'Hoe had got fighting drunk as usual

(Wish prided himself on being able to hold his liquor like a southern gentleman). This was generally safe enough, since the sight of his bodyguard looming behind him was sufficient to calm down most of Wish's opponents, and Fido's great hand held restrainingly against their chests pacified the rest. But on New Year's Eve Wish picked his fight with a drunk as belligerent as himself; and the latter had a bodyguard quite as large and formidable as Fido. So while the two bodyguards were joyously slugging it out, the drunk gave Wish O'Hoe a terrific beating. After receiving emergency treatment in the Mary Margaret MacSweeny O'Hoe Memorial Hospital, Wish had remained in seclusion at home for a week until his beauty had been somewhat restored; and Fido kept him company.

As a matter of fact, the first thing Fido did on the evening of his return to the medical school was to drive one of the bullet-proof black Buicks to Rembrandt's apartment. The artist and Rufus were just back from their meal at a Greek restaurant, where Mr. Bigginson ate as though he feared every mouthful were poison, and Rufus as though he hoped so.

"Hullo, Rembrandt," Fido rumbled; "hullo, doc; hullo, V.J.; hullo, Kaufman." He turned to hang his hat on its usual rack, then automatically stooped down to retrieve it from the floor; but Mr. Bigginson had screwed a pair of genuine brass coat-hooks in their proper places on the painted wall-rack, and Fido's hat remained where he had placed it. Fido looked as astonished at this phenomenon as though someone had repealed the law of gravity. He retreated as far as he could go, and when he was brought up short by the opposite wall, turned round to find himself looking into an elaborately framed mirror. And the image which was reflected back at him was wearing a pork-pie hat.

"Da!" he said. He swivelled round and stared at the pork-pie hat hanging sedately on the wall-rack. He pivoted and stared at the Fido in the mirror wearing the identical hat on his head. Then he began to twist his neck in semi-circles, looking first at one hat, then at the other, until Rembrandt and Rufus grew dizzy watching him. At last he pulled out his handkerchief and wiped the perspiration from his forehead, and the delighted artist could follow on his expressive face the ponderous working of his brain: first the dim idea that the handkerchief should have met with some obstruction on his brow; then the puzzled wonder why it did not; the realisation that he was hatless; the sudden inspired grasp of the real situation. Fido moved his head back and forth before his immobile reflection in the mirror. He stuck out his tongue, made a horrible grimace, wiggled his ears; then rubbed his hand over the painted face which stared at him as though it deplored his antics and disdained to repeat them.

"Da," said Fido to Rembrandt with a grin of relief, "you almost had me fooled there for a minute."

"Did you have a good vacation, Fido?" the artist asked.

"I sure did. I hadda fight."

"Bless me!"

"Aw, the guy was bigger'n me."

"Why, bless me!" Rembrandt gasped. "It must have been like the fight between Pantagruel and Loupgarou."

"Naw, his name was Gus."

"Hey, Fido," said Rufus, "you mean you wouldn't fight a guy smaller than you?"

"I'll tell you, doc. I certainly wouldn't fight him, but I'll hit him if I gotta. I mean, if I'm on duty, see?"

"When are you off duty?"

"As soon as Wish gets his M.D." Fido's brow furrowed. "Say, doc, lemme ask you somethin'."

"Sure."

"D' you think it's right to kick a nut in the tail?"

Rufus started. Since the dean had made his infamous suggestion, he was allergic to the word "nut". "Who wants to kick me in the tail?" he demanded, flushing with temper. "Wish O'Hoe?"

"You don't unnerstand, doc. Wish has already kicked the nut in the tail."

"I'll bet someone was holding him."

"I was," said Fido simply.

"Bless me!" said Mr. Bigginson.

"I was oney tryin' to make him gimme back Doc Slipstream's nose he bit off," he said apologetically.

"Rufus," said the artist faintly, "my cognac!" Shakily he poured himself a tumbler of cognac and sipped it, his shudders gradually subsiding; for he was a rather squeamish man. "Speaking of noses," he said when he had sufficiently calmed his nerves, "I'd like to paint a green-rumped horse-fly on the nose of the Chouse."

"On Doc Chouse's nose?" Fido asked, puzzled.

"On the nose of his portrait, the saboteur."

"I get it," Fido announced. He was by way of becoming an authority on *trompe-l'oeil,* not of course as a *trompeur,* but as one of the trompees. "Doc tries to brush the horse-fly off his schnozzola," here Fido made shooing motions with a great hand, "and—WOW!" He burst into deep bass chuckles. "Let's us do it, Rembrandt, huh? How about it, doc?"

To Rufus this smacked of unprofessional conduct towards a colleague; he hesitated. "Where's Suze?" Fido suddenly demanded.

"Susan," Rembrandt remarked with a sympathetic glance at Rufus's stiffened features, "is honouring us for the nonce with her absence."

"I get it," said Fido, after a diagnostic look at Rufus's face. "Suze ain't doc's girl no more." He smiled happily, got up, pulled his hat from its hook, and left the apartment. But a moment later he thrust an apologetic face through the half-open door. "So long, Rembrandt; so long, doc; so long, V.J.; so long, Kaufman."

With Wish and Doc Crotey both out of the running, Fido had figured to make a play for Suze himself.

Chapter Thirteen

TO THE UNIVERSAL astonishment of Zebulon University (and with consternation in several quarters of it), Fido's play for Dean Nimblewit's daughter was immediately and spectacularly successful. Strangely neglectful of his duties as Wish's bodyguard, he began to squire Susan to movies, basket-ball games, boxing-matches, and social functions.

The dean was in a quandary. Having contrived by a master-stroke to detach his daughter from a paraphrenic, he saw her immediately attach herself to an idiot savant. And there was no use thinking of sending Fido to Slip-stream; in their encounter three years before it had been the psychiatrist who was routed. Nor was the dean any happier in his passages with Susan. When he slyly brought the conversation around to Fido's background and lack of culture and social graces, she had retorted: "Well, then, why did you ever admit him to your medical school?"

(Everyone knew it had been under pressure from the chancellor, who had had the finger put on him by one of the trustees of the university, high in Democratic councils; but only his daughter had ever been gauche enough to ask the dean this embarrassing question.)

"Besides," she said, opening her eyes very wide, "Fido is so big and strong."

The dean paled; he had recalled parts of the three books by Doctors Foilove, Letcher, and Dildo respectively, which he was now engaged in studying. The siren of the bullet-proof sedan wailed outside; Susan grabbed up her fur coat, blew a kiss to her parents, and ran off.

"Poochie," said Mrs. Nimblewit. The dean closed his eyes, but when he re-opened them, his wife was still there. "You certainly loused that up," she said.

"I have done the best I could," he said with dignity. "It is hardly my fault that your daughter inherits a taste for low company." He escaped into his study and slammed its door before she could think of a fitting reply; and resumed his work on "The Physiology of Sex." He was finding this second chapter hard, but not impossible going.

As soon as the shock brought on by Fido's treacherous behaviour allowed him to remonstrate, Wish O'Hoe cursed him one night in their joint room in the fraternity house for having stolen his girl.

"Suze says she ain't your girl, Wish," Fido rumbled. "She ain't doc's girl either. She's mine."

"The hell she is! You stay away from her, Fido, you hear me?"

"I couldn't do that, Wish," said Fido, shaking his head.

"I'll tell my old man on you."

"That ain't right, Wish." Thought wrinkled his forehead as he sought to explain why. "If a girl thinks a guy is a nasty little rectus abdominis," he said at last, "he shouldn't ought to sing to his old man about it."

"Who called me that?" Wish yelled furiously. "Suze?"

"Naw," said Fido, shaking his head again. She had, in fact, miscalled Wish a rectus abominalis, and Love was teaching Fido cunning; and since he had never been known to tell a lie, Wish was forced to believe him.

"Well, I warn you, Fido," he blustered, "you stay away from her if you know what's good for you."

Fido merely shook his head, and began to unlace his size 15 shoes.

The next day Wish dropped into the anatomical laboratory to have a word with Crotey. A politician always prefers to have a double motive for his actions, and the son of Patrick Aloysius O'Hoe was engaged in mending his fences for that final Faculty meeting, now only four months away, at which the medical degrees were to be voted. At the beginning of the session in September he had grossly antagonised Crotey (needlessly, as it turned out); he had smashed his Ford (although he had paid for its repair); and it was now high time to offer the hand of friendship and alliance. As his second motive Wish had in mind enlisting Crotey's support in separating Fido from Susan Nimblewit. In O'Hoe's view, any reasonable man would prefer to see his girl in Wish's arms rather than Fido's, and he had not often found the medical Faculty of Zebulon University unreasonable.

"Hi, Rufe," he said after he had called the instructor into the corridor, "got a few minutes to waste?"

Rufus found himself in a sudden dilemma. It was an impertinence not silently to be borne for a student to hail an instructor thus freely and easily; but on the other hand, he remembered his own student days when nothing disgusted him more than a shirty young instructor. He avoided the difficulty by saying: "Hi, Wish," which established a factitious sort of intimacy and drew the fangs of O'Hoe's familiarity. He added, not too cordially, "Come over to my office."

"Have a cigarette, Rufe," said Wish after plopping down uninvited in the best chair. He held out a silver cigarette-case. "They're made especially for me by John Middleton."

"Thanks," said Rufus. Wish asked him how he liked it. "Okay," he said.

"I'll have a dozen tins sent down to you, then."

"Thanks all the same; I'm too used to Camels to change."

Wish shrugged. "Have a good Christmas?"

"Quiet. You?"

"Holy Mother of God! The only time I was quiet was once I passed out on the second fifth. On New Year's Eve Fido and I had a hell of a fight with a couple of drunks. Did I give my man a beating! He added candidly: "I'll admit he marked me before I laid him out, but you ought to have seen him. I've seen better-looking guys than him on one of your stone slabs."

"How'd Fido make out?"

Wish scowled. "He and his man only patted at each other like they were dabbing their faces with powder-puffs. To tell you the truth, Fido's beginning to get a little above himself."

"Fido's a good guy."

Wish gave a mirthless laugh. "Suze thinks he's a better man than you and me, anyway."

"We won't talk about Susan, if you don't mind," said Rufus shirtily.

"Well, if you see her, tell her Fido's old man works for the garbage department back home."

"Yeah; she told me he did. Well, I've got to get back to work now. Anything else on your mind?"

"Well, no," said Wish, "except I heard from one of the boys up home that Scabiosa is a cinch in the fifth at Hialeah tomorrow. I'll give my bookie a ring, and have him put a sawbuck on the nose for you——"

"No, thanks." This sounded insufferably prissy, so Rufus went on with a grin: "This long after pay-day I haven't got ten bucks left."

"No need to put up any dough."

"No, th——"

"It's a sure thing, I tell you."

"I never bet on a sure thing," said Rufus. "I like a 50–50 chance. As Mrs. Boone said when she saw her husband fighting the bear: 'Oh Lord, if you can't help Dan'l, please don't help the b'ar.'"

He repeated the non-Susan part of this conversation to Mr. Bigginson later. At first Rufus was completely puzzled why Wish O'Hoe should be sucking up to him, but all at once the reason dawned. "Rembrandt!" he exclaimed. "Wish thinks I've got a vote in Faculty meeting; he doesn't know instructors can't vote."

"Bless me," said the artist, "I believe you must be right. Rufus my boy, the scoundrel has been delivered into your hands. Tomorrow you must summon young O'Hoe, indicate to him that you have had a change of heart about the dozen tins of custom-tailored cigarettes; and incidentally you may take this opportunity to hint that you are fond of smoking imported corona-coronas after dinner; and ask him if he has anything hot on the day's races. If he has, do not allow him to bet less than fifty dollars for you. With proper handling, my boy, young O'Hoe will support us in luxury until the Faculty meeting you speak of. After that meeting it will be necessary to inform him that you never possessed a vote. That will teach him," said Mr. Bigginson righteously, "to attempt to bribe an honest man."

"That ain't right," said Rufus, shaking his head.

"Indeed it is not; and we might impress the extent of his wrong-doings upon him by asking from time to time whether he has anything really good from the Morgan feed-box too."

"I mean, it wouldn't be right for *me*."

"Bless me," said Rembrandt feebly. Then he went on, his voice growing stronger and stronger until at the end it was quivering with the force of his indignation: "Rufus, do you mean to imply that I, Rembrandt Bigginson, would counsel you to do anything unworthy, immoral, or illegal?"

"Yes, sir."

"Well, then," said the artist, mollified. "I trust the elder O'Hoe has a better taste in cigars than most of the politicians I have painted. By the way, Rufus, I wish you would run a small errand for me this evening."

Rufus nodded; he was pathetically eager for anything at all to help fill the evenings which yawned so emptily ever since Susan's disappearance. Being young, he did not have Mr. Bigginson's inner resources (memories of a gloriously mis-spent life), nor could he while away hours playing with Vigée-Lebrun, her four tumbling kittens, and Angelika Kauffmann, the white mouse.

"I wish you to take Susan her kitten."

"But—well—all right." Rufus had the air of an errand-boy being asked to deliver a pound of steak to Mrs. Jones.

Mr. Bigginson got his largest pottery casserole, lined

and padded it with linen napkins, grumbling audibly the whole time. "I suppose we won't need this any more. I suppose we'll never use these again." Then he placed the round-eyed fluffy red kitten into the casserole, kissed him on his pink nose, bade him be a good cat, cleared his throat gruffly, and told Rufus to be sure and tell Susan his name was Bamboots.

When Rufus had taken himself off with Bamboots en casserole, Mr. Bigginson lighted a cigar, and sank down in his easy chair with a sigh. If Rufus chose to act like a red-haired man, and Susan like a woman, he thought it was high time a little kitten should bring them together again. Besides, he was getting heartily tired of restaurant food. Vigée-Lebrun sprang on his lap and settled down, purring. Her three remaining kittens, whose names were Botticelli, Gaddo Gaddi, and Marietta Tintoretta, scrambled all over him, playing hide-and-seek; and the white mouse took refuge from them within the gaping front of the artist's smoking-jacket.

Rufus rang the Nimblewits' door-bell. The dean himself opened the door. "Good-evening, sir," Rufus stammered. "Is Susan in?"

"No," said the dean bitterly; "she is not."

This was a contingency the astute Mr. Bigginson should have anticipated. Rufus thrust the casserole containing the Persian kitten into Nimblewit's hands and said: "Will you p-p-please g-g-give her this when she comes in, s-s-sir? His n-n-name is B-b-b-b—BAMBOOTS."

Five minutes later he was back home. Rembrandt lifted his eyebrows in surprise. "Susan wasn't there," Rufus explained. "I left the kitten with her father."

"*Merde!*" said Mr. Bigginson.

Meanwhile, Susan was out with Fido. While on a date with him, she did not look upon him as a dope with a genius for medicine, but rather as an extraordinarily intelligent dog. Viewed in this light, Fido was splendid company, and her father's reproaches were as irrevelant as though one were to complain that a Great Dane did not bark according to the rules of grammar, and could not tell a Bigginson from a Rembrandt. Indeed, Fido talked less than a Great Dane barked. He was content to look at Susan, and wag his tail whenever she looked at him. Often enough in the past, the star full-back of Byrlady and the revelling companion of Wish O'Hoe had not been satisfied with so little from a girl-friend; and Fido did not altogether understand his present novel feeling for Suze. It somehow reminded him of his sensations when he accompanied Wish to High Mass; Fido was a Protestant, as the Mamelukes were Christians.

Susan herself could not help feeling slightly uncomfortable at treating Fido like a dog and using him like a man—or was it the other way round? Anyway, it was all the fault of Rufus's temper. And he did stammer. "Fido," she asked, "what makes people stammer?"

In his slurred amiable voice Fido succinctly epitomised the various theories of the causation of stammering.

"Well, suppose a person stammers only when he's talking to a certain other person. In that case, what's the best thing to do?"

"The best thing to do," said Fido superbly, "is da for the guy never to talk to the other guy no more."

She gazed up at him, speechless with admiration. "Fido," she said at last, "you're a genius. Doctor Slipstream would never in this world have thought of that."

"Psychiatrists," said Fido, "they're dopes."

Chapter Fourteen

CEDRIC OSBERT DEE was giving a party. The guest of honour was his old friend, the eminent artist, W. C. Tarbush; but the guests of equal or greater importance were Doctors Carnifex, Tippett, Drumslager, and Wanion, for at least two of these had to be convinced that Mr. Tarbush was the answer to a portrait committee's prayer. Dee was already convinced.

Tarbush was tall, leathery, and lugubrious. He alone was not wearing a dinner-jacket, perhaps because he thought the black-and-white uniform less artistic than his fawn-coloured spats, Tattersall waistcoat, and flowing Windsor tie; perhaps because Dee had suggested that he try to look as much like an artist as possible. If this be interpreted to mean dressing unlike everybody else, and looking very unhappy over it, Tarbush had perfectly fulfilled his instructions. Those doctors who had got the idea from tales of Beaux Arts balls and *La Vie Parisienne* that painters were cheerful fellows and gay dogs, had to revise their opinions hurriedly in the face of Tarbush's solemn countenance, measured words, and mournful accent. There was no Latin Quarter frivolity about him; anyone could see that Tarbush took his calling most seriously, and would no more joke about losing a commission than a physician about losing a patient.

Willoughby Chouse, keeping the conversation on an artistic level, said he himself had recently had his portrait painted by Rembrandt Bigginson. Smoothing his moustache, he waited for the expected tribute from a brother-painter.

"Never heard of 'im," said Tarbush heavily.

Chouse deflated like a punctured rubber glove: Tarbush's stock went up noticeably among the administration men. Someone put in maliciously: "And he paid him fifteen hundred dollars for it, too."

"That include supplies?" Tarbush asked, with a glimmer of animation. "Or labour alone?"

Dee laughed loudly, clapped his old friend heartily on the back of the neck, and dragged him away to meet the dean. "By the way, Tarbush," he remarked to the artist after the preliminaries were over, "you'll be interested to hear that Doctor Nimblewit is to have his portrait painted as a testimonial from his many friends and admirers."

The dean modestly looked off into the distance. "Is that so?" said Tarbush.

"By the way, Tarbush," Dee said, "if you were painting the dean, how would you do it?"

Tarbush stepped back, half closed his eyes, and considered the self-conscious dean with grave deliberation. All the other guests crowded around in a respectful circle, eager to watch an artist in the throes of creation. "I'd paint 'im on a 36 by 54 canvas," he said at last, "stretched with a centre brace across the back made up with half-inch flanges, close nipples, ells, and——"

"I mean, how would you pose him?" his sponsor cut in.

Tarbush scraped his leathery chin with a horny palm. "Any way he likes."

"I have been unable to make up my own mind, Mr. Tarbush," said the dean. "Academic robes are of course *de rigueur,* but whether or not to wear the cap—— What do you think, sir?"

"Well, I'll tell you," said the artist. "It all depends." He spoke in such portentous tones that the heads encircling him nodded as one. "Some prefer it one way, some likes it another. Just like," he once more became slightly animated, "some likes brass, some galv——" Dee gave a hacking cough, and Tarbush hastily concluded: "It all depends."

Drumslager managed to catch Wanion's eye, and a glance of understanding passed between them. This interloping artist was getting along altogether too well, and it behoved each of them to forget for a moment his own pet painter, and combine forces against a formidable rival. So Drumslager seized the dean by the arm and asked him how he had made out with A.T.; and Wanion placed himself in front of Tarbush and asked him what he, as an artist, thought of the architecture of Zebulon University. The rest of the company also broke up into small groups, and began to talk shop.

"Well, I'll tell you," said Tarbush. "I've had some

experience with old buildings, and I can tell you it's a job to install modern fix——"

"Excuse me, Albert," said Dee, grabbing the artist by the sleeve. "I want Tarbush to have a little chat with Ashby." With this he led him over to where the professor of urology was holding forth to Tippett and Furbelow.

". . . so I flushed it out," the urologist was saying, "with warm saline."

"Damn plumber!" Furbelow snorted.

Dee threw an affectionate arm around his old friend's neck. "Ho, ho, ho," he laughed. "No doubt you know, Tarbush, that urologists are facetiously termed plumbers?" He removed his arm with a final friendly squeeze of the artist's wind-pipe, and Tarbush stretched his neck cautiously, like a rooster swallowing an over-size grain of corn.

"No," he croaked, "I didn't know that."

"And they call plumbers, urologists," said Furbelow, trying to get a rise out of his colleague.

"I'd just like to hear 'em once," said Tarbush.

"Excuse me, gentlemen," said Dee, hauling him away. "I'd like Tarbush to have a little chat with Doctor Carnifex."

"He'd diagnosed it as branch-bundle block," the hospital pathologist was telling the old professor of surgery, "but when I opened him up, there was a lesion on the mitral valve."

Tarbush had been in time to hear the last words; his lugubrious expression lightened. "I'll tell you," he said confidentially, "I don't find any of them new types stand up like the good old globe or gate va——"

"All these medical terms must be very confusing to a poor artist, eh, Tarbush?" Dee cut in. "You'll have to get us doctors off in your studio some day and bombard us with—with terms of art, like—uh——"

"Chiaroscuro?" Carnifex suggested.

"Light, shadow, colour," said Dee, looking annoyed. "Patina."

"Litharge and glycerine," said Tarbush.

When the other guests had departed, Dee said to the artist, who was spending the night with him before returning to his home up north: "Well, we can't expect anything from Drumslager and Wanion, but you made quite an impression on Tippett and old Carnifex."

"Two thousand, ain't it, doc?" the artist said.

"Split two ways."

"Well, I'll tell you," said Tarbush heavily. "I been thinking. When I made the deal with you up at the convention, I didn't figure it would cost me so much in expenses, like this here trip for example and keep me out of the shop so long. I figured on doing the work Saturday afternoons and Sundays, like I done the picture of Shorty Mannis—you ever met Shorty, doc? Best man with a suction pump in Mercia. The boys up there asked me to do it as a special favour."

"How much did you get for it?"

"Cost plus fifty."

"Per cent?"

"Bucks. You got to remember it was a union job. When those fellows I met tonight carve each other up," Tarbush said shrewdly, "they get special rates too, don't they?"

"Well, I'm president of the Zebulon Plumbing and Heating Company."

"That ain't the same thing as being a union man. I'll tell you, doc. I'll do it for sixty per cent of the gross, and supply my own materials and helper."

"What do you mean, helper?"

"Pardon me; just a slip of the tongue. Sixty per cent of the gross," he repeated, "or no dice."

"Fifty per cent," said Dee, "or I'll get another artist."

After haggling most of the night, they finally agreed to split the difference.

The testimonial portrait of the dean was to be ceremoniously unveiled and officially presented to the medical school during Finals Week in June: and time was passing. Ashby Tippett called a meeting of his committee to receive a report on, and if necessary speed up, progress.

Drumslager announced that he had already collected $335 from the senior class. Dee said that 58 times 5 was only $290, and he looked at Drumslager as though accusing him of under-handedly making up the difference from his own pocket. Denying the insinuation, Drumslager explained that O'Hoe had contributed $55, $50 for himself and $5 for his bodyguard. Furthermore, Drumslager's agents had collected $136 from the freshman class, $126 from the sophomores, and $122 from the juniors, making a total from the entire student body of $719.

"Bzmbzm Bzmbzm?"

After an embarrassed preamble, Wanion confessed that the sum of contributions from the medical faculty still stood at fifty dollars. Immediately Drumslager and Dee jumped on him for lying down on the job. Wanion feebly defended himself, but was finally stung into retorting: "All right. I'm open to contributions from you gentlemen right now."

"I haven't got my cheque-book with me," they said.

"Bzm bzmbzmbzm—ER—bzmbzm," Tippett again took control of the proceedings.

"I agree, Ash," said Drumslager. "It is time to choose the artist. I'm sure Albert will have the money for him when the time comes."

In the course of the ensuing discussion, it appeared that Drumslager had found the ideal painter, whom, however, he neglected to identify as his cousin; Tippett knew just the man, who he quite forgot to mention was his nephew; Wanion had discovered the perfect artist in a Miss Thirkill, though he decided not to reveal that as the name of his wife's aunt; and of course Dee advanced the claims of Mr. W. C. Tarbush, who had already made such a favourable impression on the committee. Only Doctor Carnifex had no artist of his own, and he didn't count; that is to say, even with Carnifex voting for any one of the four proposed painters, that artist would then receive only a maximum vote of two, or one less than was democratically necessary to clinch the commission.

The impasse was complete. If none of the four committee members could have his own artist, all would be damned rather than vote for a colleague's. Carnifex moved that the dean himself be empowered to select his own portrait-painter. The vote on this motion was a grudging 5–0, and the committee adjourned.

Once more the committee-men passed by Nimblewit's office in single file, a long space between each. The chairman, last in line, stopped to inform the dean of his committee's decision.

"This is what always happens, Ashby," Nimblewit grumbled. "Whenever you people can't decide anything for yourselves, you dump the matter into my lap, and wash your hands of it."

"Well, just between ourselves, Mr. Dean," said Tippett, making an effort and filling his voice with sympathy and sound, "the members of my committee have let us both down—ER—in passing the buck to you. As chairman, I am—ER—prepared to take the burden off your shoulders. I am well acquainted with a rising young painter——"

"Fortunately, Ashby," the dean interrupted, "I need not presume upon your kindness. I have a painter already in mind."

That evening at home, Nimblewit could not forbear to boast that he had once more had his own way. A dean leads a lonely life, after all, and never more so than when he is celebrating a triumph over his Faculty. Except during the annual convention of deans, when they may safely boast to one another of their victories over their colleagues back home, a dean has either to bottle up his triumphs within his own breast (which is contrary to human nature), or else to parade them in the bosom of his own family (which, when one's wife is Gloriana Nimblewit, is contrary to horse sense).

"Indeed?" she remarked at the conclusion of her husband's tale. "I must ring up Major Moon at once."

"What for?" the dean rashly inquired.

"To learn the name of the artist who painted Dick."

"Who's Dick, Mother?" Susan asked curiously, pausing in her romp with the red Persian kitten her father had given her, along with a sermon, the night before.

"Thank you, Pussy," said the dean, "but I have already chosen my own painter."

"Who is he, Daddy?" Susan asked. She had not forgotten her promise to Rembrandt Bigginson, but she knew better than to advance his candidacy in this atmosphere.

"His name is Geoffrey Lanyard," said Nimblewit, "and he was my best friend at college. When I went off to medical school, Geoffrey went abroad to study art. We used to see a good bit of one another before I married. You never did like Geoffrey, did you, Gloriana?" he said bitterly.

"He was a bum!"

"My best friend," said the dean dramatically, "and my wife calls him a bum!"

"Well, do you know what he called me, Poochie?"

"Not before Susan!"

"So you see, Susan," the dean continued to his daughter, "outside of getting a Christmas card from Geoffrey every year, and sending him one, we've lost touch. But he was—is, a fine painter, and he's the man I want to do my portrait."

"Why, that's really awfully sweet of you, Daddy," she said, touched by his lasting attachment to the friend of his youth. And her heart sank as she recognised that Geoffrey Lanyard had a sort of moral mortgage on her father's face, and that the lovable Rembrandt Bigginson was just out of luck.

"Bah," said Mrs. Nimblewit. Turning her back on this sentimental scene, she went off to telephone. Five minutes later she returned, crowing with laughter. As soon as she could speak, she gasped: "That was Major Moon I was talking to just now. And what do you think is the name of the artist who painted Busby's Pride of Kilsyth's Dick? Geoffrey Lanyard!" she shrieked. "Geof—frey Lan—yard!"

"Who is Busby's Pride of Kilsyth's Dick, Mother?" Susan demanded.

"A Llewellin setter. Geoffrey Lanyard is an *animal* painter! Oh, Poochie, loose my corset or I'll die!"

Chapter Fifteen

THE DEAN HAD fled to his study; Susan was loosening her mother's corsets; when Fido sounded his siren outside. "Mother," she said, "I'm going out. Will you take care of my kitten for me until I come back? I won't be late."

"Wah wow wuh woo!"

"Really, Mother," said Susan disapprovingly, "it isn't all that funny."

"Wuh woo wow wah!" Mrs. Nimblewit waved Susan towards the door in sign she might safely leave her kitten and father to her tender mercies. Susan slipped into her fur coat, picked up the casserole in which her kitten had been served up to her, and left the house.

"Hullo, Suze," Fido rumbled from within the Buick. Susan slid in beside him and said:

"Take me over to Rembrandt's."

As she had once told Rufus, Fido was a superb driver, for whom, thanks to his official status, even stop-lights held no inhibitions. He pulled up before Rembrandt's house (by now even Rufus felt and acted as though he were the artist's guest) before she had time to arrange in her mind what she was going to say to Rufus.

She knocked on the apartment door, and Mr. Biggin-son called out: "Come in, Susan; come in!" The light from the ground-level windows shone out directly on the legs of whoever approached; and Susan's legs were unique in Zebulon. "And Fido too, bless me!"

Then Susan and Fido were inside the apartment, blinking in some embarrassment, for they felt they had shamefully deserted their old friend. The artist held out a plump hand to each of them. "Bless me! I thought I should be having to leave town without telling you goodbye."

"Hullo, Rembrandt," said Fido, pumping his hand. "Hullo, V.J.; hullo, babies; hullo—Aw, Rembrandt, you ain't goin'?" he rumbled in delayed consternation. "Aw, Rembrandt—where's doc?"

"Rufus has gone to the movies," said Mr. Bigginson, injecting a walloping dose of pathos into his voice. "I'm a lonely old man, my dear Susan and Fido, and I'm off to the stews of New Orleans, by which I think I mean the bouillabaisse."

"But you can't leave now," Susan cried; "you have to paint my father!"

"You can't go, Rembrandt," Fido protested in turn. "We ain't painted the fly on Doc Chouse's nose!"

"Hrrmph, hrrmph." Mr. Bigginson took the napkin folded inside the forgotten casserole Susan was still holding and blew his nose. "Hrrmph."

"I'll come over and cook for you, so you won't have to eat in Greek restaurants any more," she offered.

"And you can draw my pitcher," said Fido.

"Bless me. Hrrmph." He collected himself and went on: "Sit down, Susan my dear; sit down, Fido. Have a cigarette. These are rather special."

"They look like Wish's brand," said Fido.

"He has presented Rufus with a dozen tins. I think, Susan, you once under-estimated that estimable young man."

"You mean, he ain't a rectus abdominis?" Fido asked.

"Rectus abominalis," Susan corrected.

"Without knowing the terms of Rufus's art," said Rembrandt, "I would term him a *rectum equinus*. Do you really think, Susan, you can get me that commission to paint your father? Two thousand dollars, is it not?"

"According to Daddy, that's how much the committee has appropriated. And they've left the choice of painter up to him. If he doesn't pick you, Rembrandt, I'll—I'll threaten to marry Fido."

A minute later this bomb-shell exploded in Fido's brain. "Who, me?" he cried out in alarm. "Aw hey, Suze! I couldn't get married, Suze. My mamma and my old man got married, and looka what happened to them."

"What?"

"Da," he said in disgust, "they had me."

"And I'm very glad they did, too," said Susan. "At present Daddy hasn't anyone in mind," she went on to Rembrandt, "and you can be sure he won't agree to any of the friends and relatives his professors are trying to palm off on him. He had been planning to have an old friend of his paint him, but it turned out that Geoffrey Lanyard——"

"Geoffrey Lanyard! Bless me!"

"Why, do you know him?"

"Know him! My dear Susan, he was once my dearest friend. Before the Great War Geoff and I spent a number of years in Paris together, studying art and hrrmph life. But we quarrelled at last," he ended on a melancholy note.

"Oh dear, what about?"

"I had bought the first of my Persian cats, a beautiful silver-grey named Watteau——"

Fido had been following Mr. Bigginson's tale with close attention. He now interrupted it with: "He musta been an English cat, Rembrandt, not a Persian."

"How do you figure that out?"

"I seen an English movie once. Wot 'o," said Fido. "Watto!"

"What ho!" said Mr. Bigginson politely. "Well, Geoff refused to live in the same flat with a cat. Dear old Geoff, how he hated animals!"

Susan said, puzzled: "But Mother says he's an animal-painter."

"Why not?" said Rembrandt bitterly. "My dear child, people will cheerfully pay several thousand dollars to have a picture painted of some blue-beribboned pooch, or some fugitive from a glue factory or packing-house, when they wouldn't spend as many hundreds to have their wives painted, or alternatively their husbands. In his day Paulus Potter got more for painting a cow than Jan Steen for painting a man. Landseer got more for painting Fido than Alfred Stevens for——"

"Who, me?" said Fido, pointing to himself.

"But, Rembrandt, you can paint animals too," said Susan. "Look at your *trompe-l'oeil* of Vigée-Lebrun."

"Vigée is my cat. Personally, I dislike all other animals than my own, and I abhor all other cat-lovers than myself. I'd rather eat a bull than paint him, and I'm not sure I wouldn't say the same thing about a horse."

"I could eat a horse myself," said Fido. "What say we go down to the station restaurant for a steak and French fries? On me."

"Well, I don't know," said Susan. She really wanted to see Rufus, and in her indecision twisted Mr. Bigginson's casserole around in her hands, which reminded her of the ostensible reason for her visit. "I don't know what's the matter with me, Rembrandt," she exclaimed; "waiting until now to tell you I simply adore Bamboozle."

"Who?"

"Bamboo——" Her voice faltered. "Anyway, that's what Daddy told me Rufus said his name was."

"Bamboots, my dear; Bamboots. Bamboots was the name of an old Dutch painter. Or, to be precise, it was his nickname, like Fido——"

"Who, me?"

"Well, Fido is not your official patronymic or cognomen, is it?"

"Rembrandt means, Fido's not your real name," said Susan.

"Da course not. They call me Fido on account of when they call Fido, I always come."

"That's just the way it was with Bamboots," said Rembrandt.

"Will you thank Rufus for bringing me the kitten?" she asked him. "And here's your casserole; you might need it again."

Mr. Bigginson sighed gustily. "No; I'll never fill it again with veal cutlets, cooked slowly between layers of thin-sliced potatoes, onion rings, fresh mushrooms, and the smallest tenderest carrots, in a thick sauce containing the Pythagorical number of capers; no, Susan my dear, I should only see your lovely fresh young face through vapours redolent of past *soupers à trois,* and drop a tear into the gravy—hrrmph, hrrmph—where the hell was I?"

"You were feeling very sorry for yourself; and trying to make me feel like a heel."

"Did I succeed?"

"You did, my ham-in-casserole," she said, kissing him. "Tell Rufus I'm truly sorry."

"Why, I was just about to whip up an omelette."

She hesitated. "What kind?"

"Since you deserted me, I'm afraid I've allowed my cupboard to get bare as Mother Hubbard's. I can only offer you the choice of a Spanish, cheese, or jelly omelette," said Mr. Bigginson apologetically. "I only prepare breakfast here, and lunch on occasion, and now and then a *bonne bouche* at midnight."

"But you've given up cooking," said Susan ironically.

"My dear young lady," said Rembrandt with dignity; "I've given up dining."

Susan blushed. "I think a jelly omelette would be lovely," she said in a small voice.

When Rufus returned from his movie, he walked in upon Susan seated at the card-table between Rembrandt and Fido, and only a yellow crumb of egg and red smear of jelly on three plates and Vigée-Lebrun's whiskers to show for their feast. He felt a pang of jealousy sharp as hunger.

"Hullo, doc," said Fido amiably.

"Hi," said Susan.

"Hello," said Rufus, and to Mr. Bigginson: "I didn't know you had company."

"Surely Susan and Fido do not deserve that formal appellation?"

"Thank you for bringing me the kitten last night, Rufus." She added with a smile: "Daddy told me his name was Bamboozle."

"No doubt he couldn't understand my stammer."

"Rufus Crotey!" she exclaimed. "You're a brute!"

"Hey, Suze," Fido asked in a hoarse whisper, "you want I should sock him?"

"Yes!"

Fido socked him.

"Hrrmph," said Rembrandt. "Lay him on the couch, Fido."

Susan, her face white, eyes enormous, sat biting her knuckle while Fido stretched Rufus out on the day bed, felt his pulse, lifted his eyelids with great gentle thumbs, and examined his rolled-up eyeballs. "He'll be around in a coupla minutes," he announced, wise in the lore of doctor and socker.

"Bless me," said Mr. Bigginson. Then, rousing himself, he said in an energetic voice: "Get out, you two!"

Fido clapped his pork-pie hat on his head (he wore no overcoat, even in the coldest weather), then bundled Susan into her fur coat, and carried her out of the apartment. Rembrandt sat back in his easy chair, and waited for Fido's prediction to come true.

Rufus moved his head from side to side. His arms made small purposeless movements, which became purposeful as he recovered full consciousness and felt his chin.

"What happened?" he asked.

"Rufus," said Mr. Bigginson, "can you hear me?"

"Yes."

"Can you comprehend?"

"Yes."

"Well, then, I may tell you that you got just what you asked for. You were completely in the wrong, my boy. Susan had come over here to make up, as we used to say in my childhood, and you repulsed her in a manner which I agree with her was brutal."

Rufus sat up on the day bed, looking miserable as a whipped cur. "I deserved to be socked," he muttered.

The artist chuckled. "I think Susan was as surprised as you that you actually were. When Fido's reflexes are slow, they are very, very slow; and when they are fast, they are torrid."

"What'll I do now, Rembrandt?" he asked pitifully. "Do you think she will ever forgive me?"

Mr. Bigginson leaned back in his chair, and carefully lighted one of the corona-coronas made especially for Big Pat O'Hoe. "My boy, when you ask me a question on the female sex, you are inquiring of one who is the world's most unsung authority on women. Look at me: sixty, and still happily unmarried. To have reached my venerable years without ever having committed matrimony, a man must know everything about women, or nothing. As one who, to put it chastely, graduated from the latter category forty-five years ago—er—where the hell was I?"

"I asked you, if Susan would ever forgive me."

"Thanks to Fido, she will."

Fido drove Susan swiftly home, and only when he had parked before her house did she seem to rouse from her state of shock. Then she demanded fiercely: "Why did you hit him?"

Fido looked surprised. "You told me to, Suze."

"I never want to see you again!" she cried. She jumped out of the car and slammed the door violently to behind her.

He scratched his head. "I ast her should I sock him,"

he muttered aloud. "She says yes, so I sock him." He turned the proposition over and over again in his mind, and still he couldn't figure out why his girl got so sore.

"Suze, that ain't right," he called plaintively to the Nimblewits' door, through which Susan had disappeared fifteen minutes before.

Still worried, still puzzled, Fido stopped by the anatomical laboratory the next day to consult Crotey. "Say, doc, listen," he rumbled. "Last night I ast Suze: 'Suze, you want I should sock him?' didn' I?"

"Yes," said Rufus.

"So Suze says yes, don' she?"

"Yes."

"So I sock you."

"And how," said Rufus, feeling his chin.

"So why should she be sore at me, doc? I ask you that."

"What!"

Fido hung his great head, abashed. "She said she don't ever want to see me no more. I don't get it, doc. I ast her should I sock you. She says yes. I sock you. Now she don't want to see me no——"

He stopped in astonishment; Rufus was shaking the great hand which the night before had knocked him cold.

Chapter Sixteen

DEAN NIMBLEWIT WAS writing in his study behind closed doors when he heard a knock on the panel. "Who is it?" he called.

"Susan. May I come in, Daddy?"

"One moment, dear." Hastily the dean shovelled the works of Doctors Foilove, Letcher, and Dildo into a desk drawer, and shoved the notes for his third chapter, "The Sex Act", under the blotter. (Nimblewit refused to let his mind dwell on the fact that this was the last of the sixteen subjects dealt with in all sex manuals with which he had any real first-hand knowledge.) "Come in, Susan."

She entered, carrying her kitten: the opening gambit in her campaign to induce her father to select Rembrandt Bigginson as his official painter. "Daddy," she began, perching herself on the top of his desk, "my kitten's name isn't Bamboozle——"

"Ah," said the dean, doubting as he looked at his lovely daughter that he could have done any better had he possessed, on the critical night, all of Philander Foilove's deep science, "I thought Doctor Crotey must have been trying to bamboozle me."

Susan laughed merrily at her father's jest, and the dean, who had not been quite sure whether he was being humorous or caustic, was persuaded he had been witty. "It's really Bamboots," she said. "Mr. Bigginson says that was the name of an old Dutch artist. Don't you think it was sweet of him to give me a kitten?"

"Perhaps he was following the Biblical advice, and casting his kitten upon the waters," Nimblewit quipped.

"Why, Daddy!" She was shocked. "He had promised me a kitten long before he ever knew you were to have your portrait painted. Besides, even if Mr. Bigginson were the best artist in the country, you couldn't have him paint you after he had painted Willoughby Chouse, could you?"

This was a shrewd stroke on Susan's part, the fruit of intimate knowledge of her mother's technique and her father's reactions. "My dear Susan," said the dean in almost the same tone he used to his dear wife, "scientific training teaches us to be objective and impartial. If, after scientific examination, Mr. Bigginson should be found worthy of painting me, the mere fact that he has previously painted a stinker would be immaterial and irrelevant."

"Mr. Bigginson thinks Doctor Chouse is a stinker too."

"Susan, you should not say such things," said the dean sternly. "You sound just like your mother."

"Poor Daddy." Susan leaned over and kissed him. "By the way, did you know that Mr. Bigginson too was an intimate friend of Geoffrey Lanyard's? They shared a flat in Paris for years before the Great War."

He looked up with quick interest. "With Geoffrey?"

"Uh-huh," she said, sliding down off her father's desk, satisfied that she had left him sufficient food for reflection. "Well, I must run now."

"You've got a date with Fido?" the dean asked with curiosity alloyed with hopelessness.

Her eyes flashed. She was on the point of saying she never wanted to see Fido again, when she realised that she still needed him for purposes of threat or blackmail. "Why, Daddy," she said, "you know fourth-year medicine isn't all that easy, even for a genius like Fido. He has to stay home and study some time."

Alone in his study again, Nimblewit sighed helplessly, and groped in the drawer for the *Sex Manual for the Married,* by Philander Foilove, B.A., M.D., D.Sc., LL.D. A married man's troubles really began, he thought gloomily, where Foilove's book left off.

Fido actually was studying. In his room in the fraternity house, seated in a Morris chair whose springs had long since succumbed to his weight, he was reading Cecil's *Textbook of Medicine,* his lips laboriously forming each word as he read, his mind mysteriously distilling the essence like an alchemist's alembic. But his heart was not in his work.

Wish O'Hoe came in from shooting a game of pool in the billiard-room downstairs with a freshman from whom he had won three dollars. He affected exaggerated surprise on seeing Fido. "Well, look who's here! What's the matter, Fido? Suze find someone whose head came to a sharper point than yours?"

"Aw cut it out, Wish," he said unhappily.

Wish peered at him with suddenly crafty eyes. "She didn't really give you the air, did she?"

"Da look, Wish: last night."

"Yeah?"

"Last night Suze and I go over to see Rembrandt. He cooks up some eggs. I and Suze and Rembrandt and V.J., we've just finished the eggs when Doc Crotey comes in."

"Yeah, Rufe. Go on."

"He's sore at not gettin' in on the eggs, see, and makes a dirty crack at Suze."

"Go on," said Wish impatiently.

"So I says, Suze, you want I should sock him? She says yes. So I sock him."

"Holy Mother of God!"

"Then," said Fido unhappily, "she tells me she never wants to see me no more. Look, Wish: I ast her should I sock——"

"Wait a minute. You say Suze is sore at Rufe now. Right?"

"Right."

"She's sore at you too, right?"

"Yeah, but——"

Wish began to sing "When Irish Eyes Are Smiling" as he brushed his curly tenor's hair and adjusted his hand-painted necktie before the mirror. Then he grabbed up his polo coat and hat, and said blithely to Fido: "Don't wait up for me tonight, old lady. So long."

"Hey, wait up, Wish!" Fido bawled in the voice of Duty once more on duty. He placed his Cecil carefully on the floor and lumbered downstairs after his ward. Following Big Pat's instructions, Fido would permit Wish to go off alone only when he was bound for a safe haven; but with the young master tearing off in this hyperphrenic mood, perhaps to Sadie's, Fido felt his services might be needed before the night was over. When he reached the street, one of the black Buicks was already a hundred yards off, and picking up speed. Fido jumped into the other one and followed.

.   .   .   .   .

Had Susan Nimblewit, impressed by the great O'Hoe name, and eager for a share of the plunder of Mercia, been the same easy conquest as all his previous women, by now Wish O'Hoe might have been thankful enough to abandon her to Fido or Crotey or anyone else. (He couldn't help grinning whenever he thought of Dean and Mrs. Nimblewit's transparent efforts to marry their daughter off to him. Holy Mother of God, did they think he would *marry* a Protestant!) But instead of succumbing to his routine manœuvres, she had met them with a disdainful amusement and a disposition to hear him on the subject of Big Pat which had finally stung him into attempting to convince her that Patrick Aloysius O'Hoe Junior was everything Wish believed him to be.

Then, after all his trouble to seduce her mind, she had ungratefully repaid him by taking up with an insignificant instructor of anatomy. But it hadn't taken her long to find out that Rufe was a jerk. And then (Holy Mother of God!) she had to take up with Fido! Wish had had a number of girls who had been momentarily attracted by his bodyguard's size and strength, and, like Suze, they too had soon discovered he was just another muscle-bound dope. Now, with Suze disillusioned at last with Rufe the jerk and Fido the dope, Patrick Aloysius O'Hoe Junior decided to move in for the kill.

Wish parked his car before the Nimblewits' house, and knocked on the door—shave-and-a-haircut-two-bits. When Susan opened the door, he said: "Hi, Suze," and pushed past her into the entrance hall.

"Hi, Wish," she said, backing away from the partially-open door, and surreptitiously sniffing to see if she could smell the reason for his strangely exalted manner. But he smelled, even if he didn't act, entirely sober. "Do you want to see my father?"

"Not for a while," he said ambiguously; but there was only one meaning in his wolfish grin. As he continued to advance on her, she retreated into the empty living-room. "I came to see you, Suze."

"You might have phoned me first, so I could have been out."

"I knew you'd be here waiting for me."

"Apparently," said Susan, her eyes beginning to flash, "you know as much about me as you do about Medicine."

"Yeah," said Wish, who privately and publicly considered himself destined to become the Mercian Hippocrates; "I do." With this he swiftly moved in on the astonished Susan, grabbed and kissed her.

She tore herself away, her face scarlet. "Why, you nasty little reptile!" she gasped.

"You want I should sock him, Suze?" Fido rumbled from the doorway.

"Yes!" she cried.

"Fido!" Wish screamed like a rabbit in agony. "Fi——"

The rest was silence.

Wish O'Hoe's anguished scream had jerked Dean Nimblewit upright in his study chair, and in her sitting-room had made Mrs. Nimblewit leap convulsively and tear her *Racing Form*; and each rushed towards the source of the sound. There, in the centre of the living-room carpet, lay the only son of Patrick Aloysius O'Hoe, unconscious, with Susan and Fido staring down at him. If he was not actually unconscious himself, Fido was in a state of shock; for he had just been through that conflict between Love and Duty which had proved too much for even Mark Antony and Edward VIII.

"He's had a fit!" the dean cried. "Call a doctor, quick!"

Narrowing her eyes, Mrs. Nimblewit said: "He's been chilled."

"Fido socked him for me," said Susan in a proud happy voice.

Fido shook his head as though to clear away the divine mist which had obscured his eyes, and rumbled reassuringly: "He'll be okay in a minute, dean."

Nimblewit wrathfully rounded on Fido, like Jove

about to annihilate a Titan. "Father," Susan pointed down at Wish like some heroine of melodrama, "he attacked me; and," she turned to Fido, reached up her arms and clasped around the neck, "*he* saved me!" She drew Fido's head down, and kissed him. "My hero! My knight in shining armour!"

"Da who, me?" Fido swayed on his legs like a Titan who had just received one of Jupiter's thunderbolts in a tender place; then tottered over to a fragile gilt chair, sank down on it heavily, and landed on the floor in the midst of a crash and tangle of splintered wood.

"Poochie," said his wife, "scram. This is no mess for a dean to be mixed up in."

Nimblewit darted back into his study and locked the door behind him. Wish sat up, shook his head, and stared around him. His still-glazed eyes focused on Fido sitting amid ruins on the floor. "You're fired!" he shrieked.

Fido didn't even hear him. He was mumbling to himself: "Last night I ast her, should I sock him. She says yes. . . . So I sock him and she tells me she don't want to see me no more. Tonight I ast her should I sock him. She says yes. So I sock him and she kisses me. Tonight I'm a hero, last night I'm a bum: I don't get it."

"You can't fire him," Susan told Wish. "He works for your father, not you."

"I'll tell my old man." Wish glared balefully up at her.

"You wait until Mr. O'Hoe hears why Fido socked you," she said. "Your father is a good man. Wait till Fido tells him you were attacking a respectable girl."

"Aw, I wasn't attacking you, Suze," Wish mumbled, dropping his eyes, not so much in shame as because he knew Suze had him cold: the old man did draw an unnecessarily rigid line between floozies and nice Catholic girls, and if the daughter of the dean were not in the latter, only the most bigoted could include her in the former category.

"What were you doing?" Mrs. Nimblewit asked Wish.

"Aw, I was just kissing her."

"Even when I was a girl, Susan," Mrs. Nimblewit tartly remarked, "one didn't have a young man chilled by a gorilla merely for stealing a kiss."

Susan's jaw dropped at this unexpected maternal reproof, and Wish's spirits rose with his body at such welcome support. He brushed himself off, smoothed back his hair, and said: "I'm sorry we both forgot ourselves, Suze."

"A gentlemanly apology," said Mrs. Nimblewit, grimacing behind Wish's back a command that her daughter accept it.

"So am I," said Susan.

"Kiss and make up?" he suggested.

"Kiss Fido."

Hearing his name, Fido rumbled from the floor: "I resign."

"I should think so," said Mrs. Nimblewit, "after forgetting your place as you did." She thought this a most ingratiating remark, and glanced at Wish O'Hoe for a return of the approval she had given him. But Wish was looking green in the face.

"I resign, Wish," Fido repeated.

Wish's quick mind and active imagination could foresee what would inevitably happen when news of his bodyguard's resignation became known: seven of his fraternity brothers, thirty-three of his fellow medical students, and the brothers and boy-friends of an unknown number of town-maidens would yell joyfully, and rush to be the first to beat him up. And by the time his old man could send down a replacement for Fido, Wish would be needing only trained nurses. So, to Mrs. Nimblewit's amazement, Wish knelt down beside Fido, and began to plead with him to withdraw his resignation.

"Well, if Suze says so," he said at last, "I will."

"Kiss and make up, Fido," she said.

"Shake hands, Fido," said Wish, and the one kneeling, the other sitting on the floor, they shook hands.

"Get up off the floor, you," said Mrs. Nimblewit

crossly to Fido. "Look what you did to my chair."

"I'm awful sorry, Mrs. Dean," he mumbled, picking himself up from the ruins.

"And take your hat off in the house!"

Fido snatched off his pork-pie hat, blushing. "Put it back on, Fido," said Susan; "we're going out." She tucked her hand in the crook of Fido's powerful arm. "Good-bye, Mother. Good-evening, Wish."

"Da Wish," said Fido.

"Yeah?" the young master growled.

"Don't wait up for me, old lady."

As soon as Wish too had left the house, Mrs. Nimble-wit knocked on her husband's study door. "Let me in, Poochie," she demanded.

The dean shuddered at her tone of voice, cached his incriminating books and papers, then admitted her. "Well, Poochie," she said, "what do you intend to do about this mess?"

"What mess?"

She gestured towards the living-room. "That big ape slugging your daughter's future fiancé right in your own home."

"I don't understand."

"I mean, Fido chilling Wish O'Hoe; you know very well what I mean."

"I haven't the faintest idea what you're talking about," the dean declared. As he had earlier told Susan, if a scientist found something good, he embraced it without prejudice and regardless of its antecedents; and Nimble-wit conceded that his wife's advice had been admirable. She had warned him not to get mixed up in this mess, and he agreed with her 100.00 per cent. "Did Susan have callers while I was busy working in here?" he said blandly.

After twenty-five years of married life, Gloriana Nimblewit had just had her first dose of the same medicine the dean fed daily to his Faculty. She made a face as though it tasted like castor oil. Then she said:

"You were working on your new book on sex, I suppose?"

It was now the dean's turn to gag on his dose. "Are you ready for me to tell you about the birds and the bees yet?" she asked; and waited tigerishly for the poor dean to say yes or no.

"Get out of here, you old bat!" he yelled.

Chapter Seventeen

ALBERT WANION WAS finding the solicitation of gifts to the Dean Horace Nimblewit Portrait Fund a thankless task. Though he was only the *Servus Servorum Decani,* he was treated by his dunned colleagues in the immemorial manner of the tax-collector, physical violence restrained only by the knowledge that behind this contemptible creature loomed the power of a theocratic State. In the end, grumbling like peasants, twisting like Proteus, they shelled out; and Wanion made a small mark opposite their names in his notebook before he proceeded to the next on his list.

This was Doctor Lanthorn, the busiest surgeon on the hospital staff. Like all surgeons, Lanthorn had served a long, hard apprenticeship, which his colleagues in less rigorous specialities conveniently forgot when they envied his fabulous income. A skilled surgeon, however, thoroughly deserves all the money he earns. He is in such demand for really serious cases that he has no time to perform unnecessary operations (the classic reproach against his guild); and Nature, who is generally on the side of the internist even before he appears on the scene ("Happy is the physician whose coming is desired at the declension of the patient's disease," runs the old proverb) —Nature exerts his *vis medicatrix* for the surgeon only if and after he has well and properly done his work.

Wanion was lucky to catch Lanthorn in his office immediately following the lunch hour. As usual, the surgeon was dressed in his white operating trousers and gown, his white operating cap pulled down on his head. He had not been seen in any other garb for so long that it was two years before anyone besides his wife discovered he had gone quite bald.

"Good afternoon, Doctor Lanthorn," said Wanion respectfully.

"Good afternoon, er—Wanion." The faint note of interrogation in the surgeon's voice may have been because he wondered at the small fry's business or his name.

"As you've no doubt heard, we are having a testimonial portrait painted of Dean Nimblewit."

Lanthorn glanced at his wrist-watch. "Yes?"

"And I have been appointed by the committee to collect contributions from the Faculty."

"Very happy to contribute, doctor," said the surgeon briskly. "Can you come back later?" He indicated his operating-room habit. " I haven't got my cheque-book with me now."

Wanion had learned by hard experience. He pulled three cheque-books from his pocket, one for each of the Zebulon banks. "Which bank, Doctor Lanthorn?"

"Third National." Wanion handed him the proper cheque-book and his uncapped fountain-pen. "Er, doctor," Lanthorn hesitated, "how much are they giving?"

To this invariable question, Wanion made routine reply. "Well, Doctor Carnifex gave fifty dollars."

"He can afford it. How much did Tim Wimbledon and Billy Nudge give?"

"I haven't seen Billy yet; Tim gave fifteen."

Still Lanthorn didn't set pen to paper. "This has been a hard year, doctor. Texas! By God, I wish I had my knife in that fellow as deep as he has it in me."

To this invariable complaint Wanion had a stock answer. "You can deduct your contribution from your income-tax."

"You know, doctor, when I first heard the dean was to have his portrait painted, I thought how many of his former students would be delighted to have the opportunity of showing their affection for old Poochie. The broader the base the contributions rest on, the greater honour to the dean, you know."

"I know; but the goddam Alumni Association refused to let us circularise the medical alumni." In view of the mimeographed letter he had been stuck with, Wanion felt particularly bitter about this; and his tone reassured Lanthorn that everything possible had been done to save the Faculty pocket-book, so the surgeon swiftly scribbled off his cheque for fifteen dollars.

"Very happy to make my small contribution, doctor," he said, returning Wanion's pen; "wish it could have been larger, but taxes . . . Still, it's the spirit that counts."

"It certainly is," said Wanion, and respectfully left the presence.

Consulting his list, which had been copied from the medical school catalogue in which the professors were listed in order of seniority, Wanion came next on the name of Cedric Osbert Dee. Dee was a fellow-committee-man, but even tax-collectors must pay taxes. When Wanion entered his office, Dee was talking into his red telephone, and motioned his visitor to have a seat and wait.

"I can do better than that for the same type of soda-fountain in Philadelphia," he was saying, "even allowing for differences in freight." He listened for a moment, then said: "Well, confirm it in writing, then." He replaced the red phone, and said: "Well, what can I do for you, Albert?"

"Today it's what I can do you for," he said with a grin. "I'm collecting for the dean's portrait."

Dee reached for his orange phone and said: "Come back later; I haven't got my cheque-book with me."

Wanion displayed his collection. "Which bank?"

145

This simple question seemed to give Dee trouble. He banked in different places according to whether he was acting as president of the Zebulon Plumbing and Heating Company, Zebulon Beehive Industries, or still another of his profitable enterprises. At last, with Wanion growing visibly impatient, Dee seized his green phone, dialled a number, and then said: "C. O. Dee, Incorporated, C. O. Dee, president, speaking. Let me talk to Mr. Brabble."

Dee and Brabble held a long conversation concerning the optimum tax benefits to be derived from a deductible contribution, and finally agreed that in this particular instance C. O. Dee, Inc., was the best contributing agency. When he had replaced the green phone in its cradle, Dee explained: "Brabble is my lawyer. I pay him an annual retainer to handle my legal affairs, and I never make an important move without consulting him. Give me a blank on the Farmer's and Planter's." Wanion handed him the proper cheque-book, and Dee asked: "How much are they giving?"

"Well, you know Doctor Carnifex gave fifty dollars."

"He can afford it."

"Lanthorn just gave me fifteen."

"So can he, the tight-wad." Just then one of Dee's phones began to ring. Of course Wanion, his ears unattuned to their individual vibrations, could not tell it was merely the black, or medical school, phone; but as it continued to shrill, unanswered, it got on his nerves.

"Your phone is ringing," he said.

"It'll stop," said Dee; and it did. He then wrote out a cheque to the Dean Horace Nimblewit Portrait Fund, signed it C. O. Dee, Inc., per C. O. Dee, president, and handed it over to the tax-gatherer.

Wanion glanced at the cheque. Then he stared. "Didn't you make a mistake here, C.O.D.?" he asked.

"Five is more for a bacteriologist than fifteen for a rich surgeon," said Dee. "Besides, if I figured in the value of my time spent serving on the committee, my contribution would top Carnifex's." He flicked the switch on his intercom. system, and after Mrs. Dee had reported, her husband said: "Ethel, compute the value of the time I've spent attending meetings of the Dean Horace Nimblewit Portrait Committee at the rate of twelve dollars an hour, portal-to-portal, and enter it as a deductible contribution on the books of C. O. Dee, Inc."

"Yes, dear."

"It's advice like that," said Dee to Wanion, "that makes Brabble worth his hire. I wouldn't have thought of that, myself."

"That's hard to believe. Did Brabble think of incorporating you, too?"

"No," said Dee; "that was my own idea."

The door to Willoughby Chouse's office was closed, and through it, as he knocked, Wanion could hear the murmur of voices. At a shouted invitation from Chouse, he entered. Wish O'Hoe arose politely from his chair, greeted Doctor Wanion courteously, bowed to Doctor Chouse, and discreetly withdrew.

"O'Hoe must be mending his fences for finals," said Wanion. He sounded put upon; none of the gravy Wish had ladled around in the past three years had ever splashed on his waistcoat.

"He has been conferring with me about his studies. He's not as strong as he might be, of course; but he's safe enough."

"No doubt."

"What d' you mean by that?" Chouse demanded.

"Nothing; I was just agreeing with you, that's all."

"What did he do in your course last year?"

"Well, he never did learn much dermatology," said Wanion, "but he got very much interested in syphilology; attended all the lectures and clinics, worked up his cases, wrote a pretty fair examination paper; so he averaged through the course as a whole without any trouble. I often wondered if he mightn't have—er—a gift for syphilology himself. That's beside the point, though. I stopped by to see if you wanted to contribute anything towards the dean's testimonial portrait?"

"Indeed I do. Nothing would give me any more pleasure." Chouse began looking around, in all sorts of unlikely places. "I can't seem to find my cheque-book, though. Can you come back later?"

"Which bank do you deal with?"

"Third National. What a pity——"

Wanion produced a cheque-book like a magician pulling a rabbit from his hat: Chouse accepted it as though it were a summons tendered by a deputy sheriff.

"How much are they giving?" he asked.

"Well, Doctor Carnifex gave fifty dollars."

"He can afford it. How about Lanthorn and Nudge and Drumslager and those fellows?"

"Fifteen." The tax-collector was getting tired. "And you can deduct it from your income-tax, and we wanted to circularise the medical alumni, but the goddam Alumni Association wouldn't let us."

"Perhaps it's just as well," Chouse remarked as he scribbled off his cheque. "It would be quite a blow to old Poochie to discover what his former students thought he was worth in terms of dollars and cents."

Wanion pocketed the cheque and said thanks. "I suppose the safest way to have a portrait painted by your admirers is to pay for it yourself," he observed.

"What do you mean by that?"

"Why, nothing; nothing at all. I was just agreeing with you again."

Chouse was the last of the full professors on Wanion's list; Pietro Spandone, the first of the associates. Wanion found his colleague admiring his newest press notice, a humorous one-line filler from the Pretoria, South Africa, *Gazette*. After reading the item to Wanion, Spandone went on to say that when they began to joke about your work in the lay press, it was a sure sign you were one of the select circle of the really great. He instanced Einstein and his theory of relativity, the Mayo Brothers and their clinic, the famous psychiatrist Coué.

"But how come you ever saw it there in the first place?" Wanion asked.

"Oh, I subscribe to the best clipping bureaus, of course," said Spandone; and as a member of the dean's own department made only a token resistance to the inevitable. But after accepting the proper cheque-book, he suddenly asked whether the list of subscribers and their contributions was to be made public. Wearily Wanion asked what difference that made. "Well," said Spandone, "I owe a definite duty to my public. If the list is published, my public will naturally expect me to head it."

"Fine. Doctor Carnifex gave fifty dollars."

"On the other hand, though, the greater your scientific attainments, the more you need to be really modest, like I am." Spandone wrote out a cheque for ten dollars.

Returning dog-tired to his office after forcibly extracting ten dollars from the last of the assistant professors, Wanion met Johnnie Mazzard in the hallway. "For God's sake," the latter exclaimed, "what's the matter, Albert?"

He groaned. "I've been all over, collecting for the dean's portrait."

Mazzard, like Rufus Crotey, merely a voteless instructor, reached for his wallet. He gave the tax-gatherer a five-dollar note. Wanion made a shaky entry in his notebook, then murmured brokenly: "You'll go to heaven for this."

"That's a long ride for five dollars."

"Well, you're the only man I've seen all afternoon who shelled out without a squawk; and the Lord loveth a cheerful giver."

"Cheerful giver, hell!" said Mazzard. "I'm a good loser, that's all."

Chapter Eighteen

WHEN, AFTER CHECKING the last and rawest instructor off his list (Rufus Crotey), Wanion reported to Tippett, the chairman promptly summoned his committee into extraordinary session.

Wanion read them his figures: 20 contributions of $5 each, $100; 22 contributions of $10, $220; 9 contributions of $15, $135; and one contribution of $50. (Here Drumslager and Dee glared at Carnifex, who had the innocent air of a hound with egg yolk on his chops.) In all, the medical faculty had contributed the sum of $505.

"*I* collected $719 from the student body," said Drumslager.

"But students have no tenure," said Carnifex.

"That makes a total of $1,224, gentlemen," the chairman bumbled. "I am open to suggestions as to the next—ER—step to be taken to raise the balance needed, which, including the frame, will be—ER—$1,000."

"Albert, you make another round of the Faculty," said Drumslager officiously. "Point out to Lanthorn and Nudge and Chouse and all those fellows——"

"Not me!" said Wanion.

"I propose the committee itself make up the difference," Carnifex suggested; and sat unmoving through the storm which raged about his head. When the chairman had succeeded with considerable difficulty in establishing a precarious calm, Carnifex said: "I withdraw my proposal."

"Doctor Carnifex's heart is, as always, larger than—ER—our purses," said Tippett. "I personally feel it is—ER—desirable to keep the base of the contributions as—ER—broad as possible. We owe that much to the dean, gentlemen."

"If you will permit an unpractical scientist to make a suggestion, Mr. Chairman," said Dee. Tippett nodded warily. "There are but two ways of getting out of this fix Byron and Albert have got us into——"

Drumslager and Wanion bitterly protested.

"Well, if you two had collected all the money you were supposed to, we wouldn't be in trouble now, would we?" Dee said with inexorable logic. "The first way is to send them back to collect another thousand——"

"Gentlemen!" cried the chairman, just in time to prevent Dee from having to sue his colleagues for assault and battery. "Gentlemen!"

"All right, all right," said Dee.

"I just want to ask C.O.D. one thing," Wanion broke out in spite of Tippett's efforts to restrain him. "If I went back, would he give me another five bucks?"

"All right, all right; why don't you let me finish? I was just going to say, I admit this way is impracticable. The second way is to advertise in the newspapers, saying we have $1,224 to spend on an oil-painting, size 36 by 54, complete with genuine gilt frame, and inviting bids." (In this familiar kind of competition, Mr. W. C. Tarbush might have the edge on less accomplished artists.)

"What!" Drumslager shrilled. "After publicly boasting how much we were going to spend on the portrait, to publicly admit we couldn't swing it? We'd be the laughing-stock of the university, not to mention Willoughby Chouse. C.O.D., you're crazy!"

"Mr. Chairman, I demand that Doctor Drumslager withdraw his offensive remarks!"

"I withdraw them," said Drumslager sulkily, "but——"

"Will you please let me finish, Byron?" Dee asked with exaggerated politeness. "We can arrange the whole matter through a lawyer, without appearing in it ourselves or letting the school be mentioned. I'll lend the committee Brabble on a pro rata basis. He can settle with the successful bidder to intimate that he has received $2,000 instead of $1,000."

This proposal was met with that reluctant admiration Dee exacted from even his most hostile critics in matters of high finance. "I move Doctor Dee's suggestion be adopted in toto," said Drumslager; for one may hate the traitor, and still love the treason.

"Second the motion," said Wanion, willing to agree to anything rather than resume his role of tax-gatherer.

"Gentlemen," Carnifex reminded them, "you are forgetting that this same committee has already authorised the dean to select his own painter."

"Yes, gentlemen," said Tippett. "Byron, your motion is out of order."

"I move we withdraw the dean's authorisation to pick his own artist," said Dee.

This motion received four disdainful glances, but no seconder. "If you will pardon a practical old surgeon," said Carnifex, "our only recourse is to raise another thousand dollars."

"Albert, you go back to the Alumni Secretary again, and put it up to——"

"Not me!"

"Dean Nimblewit will be hurt and astonished at your lackadaisical attitude," Drumslager threatened.

"My God," said Wanion, giving him a reproachful look. "Whose idea was it, anyway, having the dean's portrait painted in the first place?"

"Mine," said Drumslager in his clear candid voice.

Wanion subsided.

"In any event, gentlemen," said Carnifex, "the time is now too far advanced for the slow process of raising money outside the medical school."

"Make a motion," Dee said suddenly. "Make a motion this committee refer the matter of finances to the dean for action."

"Great Scott, man," Carnifex exclaimed, "you can't do that."

"Make the motion," Dee said stubbornly.

"Gentlemen," said Carnifex, looking around at the rest of the committee as though appealing to a majority to live up to his epithet.

"Does anyone second Doctor Dee's motion?" the chairman asked. With old Carnifex's eye upon them, no one seconded.

"I don't see why I'm wasting my time here," Dee said, rising angrily from his place at the committee table.

"Wasting it?" Wanion asked. "With portal-to-portal deductions at the rate of twenty cents a minute?"

Dee sank back in his chair. "I withdraw my motion," he said in a sullen voice. "Now let's see what better anyone else can do."

"I'll tell you what," said Drumslager; "we don't have to do anything officially. Ashby can stop by the dean's office and kind of hint to him what a spot we're on. Nothing official. How about it, Ash?"

"Not me," said Tippett, with perfect distinctness.

"Well, you're chairman of the committee, after all. Make a motion," Drumslager said; "make a motion Ashby consult informally with the dean on the matter. Use tact, Ash; finesse."

"Second the motion," said Dee.

"Question," Drumslager began to chant. "Question, question, question."

The chairman despondently put the motion, which was carried, three to two. Drumslager leaned over and slapped Tippett on a bony shoulder. "Remember, Ash," he cautioned; "tact—delicacy—finesse!"

Dean Nimblewit had propped his office door wide open to ensure a good view of the returning committee, for he too was conscious that time was growing short. First came Dee, rushing back to his telephones. Then Carnifex, wearing the sad expression he reserved for all Faculty meetings and inoperable tumours. From neither of these committee-men could the dean draw any deduction. Then Drumslager passed by with his arm flung across Wanion's shoulders: a good sign, the dean thought. Finally, the chairman of the committee, turning as expected into Nimblewit's office.

"Good-afternoon, Mr. Dean," said Tippett in a low voice.

"Good-afternoon, Ashby."

"ER—we've just been holding a meeting of the portrait —ER—committee."

Nimblewit removed his horn-rimmed glasses and swung round in his chair so that he gazed out over High Street as Tippett continued to the back of his head: "I—ER— received Byron's and Wanion's report on financial—ER— progress."

"It has occurred to me, Ashby," the dean's words came floating behind him, "that the extra money might be expended on a dignified brass tablet to be affixed to the frame. Something simple, and yet——"

"ER—as a matter of fact, Mr. Dean," said Tippett with tact, delicacy, and finesse, "we're a thousand dollars short."

And now even Willoughby Chouse's tough heart might have bled for Horace Nimblewit had he been fortunate enough to see the dean's stricken face. For Nimblewit's perceptions had been sharpened by long and deep experience. In his day (which had extended even unto this moment) he had organised too many massacres of the innocent himself not to be familiar with the shadow of an upraised tomahawk on the wall, the odour of prussic acid in a cocktail, or the purport of Tippett's brief announcement. As in a crystal ball or nightmare, Nimblewit saw everything that had happened during the late committee meeting: ordinary means had failed completely to raise the necessary sum, and the committee had democratically refused to adopt extraordinary measures. And he thought he knew what Tippett was hinting at: that, having been given *carte blanche* by the committee to select his own painter, the dean should now limit his choice to one who would work for half price. Here the subtle mind of the wily dean went quite beyond the clumsy reasoning of his henchmen to arrive at a false conclusion. But it made no real difference; there was no hiding now from a snickering university the humiliating fact that the medical school, in spite of blackmail, *peine forte et dure,* and the Hippocratic Oath, had placed exactly half the value upon its dean that Nimblewit had too publicly set upon himself. Had he only been able to forbear boasting to his fellow deans of law, engineering, education, and arts that his testimonial portrait was to cost $2,000 exclusive of frame, Nimblewit would not now be in the horrible position of having to eat crow. He might then have had his portrait at half price and full credit, but as it was . . . As Carnifex had warned the committee, so now the dean told himself: the only recourse was to raise another thousand dollars before it was too late. He shuddered at the thought of the evil tongues panting to wag.

Nimblewit was aroused from these melancholy reflections by a knock on the opaque glass panel of his open office door. He whirled round to see George Slipstream, officially reporting his return to duty after a long period of seclusion following upon his attack and mutilation by a madman. In an ingenious attempt to draw attention away from his truncated nose, Slipstream had grown a moustache.

"Good afternoon, Mr. Dean," he said.

"Why, good afternoon, George," said Nimblewit, unconsciously donning his spectacles for a better view of the phenomenon, then hastily snatching them off. "I'm happy to see you back." Diplomatically skirting the late unpleasantness, he asked: "Did you have a good vacation?"

"Vacation!" said Slipstream bitterly. "Vacation! A raving maniac chews off the end of my nose, and you call it a vacation!" (In modern psychiatry it is essential that the patient face facts, rather than bury them in the subconscious, there to fester and rot.)

"I was very sorry to hear about your accident, George," said the dean, now that the subject was brought into the open.

"It wasn't any accident; he did it on purpose."

"I'm sorry. I trust you are fully recovered by now?"

"Perfectly, thank you, Mr. Dean."

"By the way, George, that's a handsome moustache you're sporting," Nimblewit remarked to cheer up the psychiatrist.

"Thank you, Mr. Dean," he said gratefully. "The only trouble is, it tickles the end of my nose." Nimblewit smiled faintly at the joke. "And when I scratch it, it isn't there," he concluded seriously; he hadn't been joking.

The dean was also an anatomist. "Probably the severed end of the nasal branch of the infra-orbital nerve is irritated," he diagnosed.

"I'm sure I don't know what could be irritating it," said Slipstream plaintively. "I am perfectly free of inhibitions, complexes, and psychoses; my id is blossoming, my ego is blooming; my mental health is superb. My secretary tells me you wanted to see me some time ago."

The transition was too abrupt; for a minute the dean couldn't remember what the psychiatrist was referring to. Then he recalled Rufus Crotey. Nimblewit had long since relaxed his pressure on Rufus; at least, ever since his daughter had dropped Crotey and whistled up Fido; and there was now no stronger reason than philanthropy for the dean to seek his instructor's cure. "Oh yes," he said at last. "Young Crotey, one of my instructors, stammers——"

"Aha!"

"And I thought it might be a good idea for you to give him the works—a course of psychotherapy, you know. However——"

"Please," the professor of psychiatry said with offended dignity. "If *your* instructor stammers, Mr. Dean, *my* instructors are the proper men to handle him."

"Yes, yes; of course. I appreciate that. I was just thinking of your remarkable success some years ago in the case of that unfortunate student who had contracted phallomania."

"A beautiful case!" Slipstream declared. "Incidentally, next week I am reporting an even more remarkable one before the Tristate Psychiatrical Association: the first case on record of human metakinesis of sex."

"I suppose you call it Spandone's Disease," said the dean coldly. No head of a department likes one of his subordinates to receive more press notices than himself.

"By the way, Mr. Dean, that reminds me. I hear you yourself are now writing a book on sex?"

The dean swivelled himself swiftly round until he was facing the window. "Where did you hear that?" he asked in a strangled voice.

"My wife told me when I returned. I understand your wife told her."

Nimblewit uttered a hoarse cry. Oh God, to be knifed on the same day by your own Faculty and your own wife!

"If you want any help when you come to sexual aberrations," Slipstream offered, "don't hesitate to refer to my department."

"Thank you, George. Perhaps in a year or two . . ." The dean allowed his voice to trail away from the painful subject.

"You won't mind if I make one suggestion now, Mr. Dean?"

"Not at all."

"Don't waste too much space on normal sex. To tell you the truth," the psychiatrist here lowered his voice to a confidential whisper, "sex is never normal; that is a physiological illusion."

Nimblewit clapped on his glasses and scribbled a note on his desk pad. When he looked up again, he was alone. A good psychiatrist has a large bump of the theatre, and Slipstream had recognised a hot exit line.

There was only one possible subject which could have distracted the dean from the fiasco of his portrait fund. This was his projected textbook of sex for medical students which, thanks to his wife and his own indiscreet tongue, now bade fair to become an even greater catastrophe. For the dean was completely unable to get beyond his third chapter. After "The Sex Act" he had tried mixing advice from Doctors Foilove, Dildo, and Letcher, and boiling the resultant mixture down two-thirds; but it still sounded like something he had uncomprehendingly copied from a book. Either Foilove, Letcher, and Dildo were more skilled plagiarists than he, or else they had done a good deal of curious research which age and modesty alike forbade Nimblewit to repeat. Had he been the master of his own fate, he would have destroyed his three books on sex and burned his own three manuscript chapters, after which no one but the Recording Angel would ever know he had been guilty of such presumption and folly. But there was his wife. Having been the innocent victim of young Horace's blundering ignorance, Gloriana Nimblewit now seemed maliciously resolved to make old Horace pay for it; and—rare dramatic irony!— pay by displaying that same ignorance before the world. Mrs. Nimblewit knew she had her husband over a barrel, and the dean knew she knew it. If he confessed he was unable to write his textbook (and failure to finish it, now she was deliberately informing every Faculty wife what he was up to, would be tantamount to confession), the university would roar with delighted laughter. And if he wrote his book, Gloriana herself would know it was a sham, and her lone laughter was more dreadful to contemplate than the university's mass merriment.

Staring glassy-eyed first out of the window, then (after revolving through an arc of 180 degrees) out of his office door, Nimblewit saw rather than perceived Fido, porkpie hat on head, walking down the corridor on his way to the medical library. Fido glanced through the dean's open door as he passed, noticed Nimblewit's eyes apparently upon him, and amiably rumbled: "Da hullo, dean" as he went by.

The dean gave a convulsive start, and promptly forgot all about such trivial matters as his portrait fund and sex-manual fiascos in the face of a really serious trouble. For his daughter had begun to mention the word marriage and the name Fido with ever-increasing frequency. She had never actually coupled the two, but the dean was a scientist, used to weighing evidence objectively and impartially, and he was as able to add 2 and 2 as Dee to subtract 10 and 10.

Nimblewit groaned aloud at his Cerberus of trouble.

"Did you call me, sir?" his secretary inquired, appearing in the doorway separating her ante-room from the dean's office.

"No," said the dean.

"Doctor Nimblewit," she said hesitantly, "if you'd like me to type your manuscript for you, I'd be awfully glad to do it. I mean, on my own time—in the evenings."

"What manuscript, Dorothy?" the dean inquired, touched by her loyalty.

She coloured slightly. "Your book on sex technique."

Chapter Nineteen

"RUFUS MY BOY," said Mr. Bigginson, "there are times in our life when one proverb speaks louder than a Fourth of July oration."

"Yes, sir," said Rufus.

"To wit: 'Faint heart ne'er won fair lady.'"

"My heart isn't faint," he said, flushing. He had been unlucky enough to drive up to the Nimblewits' to make his peace with Susan just as she and Fido, the latter having just chilled Wish O'Hoe, had emerged hand in hand, and driven off together in a Buick. "The fair lady seems otherwise engaged."

"Don't be a dope," said Rembrandt. "Promptly at six o'clock this evening I want you to invite Susan to dine with us here, and promptly at seven I shall expect you both."

Rufus seemed undecided. "He who hesitates is lost," said Rembrandt sententiously.

"Fools rush in where angels fear to tread," Rufus retorted.

"There's no fool like a young fool."

"Look before you leap."

"Nothing ventured, nothing gained."

"Haste makes waste."

"Oh, twenty-three, skiddoo," said Mr. Bigginson.

Rufus went, secretly happy to be ordered to do something only an unworthy obstinacy had kept him from repeating. He took with him a "make-up" present for Susan packed in a cardboard box. Only the dean's Cadillac was parked before her house. Rufus rang the door-bell; Susan answered it; and he greeted her with an uneasy conscience.

"Hi, Rufus," she said with extreme outward self-possession.

"Rembrandt sent me over to invite you to dinner tonight," he said. (*Merde!* muttered the hovering spirit of that authority on the female sex.)

"Rembrandt sent you?"

"Honest he did."

She sighed and smiled, and taking encouragement from the latter, he went on: "I brought you a present."

"Did Rembrandt tell you to?"

"No."

"What's he going to have?" she asked with interest.

Rufus had to tell himself not to get sore just because she was more interested in Rembrandt's menu than his present. "Sauerkraut—from a barrel, not out of a can; knochwurst; boiled potatoes; and beer. He has some imported Bavarian beer."

"Wait till I tell Mother I won't be in for dinner."

When she had settled herself beside him in the Mercedes, he said: "Rembrandt doesn't want us until seven; you know how funny he is about having anyone

160

but Vigée-Lebrun around while he's cooking. What would you like to do until then?"

"Work up an appetite," said Susan.

"That's all you think about. You'll have a pot like Rembrandt before you know it."

"Not before I know it, I hope." Susan may not have been a medical student, but she was a true girl-child of the medical school in the frankness with which she spoke her mind.

"Why don't you open your present?" he asked.

She unfastened the top of the cardboard box and lifted out a toothless skull which had been tenderly polished to an old ivory tone. "Oh, Rufus, it's beautiful!" she exclaimed. "It's just what I've always wanted." (This was a pardonable exaggeration; this ambition of hers had been gratified long since when Wilfred had presented her with her first skull, the top of its cranium sawn through and hinged. Susan now kept her dusting-powder within it.)

"It's Doctor Ruddock," he said. "I thought you might like him."

"That's awfully sweet of you, Rufus."

"Wilfred did a good job on him, didn't he?"

"Much better than his usual five-dollar skulls he sells to the medical students."

"He didn't charge me for it."

"Wilfred's nice." She looked down on Ruddock's skull on her lap, and went on reflectively: "It makes me feel like Salome with the head of John the Baptist."

"There's nothing like a skull for making you think," he said. "Rembrandt says there're times when only a proverb can express a situation. I suppose a philosopher could write a book on the subject, but when you boiled it down, all it would say would be 'Hair today and bone tomorrow.' "

"My dear Susan," Mr. Bigginson cried, welcoming her with outstretched hands, "welcome home."

She kissed him. "How are Vigée and the kittens and Angelika Kauffmann?" she said with a rush. "Bamboots is adorable; I meant to bring him along to visit his mamma and papa."

"Now that you are here, we are all happy. Bless me!" he exclaimed. "What is that you are holding, Rufus?"

"Susan's skull."

"He gave it to me for a present. Wasn't it sweet of him, Rembrandt?"

"Dispose of it at once," said the artist, shuddering. "I'll have no skellington at my feast, not even the cupola of one. I understand it was the custom of the ancient Egyptians to display a *memento mori* in the form of a mummy at their banquets, but I confess the idea takes away my appetite and gives me the meemies."

"Gosh, I'm sorry, Rembrandt," said Rufus.

"Give Doctor Ruddock to me," said Susan, and wrapped the skull in her scarf, placed the bundle on the day bed, and dropped her coat over it.

Mr. Bigginson wiped his face with the bottom of his apron, and said in a weak voice: "Do I understand the gentleman is an acquaintance of yours?

"Don't answer that!" he cried. "Rufus, the cognac!"

When he had quieted his shaken nerves with half a tumbler of cognac, Susan asked him if he hadn't been required to study artistic anatomy as an art student.

"Topographical anatomy from a living model is quite a different thing from raw heads and bloody bones," said the artist. "I was considered rather an authority on the former in my day. Rufus, you've heard of 'Bigginson's Dimple'. Well, hrrmph, that was named after me."

Rufus didn't like to admit he had never heard of this eponym; not being a professional anatomist, Susan didn't hesitate to ask what it was.

"Bigginson's Dimple," its discoverer said, "is a slight depression in the flesh of a certain region. Only two per cent of females possess it. I myself found seven cases."

"Then," said Rufus, whose mind was working slowly

but scientifically, "you must have examined three hundred and fifty——"

"Hrrmph, hrrmph, dinner is served."

Fortunately for Rembrandt's appetite, the table-talk took a less medical turn. To Susan's surprise, it centred on horse-racing, and she was even more astonished to hear that Wish O'Hoe had been feeding Rufus hot tips on the ponies, and even placing bets for him with his own bookie. By these transactions, it appeared that Rufus had already won several hundred dollars, and expected more.

"It was Rembrandt's idea," said Rufus guiltily, noticing her expression.

Mr. Bigginson explained what they were up to, concluding virtuously: "And so we shall inculcate in young O'Hoe the great maxim that crime does not pay, regardless of how much we ourselves profit by the lesson in morality."

"Well, I hope my father never hears of it," said Susan, dimpling (but not with Bigginson's Dimple; or if she were, it was not apparent). "He would never believe an honest man could accept a tip from an O'Hoe and give nothing in return."

"I suppose I'm giving Wish a certain temporary peace of mind," Rufus said, grinning.

The artist sighed. "I wish I could be in on the dénouement, but——"

"Oh, I don't mind telling him in front of you."

"But I shall be far away from Zebulon."

"Don't you dare talk about leaving," Susan scolded him. "I'll have it all fixed up about Daddy's portrait within a week, you see if I don't."

So Mr. Bigginson talked about Paris before the Great War, and Susan and Rufus sat with glassy eyes brought on by a surfeit of sauerkraut, sausages, and beer, until he was interrupted by a knock on the outside door. Immediately it opened, and Fido entered like the First Conspirator.

"Hey, Rembrandt," he hissed, "is it all right I bring it in in front of Rufe?"

"You may bring in whatever you like, Fido," said Rembrandt, "except the lower portion of that gentleman on the sofa."

Fido turned towards the day bed and politely tipped his hat to the other guest. Then he withdrew, and a moment later reappeared carrying the enormous gold-framed portrait of Willoughby Chouse.

"God bless my soul!" said Mr. Bigginson.

"Well, let's us paint the horse-fly," said Fido.

"Where did you get that portrait?"

"Out at Doc Chouse's place."

"Well—what—how!" they said together.

"Aw, he wasn't home," Fido said. "He got a lecture tonight over at the med. school, so I figured to borrow his pitcher for Rembrandt to paint a horse-fly on the nose of. Don't forget, Rembrandt, you said you was goin' to give it a green rump."

"But how did you get in?" Susan asked.

"The room where the pitcher was got glass doors. I just give one a pull and it opened."

"But where were Mrs. Chouse and the maid and the children?"

"I dunno, Suze. I never thought about no one except Doc Chouse."

"Well, God certainly looks after dopes too."

"We oughta paint that horse-fly before he gets back," said Fido. "He might notice his pitcher is missing."

"He might at that," agreed the painter, studying the portrait, which was a good four by five and a half feet in its heavy gold frame. Swiftly he shed his apron, struggled into his painting-smock, and began to set his palette, meanwhile directing Rufus to clear a working space for him, and Fido to place the portrait in the best light. "I'll use plenty of siccatif," he remarked, "so it will dry quick and shiny."

Then, with incredible speed and skill, the artist painted

a green-rumped horse-fly on the bridge of Willoughby Chouse's aristocratic nose. With two deft strokes of a brush he managed to make Chouse's eyes squint down at the impertinent insect.

Susan clapped her hands in delight. Fido went up close to the portrait, stared at Chouse's nose, then made shooing motions with his hand and said: "Shush, shush, shush."

"Fido has given it his imprimatur," said Rembrandt, laying his palette and fine sable-haired brushes on the table. "Now let's replace the portrait before he returns."

"I'm going along," said Susan promptly.

"Susan, you can't!" Rufus protested. "If you're caught —your father——"

"If I'm caught," she said, placing her hand on Rembrandt's arm, "I'll be in good company."

"Okay," Rufus sighed. "What can I lose but my job and a couple of years of my freedom?"

"Less time off for good behaviour." And she gave him a smile for which he would have braved more than a dean.

"You two will stay right here," Mr. Bigginson ordered.

"And let you and Fido have all the fun? Don't be silly!" To Rufus she sounded just like the night they had hurtled down the highway in the bullet-proof Buick at better than ninety miles an hour. She slipped into her coat, and picked up Ruddock's skull wrapped in its silken scarf.

Rufus and Susan steadied Chouse's portrait on the back seat of the Buick while the artist rode with Fido up front. Fido parked by the side of the hard-surface road from which a gravelled drive-way led to Chouse's large neo-Georgian home. He then seized the framed portrait in his hands and set off towards the house, not along the gravelled road, but through the shrubbery. Rembrandt, Susan, and Rufus had to trot to keep up with his long strides.

When they reached the house, Fido turned towards a

stone terrace on which two pairs of french windows opened. A lighted table lamp inside the room shed a warm glow through the glass. He hoarsely whispered to Rufus to hold the door open for him to pass through with the picture. When Rufus did so, he noted that the small brass bolt which was supposed to lock the doors had been pulled out by the roots as by some tremendous force. Fido entered the room, followed by Susan, Rembrandt, and Rufus. By unconscious habit, Rufus closed the door behind him. Then Fido rehung the portrait on its waiting hooks on the end wall of the room, and wiped his hands on his trousers.

Only Rufus had never before been in the Chouses' drawing-room. Mr. Bigginson had attended the fatal party in his honour there, and the dean's daughter was familiar with most medical professors' homes; while Fido had burgled the place only an hour and a half before. Rufus looked around him. In the centre of the long outer side of the room was a large fireplace flanked by french windows leading to the terrace. At right angles to each end of the fireplace, facing one another, were two sofas with valances. Chouse's portrait was perfectly hung at one end of the room; at the opposite end, between a very expensive television set and a bookcase, was a tall window. The window had long heavy curtains reaching to the floor.

Rufus had scarcely reached this point in his inspection by the subdued light of the table lamp before he heard the sound of an approaching car crunching the gravelled drive-way, and its powerful headlight beams stabbed through the french windows and illuminated the drawing-room like a star-shell over no man's land.

"Take cover!" Rembrandt hissed; a reflex acquired during the Great War. He dived under one of the sofas; Rufus under the other. Susan ran to crouch behind the television set, and Fido looked about him for a hiding-place large enough to conceal his great body. Pausing only to pick up the scarf-wrapped skull which Susan had fumbled, he disappeared behind the curtains of the window across the room from the portrait.

The car drew up under the porte cochère, and a few moments later Doctor and Mrs. Chouse entered the drawing-room. "I don't see why you couldn't have waited until I'd finished the rubber," she was complaining.

"I was tired," said Chouse.

"And Gloriana Nimblewit hadn't finished telling me about the book the dean is writing."

"You mean, his manual on sex?"

"Yes. She says he's almost to the birds and the bees. Tell me, Willoughby, what do you have to teach about birds and bees for in a medical school?"

Her husband ignored this; he said meditatively: "Old Nimblewit will make a pretty penny from that textbook. Trust a dean to keep the plums for himself." He suddenly chuckled. "Do you know what C.O.D. told me tonight?"

"No, dear; what?"

"He told me in confidence that the committee had only been able to raise half the amount needed for the dean's testimonial portrait. Ha, ha, ha, only half the money!" he cried joyfully.

"Be quiet, Willoughby; you'll wake the children. I'm going to bed now. Don't sit up too late. Don't forget to turn off the lights and make sure the doors are fastened. If you decide to get something to eat, for goodness' sake put everything away when you're through. You know it draws the bugs if you leave food around. And——"

"All right," said Chouse. "All right, *all right,* ALL RIGHT."

"Well, good-night, dear."

"Good-night, precious." Chouse drew a deep breath. "My God," he muttered aloud, "it's good to be alone."

He switched on a floor lamp beside the sofa under which Rufus was lying. He sat down, took off his shoes, then rested his head against one padded arm and put his feet up on the other, and began to read a mystery story.

167

Time passed. At last he yawned, closed his book, stood up, and walked in his stocking feet to a position before his portrait. Live Willoughby Chouse gazed in silent admiration and growing perplexity upon painted Willoughby Chouse, when, twenty-five feet behind his back, a window curtain was suddenly thrust aside to reveal Fido with Doctor Ruddock's skull gripped like a baseball in his right hand. Fido drew back his arm. . . .

Straight and true the skull sped through the air, and caught Chouse on the back of his head with the sound of two coconuts colliding. For a moment he remained upright, then slowly folded up on the floor.

"Rembrandt, Suze, Rufe!" Fido called softly.

Two heads appeared from beneath the sofas, and one from behind the television set. "Let's scram," Fido rumbled; and they scrammed, Fido once more scooping up Ruddock's skull from the floor as he fled.

"Bless me!" gasped Mr. Bigginson when they were safely back in the apartment once again. "That quite reminded me of old times."

Rufus blinked. "You mean, you're used to house-breaking?"

"Bless me, no! I was thinking of diving under the sofa when the man of the house unexpectedly returned."

"Da Suze," said Fido, "here's your skull you dropped."

"Thank you, Fido." She seemed subdued. Though like her companions she pretended to have overheard nothing, she was thinking about Chouse's remarks about her father.

"Sir," said the artist, bowing ceremoniously to Ruddock's skull, "I must beg your pardon for having treated you so uncivilly. If it were possible, I should be delighted to grasp your hand. *Que dis-je?* Rufus, the cognac!" When he had calmed himself by a draught, he continued: "Since that is fortunately impracticable, I am more than happy to shake Fido by the hand. Fido my boy," he said, shaking hands with him, "permit me to congratulate you

168

upon a brilliant analysis of the situation; a solution which merits the adjectival form of the epithet 'genius', whatever that may be; and a perfect peg."

"Aw it wasn't nothin'," said Fido, blushing. "Hey Suze," he reverted to a matter which had been bothering him ever since he had snitched Chouse's portrait, "I'm awful sorry I didn't see you tonight."

"Oh, that's all right, Fido."

"Me and Rembrandt had business."

"I know. You can come around tomorrow night," she said.

Rufus started violently. During the exhilarating ride home, he had got the impression that he and Susan had made up on the back seat. At least, he had kissed her; and she had kissed him; and they had held hands for the rest of the journey. He gave the inconstant one a look of reproach.

"Rufus my boy," said Rembrandt, "Susan is engaged in a piece of harmless deception. She is merely trying to blackmail her father the dean into commissioning me to paint his portrait by threatening to marry Fido."

"Aw Suze!"

"Oh, stop worrying, Fido. I'm not going to marry you; I'm going to marry Rufus."

"M-m-m-me?"

"But remember, Fido, it's a secret. Don't you dare tell anybody."

"Cross my heart and hope to die." An expression of worry chased the relief off Fido's face. "Rufe ain't gonna mind me datin' you every evening, is he?"

"Of course not."

"That's all right then," he said.

"Oh, is it?" said Rufus belligerently.

"Rufus Crotey! If you're going to lose your temper again, I will marry Fido."

"You want I should sock him, Suze? Hey, me? Aw, Suze, you promised!"

Mr. Bigginson commandingly cleared his throat. "If

you young people will take the advice of a man of experience—of experiences, that is to say, analogous rather than
identical; for while I have never found myself in Susan's
position, in my day I was often mixed up with two dames
at once."

"Hey, that's bad," said Fido, shaking his head. "That
ain't right."

"Rembrandt, I'm beginning to think you must have
been an old rake," said Susan.

"*Eheu! fugaces labuntur anni,*" he sighed. "Fido," he
then directed, "you call for Susan at her home at seven
each evening, and bring her here for dinner."

"I'll have to ask Suze," he said. "Suze, is it okay by you
I bring you to Rembrandt's for dinner?"

"That's okay by me, Fido."

"Okay, Rembrandt."

Susan remarked to Rufus: "You see how simple everything is when an old rake manages things? Daddy thinks
I'm dating Fido, and I'm really dining with you."

"In Rembrandt's horse-and-buggy days they seem to
have felt differently," he said ungratefully; "but we
modern jet-propelled rakes like to be alone with our girls
once in a while."

"Aw don't be like that, Rufe," Fido said. "After Suze
marries you, she'll be alone with you all the time."

"Rembrandt," cried Susan, "the cognac!"

And so Mr. Bigginson returned to his saucepans and
casseroles. He didn't mind cooking for another mouth,
even one the size of Fido's, provided he didn't have to
wash up afterwards. And Fido more than paid for his
dinners by the grotesquerie of his table-talk.

Having fought and lost Duty's battle against Love
when he had slugged Wish O'Hoe at Susan's bidding,
Fido no longer seemed concerned over deserting the
fraternity dining-room where he was supposed to eat with
his old master. Wish, however, fretted and fumed, but
dared not object to his watch-dog's absence lest he resign

and leave him a prey to the circling wolves. So every evening Fido dined at Rembrandt Bigginson's Wish drove out to Sadie's and got drunk. Ennis, Sadie's bouncer, came to the medical school and told his colleague Fido about it.

"Hey, Ennis," Fido rumbled, "take care of him for me, will you? Don't let him get bad hurt."

"Sure, pal," said Ennis. "I'll look after him like he was my own kid."

Chapter Twenty

AS THOUGH NIMBLEWIT hadn't trouble enough, his morning eggs were bad. The dean was very fond of his two soft-boiled eggs for breakfast, and prided himself on his skill in cracking their shells and spooning out the oozy contents. On this morning, the contents were not only oozy, but highly odorous. Pinching his nostrils, he nasally commanded the cook to take them out and bury them; then turned to his wife and acidly remarked that he didn't see why they couldn't have fresh eggs once in a while. Mrs. Nimblewit was breakfasting on dry toast and black coffee for her figure's sake. She set down her cup with the air of one stowing away the breakables before going into action, but only said, reasonably enough, that she didn't keep chickens. The dean wanted to know what that had to do with it. Mrs. Nimblewit said: "Wah wow wuh woo, and you're supposed to be writing a book on sex! Oh, Poochie, wuh woo wow wah!"

The dean threw his napkin savagely down on the table, and stalked from the dining-room. Seated now in his office in the medical school, he was still angry and still hungry. "I should have told her," he said to himself, for he was also beginning to think of appropriate retorts, "the way she cackles, we don't need to keep chickens. I should have told her to go to Hialeah."

Like a man drowning in a sea of troubles, Nimblewit saw his past life flash by in review. All those peaceful years during which he had complained that his wife had been neglecting her home and family—ah, that was the Age of Gold before the present Iron Age. Even more than most deans, Nimblewit loved peace and quiet, domestic and academic. Unfortunately, his wife did not. In a sudden access of affection, she had recently told her husband she had forgotten how much fun it was to quarrel with him: it had all the excitement, if none of the suspense, of a horse-race, for (she had added) she always knew in advance who was going to win.

"I should have told her," the dean said to himself, "the eggs she lays when she thinks she's being funny smell worse than the cold-storage ones she buys at the grocery."

Well, if he couldn't do anything about his wife, he could at least see about some fresh eggs. He picked up his phone and asked for Doctor Dee.

"Yes, Mr. Dean?" Dee said suspiciously into his black telephone.

"I wonder if you would be kind enough to do me a favour, doctor," Nimblewit said in his most affable voice.

Dee thought immediately of the portrait fund, which still stood at $1,224, and concluded that Nimblewit was about to apply pressure for an additional contribution to help make up the deficit. "Ho, ho," he said, "ha, ha. I have just been doing the Secretary of the Treasury a favour."

The dean smiled somewhat painfully into his phone. "I've paid my own income-tax," he said.

"I had to borrow the money to pay mine. Five per cent money, too. Cash is tight, Mr. Dean; ready money is scarce."

If Nimblewit needed any confirmation of his instinct that his Faculty had contributed their last dollar towards his testimonial portrait, Dee's tone made it a grim certainty. In a voice belying his bitter thoughts, he said: "But I trust eggs are not."

"I beg your pardon, Mr Dean?"

"Eggs. I should very much like some really fresh eggs——"

"Please call 2-2717," Dee interrupted.

Nimblewit jiggled his phone, then dialled 2-2717. In his own office, Dee picked up the yellow phone, and said: "Zebulon Poultry and Dairy Farm, C. O. Dee, gentleman farmer, speaking."

The dean grimaced; shrugged; replied: "How much are fresh eggs?"

"What grade?"

"I don't know anything about grades. I don't care what grade, so long as they are strictly fresh."

"Just a moment, Mr. Dean; I'll inquire." He received the latest quotation over the intercom. from his wife, then said: "Fifteen even, Mr. Dean."

"What do you mean, fifteen even?"

"Fifteen dollars and no cents."

"For *eggs*?" Nimblewit's voice rose until it cracked.

"Per crate," said Dee. (Ignorant old fool.) "Per thirty-dozen crate."

"How much are eggs a dozen?" the dean asked hoarsely. "Fresh eggs?"

"The Zebulon Poultry and Dairy Farm does not sell eggs by the dozen. However," Dee hastily added, just in time to keep Nimblewit from exploding, "as a special favour to you, Mr. Dean, I'll let you have half a gross at the per crate price."

"A dozen eggs! A dozen eggs! A dozen eggs!"

"Oh, they'll keep," said Dee. "And don't forget, Mr. Dean, the price I'm making you is fifteen cents per dozen under current retail price."

"I'll take the half-gross. When can you deliver them?"

"It so happens that I have a couple of crates in one of my trucks out in the parking lot. I'll send them to your office right now. That will be $3."

"Less ten and ten?"

"Net, C.O.D.," said Cedric Osbert Dee.

"I'll have the money waiting for you. By the way," the dean went on, "what progress are you making in the matter of the students' lounge and snack-bar, doctor?"

"Call 2-4748," said Dee; and hung up.

Puzzled and annoyed by this brusque action, Nimblewit dialled 2-4748. In his office, Dee reached for the new violet-coloured telephone on his desk.

"Zebulon Snack-bar, C. O. Dee, manager," he said. "I'm making very material progress, Mr. Dean. Very profitable progress. Good-bye."

The warm pleasant glow kindled in Nimblewit by his triumph in obtaining half a gross of fresh eggs at fifteen cents per dozen under the retail price of cold-storage ones lasted all too briefly before being extinguished by the memory of Dee's plain intimation that he had washed his hands of the dean's portrait. And so, apparently, had all the committee; for the dean had heard nothing further from its chairman after Tippett had dumped the problem into the dean's lap.

Nimblewit had no trouble in discovering its one theoretical solution. It was distasteful; it was damnably difficult to carry out in practice; but though his mind had twisted and turned like an eel in a bucket or a philosopher before the problem of Good and Evil, the dean had been unable to find any alternative to making up the thousand-dollar deficit out of his own pocket. The consequences of not raising the full sum were so horrific to contemplate that he was eager enough to pay $1,000 to escape them; but this was not so simple a matter as presenting the committee with his cheque for that amount, even under pledge of secrecy. Such a pledge would be given only to be broken—at the Faculty Club, and eventually at every medical convention in the country. Nor could he mail Tippett ten hundred-dollar notes from "A Friend": Nimblewit knew his Faculty too well to suppose they wouldn't jump to the false conclusion that the only friend the dean could have who considered him worth a thousand dollars in cash was Horace Nimblewit himself. For the first time in his sixty-one years, Nimblewit found himself panting to give away a king's ransom; and he was completely unable to figure out any way to do it.

Dee's technician Ulysses brought Nimblewit six dozen fresh eggs in a cardboard box. The dean gave him $3, and as soon as the messenger had left, Nimblewit carried the box to his desk, sat down in his swivel-chair, donned his horn-rimmed glasses, and commenced to count the eggs, taking them one by one from their box and laying them on his desk. One . . . two . . . three . . .

Seventy, seventy-one. That was all; there was no seventy-second egg. (Nimblewit knew his professor better than Dee knew his dean.) Just as the dean reached for his telephone to register an outraged complaint with the Zebulon Poultry and Dairy Farm, his secretary Dorothy entered his office. Her eyes widened in astonishment at the sight of the dean's desk covered with eggs. Nimblewit gave a shame-faced grin. "Fresh eggs," he mumbled.

"Goodness!" she said.

"Strictly fresh. I bought them directly from a farmer. I do not like cold-storage eggs."

"My goodness, you must eat a lot of eggs, Doctor Nimblewit."

"Oh, they'll keep."

Dorothy smiled the indulgent smile of a woman who sees a man make a fool of himself by meddling in petticoat affairs. "Well, won't they?" he sharply demanded.

"Oh yes, sir; they keep them in cold-storage for years."

The dean started. He removed his glasses, and swivelled round until he was gazing out of the window. "Would you care to have a couple of dozen, Dorothy?" he said over his shoulder. "They are strictly fresh; I just bought them from a farmer."

"I don't like to keep eggs too long, so I couldn't use more than one dozen, thank you, Doctor Nimblewit. I'd love a dozen, though."

"They are much cheaper than cold-storage eggs in the stores, too. Fifty cents a dozen."

"My goodness, that is cheap." She returned to her own office for the money, placed two quarters on the dean's desk, and removed twelve eggs. "Oh, I almost forgot what I came in to tell you, Doctor Nimblewit," she said. "Doctor Slipstream phoned to ask if he could borrow your annual report to the chancellor."

"Yes, yes," said the dean; "later. I'm busy now." He replaced the remaining eggs in their cardboard box, and when he had finished, phoned Dee.

"Doctor Dee," he said coldly, "about those eggs——"

"I beg your pardon, Mr. Dean; you want 2-7717."

"Dee!" Nimblewit shouted, losing his temper. "You hold on to that phone and listen to me! About those six dozen eggs——"

"I'm sorry, Mr. Dean," Dee interrupted again. "You know darkies aren't very good at arithmetic; I'll get after Ulysses right away for miscounting."

"There were only seventy-one eggs," said the dean angrily.

"Seventy-one? Did you say, seventy-ONE?"

"How many eggs did you think were in half a gross?" Nimblewit said nastily, and slammed his telephone back in its cradle.

"Ulysses!" Dee screamed into his squawk-box. "You carried the dean seventy-ONE eggs!"

"I'm sorry, boss," Ulysses' voice came apologetically from the speaker. "Scuse me, suh. I'll bring yo' an egg fum my own hens, yassuh, I sho will."

The dean was still fuming when Rufus Crotey entered his office with a list of grades on an anatomy quiz Nimblewit had given and his instructor had corrected. "H-h-h-here are those g-g-g-grades, D-d-d-d——" he began.

"Yes, yes," said Nimblewit, cutting short the nerve-racking performance. "Thank you, Doctor Crotey." Rufus turned to escape, but quicker than his heels was the dean's brain. "Doctor Crotey!"

Rufus stopped, turned, stammered: "Yes, sir."

The dean swung round, stared out over High Street, and said over his shoulder: "I understand from my daughter Susan that the gentleman with whom you are residing is a cook."

The fact that he was now speaking to the back of the dean's head instead of to his face was a great comfort to Rufus, and he barely stammered at all as he replied: "Mr. Bigginson is an amateur chef, yes, sir." From the dean's words, he could not tell whether he knew his daughter was once more dining nightly with Rembrandt (and Rufus and Fido), or whether he was referring to that earlier time when he, instead of Fido, called for her nightly at seven. But it was clear the dean disapproved.

"I suppose he uses eggs, then?"

"He makes an omelette, sir, that is superb."

"Then no doubt he would be glad to have some really fresh eggs. I have just been fortunate enough to procure some strictly fresh eggs direct from a farmer; more than I can use, in fact; and if you would like a couple of dozen . . .?"

"Why, thank you very much, sir. I would."

"They are cheaper than the cold-storage eggs one buys at the stores," said the dean. "Fifty-five cents a dozen. Ask Dorothy for a box to put them in."

Dorothy gave Rufus a cardboard box which had once held 500 envelopes. Nimblewit began to count eggs from his box into Rufus's: one . . . two . . . three . . .

Rufus's lips were moving mechanically as he unconsciously kept count of the transfers. Twenty-three . . . twenty-four. He gave the dean a dollar note and a dime, and received two dozen eggs. With the dean's eyes once more fixed upon him, he stammered: "Thank you, D-d-d— DOCTOR NIMBLEWIT."

The dean's eyes closed in pain. Before he opened them,

he said: "Will you be kind enough to take this report over to Doctor Slipstream's office for me?"

"Y-y-yes, sir," said Rufus.

Chapter Twenty-one

RUFUS CARRIED THE copy of the dean's report to Quackenbush Pavilion, and there entered the office of the secretary of the department of psychiatry. Boris Drubetskoy was lounging against one side of the secretary's desk, Boru O'Shawnessey was sitting on the other end of it.

"Hi, gentlemen," he said; and to the secretary: "The dean sent this report to Doctor Slipstream. Will you give it to him, please, Miss Palfrey?"

"I certainly will, Doctor Crotey," she replied.

Drubetskoy and O'Shawnessey exchanged a glance of mutual understanding, and in unison said: "Aha!" Drubetskoy straightened up and gently grasped Rufus by the left arm; O'Shawnessey slid off the desk and tenderly seized him by the right arm. They led him off between them.

"Hey!" he said. "What goes on here?"

"Come into our office and have a cigarette," said Drubetskoy.

"And a little chat," said O'Shawnessey. "Nobody ever comes to see us, 'way over here in Quackenbush. We're lonesome."

Rufus was not proof against this technique, and before he knew it he was sitting in the centre of a leather couch with Drubetskoy and O'Shawnessey on either side of him. "Have a cigarette, Crotey," said Drubetskoy.

"How can I?" he said. "You're both holding my wrists." Then he recognised with a sense of shock that the two psychiatrists were feeling his pulses. He jerked his hands away, and said again: "Hey, what goes on here?"

178

"Force of habit." "Mere reflex," they said together. Rufus took a crumpled packet of cigarettes from his pocket and stuck the end of one into his mouth.

"Well, what are you guys staring at?" he demanded.

"Do you always put the cigarette in your mouth like that?" Drubetskoy asked.

"Sometimes I put the other end in first," said Rufus.

"Aha!" said the two psychiatrists. Rufus stuck his left hand into his coat pocket for a book of matches, and lighted his cigarette.

"Aha!" said O'Shawnessey. He turned to his colleague. "Well?"

"Pfui," said Drubetskoy, shrugging his shoulders.

"No wonder you two guys are lonesome," said Rufus, starting to rise. They immediately grabbed him and pulled him down again on the couch between them.

"Tell me, Crotey," Drubetskoy said in an insinuating voice, "whatever made you become an anatomist? When you were a child, now, did you——"

"Keep rabbits?" O'Shawnessey suggested.

"Pull the legs off of insects?"

"Were you ever frightened by a corpse?"

"When did you first become conscious of the idea of death?"

"I'll make a bargain with you guys," said Rufus, after a few tugs had proved to him he couldn't release himself without an undignified struggle. "If you tell me why you picked psychiatry, I'll tell you why I became an anatomist."

Drubetskoy and O'Shawnessey stared at him in amazement. "But there's nothing abnormal in becoming a psychiatrist," said O'Shawnessey at last.

"Maybe it's listening to the answers to silly questions that causes it, then," said Rufus.

Drubetskoy shrugged. "Who listens?"

"Now, Crotey," said O'Shawnessey, "be reasonable. How can we help you if you don't answer questions? They may sound silly to you, but you must remember you are too stupid to judge their real value. All Boris and I are trying to do is cure your terrible mania for anatomy, so you can take your place once more, a sane and well-adjusted man, in the body of society."

"Exactly," said Drubetskoy.

Rufus threw himself back on the couch and roared with laughter. "A serious case," O'Shawnessey said to his colleague across the patient's convulsed body.

"Worse than the Chief told us it was."

"Gentlemen," said Rufus, once more under control, "you must have got your signals crossed. You are supposed to cure me of stammering, not of being an anatomist."

"Stammering!" the psychiatrists exclaimed. Then O'Shawnessey continued alone: "We understood we were to probe your subconscious to learn why you were insane enough to become an anatomist."

"Stammering isn't so dangerous, but it's just as serious, Boru," said Drubetskoy.

"No, Boris; stammering isn't so serious, but it's just as dangerous." O'Shawnessey turned to Rufus. "Now, Crotey——"

"I first began to stammer," he said rapidly, "when I was thirteen months old. I was the only baby known to medical science who stammered a year before he could talk."

"Please, Crotey," said Drubetskoy with a commanding gesture. *"We* ask the questions. Now, when you dream, do the characters wear clothes?"

"Yes," said Rufus regretfully.

"Aha!" said Drubetskoy, and with a movement of his eyebrows passed the patient across to his colleague.

"When did you first begin to use your right hand?" O'Shawnessey asked.

"For what?"

"Evasive," said O'Shawnessey to Drubetskoy.

"When did you first soil your underwear?" the latter then inquired.

"Well——"

"Evasive," said Drubetskoy to O'Shawnessey.

"He isn't being evasive," O'Shawnessey replied. "He's answering your leading questions about toilet training fully and frankly. I've told you time and again, Boris, that stammering is not caused by faulty toilet training. Boris, it pains me to say this, but you have s—t on the brain."

"Only a man whose early toilet training was improperly managed could be as stupid as you, Boru," said Drubetskoy. "I am merely trying to establish that Crotey's toilet training was too early and harsh, rather than too late and lenient."

"Excuse me," said Rufus. "Suppose it was just right?"

"In all my years in psychiatry, Crotey," said Drubetskoy, "I have never come across but one person whose toilet training was not either too early and harsh, or too late and lenient. It was fortunate for me that my parents house-broke me in a manner as rare as it was perfect; and consequently I am today without a single complex or inhibition—a unique example of eunoia; while Boru, obviously——"

"If you don't mind, Boris, my toilet training is not the point at issue, and furthermore it was as good as yours, so there. Now, Crotey," O'Shawnessey said to Rufus, "in which hand do you hold your dissecting knife?"

"My right one."

"Aha!" he said triumphantly. "You see, Boris? Crotey was originally left-handed; one grasps that immediately from his unconscious use of the left hand to remove matches from his pocket; but his parents and teachers forced him to use his right hand instead, and the mental conflict causes him to stammer."

"Well, I'll be damned!" said Rufus.

"You see, Boris?" O'Shawnessey said. "You see how simple it is? All Crotey has to do is use his left hand naturally; his mental conflict is resolved; he stops stammering."

"Even if I wasn't left-handed to begin with?" the patient asked.

"You must have been. You stammer, don't you?"

"Well, as a matter of fact, I only stammer when I'm talking——"

"Naturally," O'Shawnessey cut in, while at the same time Drubetskoy said: "I agree with you, Boru, that stammering is a question of mental conflict; but——"

"To the——"

"But one induced by too early and harsh toilet training," Drubetskoy went on. "The inhibitions set up by——"

"Left-handedness, Boris," said O'Shawnessey.

"Toilet training, Boru," said Drubetskoy.

"Left-handedness, Boris!"

"Toilet training, Boru!"

"LEFT-HANDEDNESS!"

"TOILET TRAINING!"

"Aha," said Rufus; and lighted another cigarette.

When the uproar was at its height, Miss Palfrey opened the door and cried: "Boris! Boru! Doctor Slipstream's coming!"

Immediately Drubetskoy and O'Shawnessey composed themselves, smoothed back their hair, and straightened their clothes which their vehemence had disarranged. They passed their tongues nervously over their lips. Then the professor of psychiatry made his entrance.

"G-g-g-good aftern-n-n-noon, D-d-d-doctor S-s-s-slipstream," Drubetskoy stammered.

"G-g-g-good aftern-n-n-noon, Ch-ch-ch-chief," O'Shawnessey stuttered.

"Good afternoon, boys." Then Slipstream caught sight of Crotey's popping eyes and fallen jaw. "Aha!"

"Good afternoon, Doctor Slipstream," said Rufus.

"Having a little consultation with my boys, doctor?" the psychiatrist asked. Rufus said he had been enjoying a social cigarette. "Well, how are you doing with him, boys?" Slipstream inquired of his assistants.

"A c-c-c-clear c-c-case of m-m-m-mental c-c-conflict from un-n-natural right-handedn-n-ness," O'Shawnessey said.

"An obvious c-c-c-case of f-f-faulty t-t-t-toilet-t-t-t-training," said Drubetskoy.

"Super-imposed upon metakinesis of sex. No, don't go," said Slipstream to Rufus. "In view of your disorder, this will interest you too." He scratched the air where the end of his nose had been, then sneezed. "Boris, Boru, I want your frank reaction to this case report."

"It's g-g-g-great, Ch-ch-ch-chief," said O'Shawnessey promptly.

"M-m-m-marvellous," Drubetskoy chimed in.

"Can't you even wait until I've read it?" Slipstream complained. He pulled a sheaf of typescript from his pocket and recited the mental history of one B. J. S.: she had not been an only child; her intelligence quotient was 100; her reaction time to the word lists was normal; her Alpha, Beta, Binet-Simon, Bourdon, Chicago, Ebbinghaus, Finckh, Freud, Herring, Kohs, Laborde, Lichtheim, Marie, Rorschach, Silvette, and Stanford tests were all normal.

"An obvious case," he interjected, "of a precariously-maintained crust of normality."

But from underneath this, Slipstream had ultimately rooted out his patient's real trouble: metakinesis of sex.

Drubetskoy and O'Shawnessey jumped to their feet and gave their chief a standing ovation. They shook hands with one another; they shook hands with Professor Slipstream; perhaps they would even have shaken hands with Crotey, but, unperceived by the three psychiatrists, Rufus had stolen from the room, a thoughtful expression on his face.

Five minutes later, he knocked on the door of the dean's office. Nimblewit was on the point of leaving for the day. In his hands was the cardboard box containing thirty-five eggs; in his pocket, ten cents honest profit.

When he saw his cacophonous instructor, his ear-drums trembled.

"Sir," said Rufus, "I just wanted to tell you I gave the report to Doctor Slipstream's secretary. Is there anything else I can do for you this afternoon, Doctor Nimblewit?"

"Your stammer?" stuttered the dean, in his astonishment relaxing his grip on the box of eggs. Rufus deftly caught the box before it hit the floor, and restored it to Nimblewit's hands.

"Sir?"

"What did you do with your stammer?" Nimblewit demanded, clutching his box of eggs as though it contained his sanity.

"Oh, that. I'm happy to say, sir, that Doctors Drubetskoy and O'Shawnessey cured me after all."

Chapter Twenty-two

LEAVING THE SHAKEN Nimblewit to wobble along in his wake, Rufus left the dean's office on his own way home. In the corridor outside he almost collided with the gentleman farmer hurrying along with the dean's seventy-second egg clutched in his fist. Just in time, Rufus dodged.

"Dean in?" Dee said tersely.

"Yes, sir."

Dee turned sharply into the dean's office. Rufus heard a startled exclamation; a cry; a crash; a despairing wail. He kept on walking.

"Now look what you've done," Nimblewit wrathfully exclaimed, staring down at the cardboard box on the floor. Yolk and white were beginning to ooze glutinously from its ruptured seams. Dee held his hand away from his body; egg was oozing from between his fingers too, and dripping gluily to the floor. "Roaring into my office like a maniac," the dean continued. "Smashing my eggs."

"I'm—I'm sorry, Mr. Dean."

"Being sorry won't unscramble my eggs."

"I'll—I'll replace them, Mr. Dean," Dee madly offered.

"Seventy-TWO eggs," said Nimblewit, grim emphasis on the two.

Rufus entertained the dinner-table that evening with the account of how he had been cured of his stammering. Then Susan told of her father's triumphant clash with Professor Dee (alas, once more the dean could not forbear to boast); of how he had got twelve dozen eggs for the price of six, and those six at the wholesale rate of fifty cents a dozen.

"F-f-f-fifty cents?" Rufus stammered.

"I thought you were cured?" she said.

"The dirty dog dug me for a dime," he said to prove his claim. It was the beginning of his disillusionment. Of this moment Rufus would later say: "It was then that I became a Man."

"Have you heard anything of the Chouse?" Mr. Bigginson asked.

"He didn' meet his class today," said Fido.

"Bless me, I trust you didn't kill him, Fido?"

"Naw. They'd have give us the day off if I'd of croaked him." Rembrandt looked greatly relieved. "Besides," said Fido, "I looked at Suze's skull. It wasn't even cracked."

Then Susan and Rufus carried all the dirty dishes, pots, and pans into the bathroom to wash up. That was their only time together these days, and they obtained it only by over-riding Fido's sense of the fitness of things. Fido wanted to do Suze's work for her. "Aw, who wants to be alone with you, Fido?" Rufus had said.

So, while Rufus and Susan did the dishes, Fido and Rembrandt smoked Big Pat's cigars in the living-room. (Wish O'Hoe realised that Rufe was milking him, and submitted with outward good grace and an inward resolution to settle scores with him the day after graduation.)

185

For all he was no older than Rufus, Fido was full of curious reminiscences, and Mr. Bigginson loved to listen to them; but when they became medical, the squeamish artist would shudder, and call loudly for cognac. But it was precisely these medical anecdotes which were the most remarkable. Apparently Fido's mind dealt with medical data as Rube Fields's lop-sided brain handled mathematics:

"Give Rube Fields the distance by rail between any two points, and the dimensions of a car-wheel," ran a contemporary account of this dope with a genius for mathematics, "and almost as soon as the statement has left your lips he will tell you the number of revolutions the wheel will make travelling over the track. Call four or five or any number of columns of figures down a page, and when you have reached the bottom he will announce the sum. Given the number of yards or pounds of articles and the price, and at once he will return the total cost" (but Cedric Osbert Dee hourly duplicated this feat), "—and this he will do all day long, without apparent effort or fatigue. Fields's answers come quick and sharp, seemingly by intuition. Calculations which would require hours to perform are made in less time than it takes to state the question. The size of the computations seems to offer no bar to their rapid solution, and answers in which long lines of figures are reeled off come with perfect ease. In watching the effort put forth in reaching an answer, there would seem to be some process going on in his mind, and an incoherent mumbling is often indulged in, but it is highly probable that Fields does not know himself how he derives his answers. Certain it is that he is unable to explain the process, nor has anyone ever been able to draw from him anything concerning it." Outside of this gift, which Fields declared to be of God, Rube was more ignorant than Fido before the latter attended Byrlady University. If he had gone to school, Rube once said: "Da he'd of become as big a fool as other people." No wonder Slipstream had been as baffled by Fido as those

186

earlier eminent professors who had examined Rube Fields.

"Rufus," said Susan, handing him a plate to be wiped dry, "Daddy is terribly upset."

"Over that little bit of money?"

"Oh, it isn't the thousand dollars——"

"Thousand dollars!" Rufus had been thinking of his ten cents.

She glanced in the direction of the living-room, and unnecessarily lowered her voice. "Don't you remember what Willoughby Chouse said when we were hiding under his furniture?"

"Well, yes."

"Didn't you grasp its significance? After telling it all around the university they were going to raise $2,000, those jealous doctors have refused to contribute enough money for Daddy's testimonial portrait."

"I'd have given more than five dollars," he said defensively, "but Wanion hinted it would be uppity of a mere instructor."

"It's not a question of five dollars now. From what Chouse said, they are a thousand short; and if you'd lived all your life in the university, as I have, you'd realise they are all waiting like ghouls for Daddy to contribute the balance himself."

"But that would be . . ."

"It certainly would," she said grimly. "That's why I said it wasn't a question of money now, but rather how we can manage to get it into the hands of the committee."

"Gosh, is that what the dean is planning to do?"

Susan gave him a soapy cup. "It's what I am planning to do."

He dried the cup; said "Poor Dean Nimblewit"; and gave a pitying look at his daughter.

"Or, rather, what you're going to do," she said. "I mean, figuring out some way to get $1,000 to the portrait

187

committee without them discovering where it came from."

"Me? I haven't got a thousand dollars. But maybe Rembrandt can raise it——"

"Now that's a brilliant idea," she said scornfully, "when it's Rembrandt who is going to paint the portrait. Besides, if he knew the committee couldn't raise $2,000, he's just unworldly enough to offer to paint Daddy for half price."

Remembering Mr. Bigginson's once standard fee of $500, Rufus thought the artist would be quite willing to paint a portrait for twice that sum. He said: "It's an idea, Suze."

"Do you think Daddy would want a bargain testimonial?" she said scathingly. "Rufus, I wish you wouldn't be so dense."

"Well, there's one advantage in being dense. I won't ever get into a mess over *my* testimonial portrait."

Susan hit him over the head with a soapy dinner-plate. The plate broke, and he had to grab the edge of the wash-basin and hold on until his knees stiffened again. "If you don't learn to control that temper of yours," she said, "I won't marry you."

"I never asked you to," he said thickly.

She broke another plate over his head. "Da, Suze," said Rufus, weaving like a punch-drunk fighter, "will you marry me?"

"Well, I'll consider it if you figure out a way to give the portrait committee a thousand dollars so they can't possibly learn where it came from."

They washed and dried the rest of the dishes in silence. From the living-room came the sound of Fido's rumbling words, and once Mr. Bigginson's frantic: "Fido, my cognac!"

"Okay," said Rufus to Susan as they were stowing the dishes away in the bedroom-cum-kitchen cabinet; "get me the thousand."

"You got it?" she asked, her eyes shining.

"I got it. My wits only wanted a little shaking up, da that's all." He rubbed the top of his head.

"Bend over; I'll kiss it and make it well." Then she said: "For a change you taste like dish-water instead of embalming fluid. How are you going to do it?"

He shook his head. "I'd better not tell you. Then if anyone asks you, you can truthfully say, you don't know anything about it."

After Fido took her home, Susan knocked on the closed door of her father's study. Nimblewit automatically swept his sex manuals into a desk drawer, but there was no longer any need to cover up his MS. Though he still kept up a pretence of working on his book, it was more in the hope of being able to take his mind off the looming catastrophe of his testimonial portrait than in any expectation of finishing his treatise. For he had virtually conceded defeat in this second encounter with Sex, which was proving hardly less fortunate in its outcome than his first encounter with his wife.

"Come in, Pussy," he said in a resigned voice.

"It's Susan, Daddy."

Nimblewit smiled wanly at her as his daughter entered his study. "I don't see much of you these days, Susan," he said.

"You're always so busy writing."

"And you're never home for dinner any more," he complained. "I can't see how you stand that moron all the time."

"Surely you're not speaking of the man who stands first in the senior class of the medical school?"

The dean sighed. This beautiful child of his was also a kitten of Pussy's; and in spite of himself he could not help feeling sorry for Fido, who seemed destined to lead a dog's life.

"Besides," she continued, touched by her misinterpretation of her father's plaintive sound, "we dine with Mr. Bigginson every evening."

"Doesn't Fido eat a lot?"

"Enormously. Daddy, why don't you have Mr. Bigginson paint your portrait?"

"Paint my portrait!" the dean cried bitterly. "How can anyone paint my portrait when that double-crossing committee refuses to collect the rest of the money for it?"

"If I were you, I'd show those stinkers," said Susan; "I'd show them."

"How?"

"Why, I'd give them the rest of the money myself. Then the laugh would be on them. They think they've sabotaged your testimonial, but you'd have out-foxed them, and they'd be too dumb to know it."

"Ha!" The dean brightened at the pleasant thought.

"Of course you'd have to do it secretly. I'll tell you what, Daddy; you give me the money, and I'll see that the committee gets it; and I promise you they'll never be able to find out where it comes from."

Father and daughter exchanged a solemn look. Nimblewit's said, my honour is in your hands; Susan's replied, your honour is my own. The dean took his cheque-book from the top desk drawer and wrote out a cheque for $1,000 payable to Susan Nimblewit. He was too cagey to ask her what she was going to do with it, guarding his innocence like a virgin. "Daughter——" he said; then hesitated.

"Yes, Daddy?"

"When your mother returns, you needn't . . ."

"No, Daddy."

"You're a good girl, Susan," said the dean gratefully. "I wish," he went on in a wistful voice, "you did dine at home occasionally."

She smiled. "If I were you, I'd show me. I'd invite Mr. Bigginson here to dinner, and then Susan would have to stay home or go hungry."

The next evening at dinner, Mr. Bigginson said:

"Rufus, you and Fido will have to forage for yourselves tomorrow night. Susan and I are dining elsewhere."

"Else*where?*" he asked jealously.

"Oh, with some dull people named Nimblewit," said Susan; and later, when she and Rufus were alone, washing up, she gave him an envelope containing ten crisp new hundred-dollar notes.

Chapter Twenty-three

ASHBY TIPPETT WAS sitting in his office when his secretary showed Fido in. "Da hullo, doc," said Fido, politely raising his hat.

"Good morning—ER—Fido."

"I unnerstand you're in charge of the pitcher of the dean?"

"Yes, I'm—ER—chairman of the portrait committee," Tippett admitted cautiously.

"I got some dough for you, doc." Fido showered the top of the chairman's desk with five-, ten-, and twenty-dollar notes, for which Rufus had exchanged the ten hundreds. "Nine hundred sixty bucks."

Tippett gasped. As soon as he could speak, he asked: "ER—whom did you—ER—collect it from?"

"Well, it was like this, doc," Fido said in some embarrassment, for this was his first lie, and only Rufus's reminder that he was Suze's knight in shining armour had made him consent to telling it at all: "when they come around collecting for the dean's pitcher that time, Wish give them five bucks for me. The dean's a good guy, doc. I wanted to give him some of my own dough. I hadda hot tip on a horse, so I put five bucks on him for the dean's pitcher. He won. So I put the tweny bucks on the next pony I hadda red-hot tip on. The dean's pitcher win again. So I put the hunderd tweny bucks on another nag, and he win too. I figure the dean's luck is about give out, so I decide to give you the dough this time."

"Nine hundred and sixty dollars!"

"Naw, doc." He shook his head. "Five bucks. I put this five bucks on a horse, see, and I parley it up to nine-sixty."

"But—ER—all this money?" Tippett said unbelievingly. "Do you want to—ER—contribute it all?"

"It ain't my money, doc," Fido patiently explained. "It belongs to the dean's pitcher. Five bucks was my money. I put this five bucks on a horse——"

"Yes, yes." Tippett was beginning to experience that slightly nightmarish feeling which any extended conversation with Fido on a non-medical subject invariably induced. "I quite—ER—understand, Fido. It will give me great—ER—pleasure to add your nine hundred and sixty dollars——"

"Oney five bucks is mine, doc."

"Yes, yes. To the Dean Horace Nimblewit Portrait Fund."

"Well, so long, doc," said Fido, tipping his hat.

"Da so long, Fido."

Tippett rushed straight to the dean's office to tell his incredible story. But incredible was a word the medical Faculty had long since ceased to apply to Fido or any of his works; and there was the evidence of $960 in genuine United States currency to prove to both of them that Tippett wasn't lying.

"From five dollars to nine hundred and sixty," the chairman of the portrait committee kept saying; and each time he did so, the dean repeated Slipstream's classic phrase:

"Fido is a genius, da that's all."

Nimblewit was personally abstemious, but he was also the perfect host. "Will you have sherry, sir?" he asked

Mr. Bigginson. "Or perhaps you would prefer a cocktail before dinner?"

The artist was dressed in dinner clothes which seemed more antiquated than they really were. That is to say, they were old-fashioned in design, but relatively new in manufacture; for Rembrandt had insisted on the style of 1912 or thereabouts, and his tailor had turned out such a period masterpiece that Mr. Bigginson was often sorry he had never paid his bill. His linen, rather than gleaming white, was softly ivory-tinted. When he had driven up to the Nimblewits' in his Mercedes, and Susan had admitted him, her eyes had widened at the picturesque and impressive sight. After showing him into the living-room, she had quickly excused herself and run off to whisper into her father's ear. With a groan the dean changed from his business suit into formal attire; and Susan slipped into a dinner dress and donned ear-rings. Then she hurried down the back stairs to tell the cook to place candlesticks on the table, which had been laid for three; for Mrs. Nimblewit was off attending the closing meet at Hialeah.

Mr. Bigginson eyed the bottle of California sherry on the tray, then the hammered aluminium cocktail-shaker next to it. The unlabelled cocktail-shaker seemed to offer at least a gambler's chance, so he said: "I should like a cocktail very much, thank you, sir."

"And you, Daddy?"

"I'll have a cocktail too," said Nimblewit. Susan poured them each a cocktail, and herself a glass of sherry. Mr. Bigginson took a sip of his cocktail and looked startled: the cocktail had come already mixed from a bottle, needing only to be emptied into a shaker and chilled to startle one's guests; or so the advertisement had said. The dean, sipping his own cocktail with the abandoned air of a Left-Bank artist swilling absinthe, was pleased to observe that the advertisement hadn't lied: his guest did look startled.

"Excellent, sir, excellent," said Mr. Bigginson, following the advertising copy as though he had written it himself. Susan choked over her sherry; Rembrandt gave her a reproachful glance.

"Ready for a dividend?" she inquired.

"After the dean, Susan," said Rembrandt. Ignoring his movement of protest, Susan refilled her father's glass. The artist raised his, and said: "As Geoff Lanyard and I used to say, *'Voici de la boue dans l'oeil.'*"

"Your good health too, sir," said Nimblewit courteously. "I suppose my daughter has told you that Lanyard and I were old college friends—room-mates, in fact, at Lehigh?"

"I knew he was a loyal alumnus," said Mr. Bigginson. "In our day, more Frenchmen knew the words of 'Down in the Lehigh Valley' than of the Star-Spangled Banner."

"What's that?" Susan asked. "I never heard of it."

"I should hope not," said the artist; "it is a very improper song."

"Hok, hok," said the dean. "It is not the college song, Susan."

"Geoff translated it into French," Mr. Bigginson said. "Gendarmes used to be summoned from the next arrondissement when he sang it. Hrrmph, hrrmph. No doubt your daughter has informed you, sir," he said to the dean, "Lanyard and I shared a flat in Paris for some years?"

"Have you seen him recently?"

"Not since the night of the Armistice, really. Geoff and I had been driving an ambulance for the French. Ah, sir, for two young men (for I was but thirty then: *Eheu! fugaces labuntur anni!*)—for two young fellows to possess an empty ambulance in Paris on the night of November 11, 1918—*c'était formidable!*"

"I can imagine it," said Susan.

"My dear voung lady," said Rembrandt, "you cannot. Well, well, Dean Nimblewit. If we elderly fellows did not have our memories . . ."

"Ah yes," said the dean.

"Why, Daddy, you must have been an old rake too!"

Nimblewit swelled out his chest. "A rake with very small teeth." His second cocktail was mounting to a head unused to one. " 'Down in the Lehigh Valley,' " he warbled.

"Hrrmph, hrrmph," said Rembrandt loudly. "Hrrmph."

"I must tell you a most amazing story, sir," said the dean, grasping Mr. Bigginson by one satin lapel.

"Daddy," said Susan hastily, "have a canapé."

"As you may have heard, sir," Nimblewit pushed away the plate his daughter had thrust beneath his nose, "my colleagues and students have generously offered to have my portrait painted as a testimonial to my years of service to the medical school."

"A well-merited recognition, sir."

"Yes. One of my students—in fact, my favourite student, if a dean in the privacy of his own home, and before his own daughter and the intimate friend of his old college room-mate may be permitted to confess himself guilty of favouritism, which a scientist no less than a dean should always subordinate to impartial and objective—where was I?"

"You were speaking of your favourite student, sir."

"Yes, of course. Fido."

At Fido's sudden incredible rise in her father's affections, Susan almost dropped the tray of canapés.

"Fido," he repeated. "The dear boy wanted to contribute a small sum towards my portrait, but instead of giving his five dollars directly to the tax-collector, he laid it on the noses of three successive nags and parlayed it to nine hundred and sixty bucks, which he then presented to the chairman of the portrait-fund committee."

"God bless my soul!" said Mr. Bigginson.

"I may tell you in strict confidence, sir," said the dean boozily, "my daughter is going to marry the dear boy."

"Rembrandt, this is awful!" Susan said as she rode back to the artist's apartment with him in the Mercedes for a private talk with him and Rufus. "How can I blackmail Daddy into commissioning you to do his portrait by threatening to marry Fido, if he's already given us his blessing?"

And it appeared as though some sort of blackmail might be necessary; for the dean, quickly sobered up by roast veal and trimmings, had resisted all his daughter's hints to get him to invite Mr. Bigginson to paint his portrait. It was not that Nimblewit hadn't been sufficiently taken by the old friend of his old friend; but instinctively a dean avoids coming to any decision unless absolutely forced to make one, and by some psychological law or statute of his guild he automatically resists any effort to push him in one direction or the other.

"Damn!" said Susan.

"Young ladies should not curse," said Mr. Bigginson.

"Well, what would you say if you were in my fix?"

"*Merde.*"

Rufus and Fido were seated at the card-table, playing pinochle. Before Rufus on the table was a quart bottle of beer; in front of Fido, a quart of milk and Kaufman the white mouse. Susan rushed into the apartment and kissed Fido. "My knight in shining armour!" She kissed Rufus. "I'll bet when Mycroft Holmes gets stuck," she said to him in reverent tones, "he comes to you for help."

"May one inquire the cause of this unseemly exhibition?" Rembrandt asked. Susan, Rufus, and Fido all shook their heads. "Hrrmph, hrrmph," said the artist. "Come here, Vigée; comfort an abandoned old man."

"Did you two have any dinner?" Susan inquired of the pinochle players. They shook their heads, letting the corners of their mouths sag dismally, like Early Christian martyrs.

"My three hams," she said. "What's that the kittens are gnawing on?" she said suddenly. "Let me see, Botticelli; let go, Gaddo Gaddi. Ouch!" Marietta Tintoretta had bitten her finger with sharp baby teeth. She straightened up and stared at Rufus and Fido, who were looking like Saints Cosmo and Damian just before the axe fell. *"Hamburgers!"*

"Before I forget it, Rembrandt," Rufus said hastily, "Chouse phoned while you were out. He wants you to call him."

"He did not utter any hrrmph threats, Rufus?" the artist asked nervously.

"Maybe he found the horse-fly on his schnozzola?" Fido said.

"More likely he had a flea in his ear," said Susan.

"Rufus, please be good enough to get my travelling-bags from under the bed," said Rembrandt. "Bring me Vigée-Lebrun's basket. Bring me my cognac."

"As a matter of fact," said Rufus, "Chouse sounded extraordinarily ingratiating. Shall I get him on the phone for you now, Rembrandt?"

"Yes, do," said Susan.

Ignoring Rembrandt's frantic motions, Rufus did so; then handed the artist the telephone. "I trust I did not get you out of bed at this late hour, Doctor Chouse?" Mr. Bigginson said.

The telephone receiver rattled, crackled, and finally purred into Rembrandt's ear, and the artist's face took on an expression of bewilderment. "Bless me!" he said from time to time. At last he said in a voice of tremendous dignity: "Once Rembrandt Bigginson has signed one of his portraits, he never touches it again, sir!" The receiver complained. Rembrandt said firmly: "No, sir; never! Good night!"

He replaced the phone in its cradle, and said: "Kick my travelling-bags back under the bed, Rufus. Vigée, my darling——"

"What did he say?" Susan and Rufus demanded. Mr. Bigginson shook his head.

"I can't stand it!" she wailed.

"My dear young lady, what is sauce for the gander is sauce for the goose."

"Why, you old blackmailer!"

197

Rembrandt calmly lighted a cigar.

"You fiend," Susan said. She whispered at length into his ear.

"Bless me! God bless my soul! Bless me!" he said at intervals. Then, when she had finished, he struggled up from his easy chair and shook hands with Fido and Rufus.

"That was the Chouse," he said.

"*Merde!*"

"The Chouse informed me that his young son was recently given a box of oil-paints on his birthday, and had been amusing himself by painting moustaches on magazine cover-girls and his mother's photograph. He went on to say that since his own portrait, thanks to Nature and Rembrandt Bigginson, already possessed a handsome moustache, his young son had painted a fly on its nose. And he offered me fifty dollars to paint it out."

"Da Rembrandt," Fido said, his brow furrowed, "I thought you painted a horse-fly on Doc Chouse's schnozzola?"

"I did, Fido my boy; I did."

"Aw, I get it. Now he got two flies on his nose."

"Possibly, Fido; but I doubt it. My children, outside of two classes of people, the fear of ridicule is the dominant emotion in most people's lives. The great are above ridicule; the bums of the world like myself are below it. But between these two extremes lie the great middle class, and in the precise centre of that is a university community, where to be ridiculous is the eighth deadly sin. Am I not right, Susan?"

"Yes."

"Rather than admit that some disaffected genius with the brush broke into his house, and painted a green-rumped horse-fly on his schnozzola, thus rendering him an object of ridicule; rather than sink down on his marrow-bones and thank Heaven for a *trompe-l'oeil* worthy of the great Quentin Matsys, whose similar feat is still celebrated in the annals of our profession; rather than—where the hell was I?"

"You was talkin' about the fly Doc Chouse's kid painted on his nose."

"Precisely. That, at least, is conventional. Kids will be little stinkers. When junior perpetrates some childish prank, papa gives him a spanking, and then calls in the appropriate workman to repair the damage." Mr. Bigginson chuckled evilly. "I wonder what the Chouse will do now that the appropriate workman has refused to come?"

At that moment, Willoughby Chouse was kneeling down in his drawing-room, the stock of his young son's .22-calibre rifle against his shoulder, its barrel steadied on the back of a chair. He took careful aim at the fly on the nose of his portrait, and gently squeezed off the trigger. The drawing-room reverberated with the sharp report of the rifle, and a small round hole replaced the fly on Chouse's painted nose. His painted eyes seemed to squint in surprise at the miraculous disappearance of the insect.

"Willoughby!" his wife screamed from upstairs. "What was that?"

Chouse did not answer.

"Willoughby, what's wrong?"

Silently Chouse arranged himself artistically on the floor, and shut his eyes. While waiting for his wife to discover him, he rehearsed his story: "I was reading. Suddenly I felt there was someone in the house. I seized Junior's rifle and went downstairs, and in the drawing-room was a burglar; his face was completely covered by a black mask. I fired one shot at him before he sprang on me. He hit me with a blackjack, and I knew no more." At this point, in his imagination Chouse chuckled and pointed out his portrait to a succession of enthralled audiences. "And would you believe it, I had shot myself!"

"Rufus, will you drive me home now?" Susan asked.

"Aw, Suze," Fido protested, "I always drive you home."

"Well, I'd like you to," she said, "but if my father

199

catches us together, he'll make you marry me. Isn't that so, Rembrandt?"

"His gratitude certainly seemed to know no bounds."

Fido said in a worried voice: "Aw, you know I can't marry you, Suze. But I'll be a brother to you."

"You're the sweetest brother in the world, and I love you, Fido." She kissed him and Rembrandt, then left with Rufus.

"Don't think you can rest on your laurels now," she told him in the Mercedes. "You've still got to figure out a way to make Daddy give Rembrandt the commission."

"Well, I know a sure way," said Rufus.

"What is it?"

"Tell your father Rembrandt will split the take with him."

Susan slapped him hard, and said: "Temper, temper! Daddy thinks fee-splitting is unethical, and besides——"

"Yes, Susan." He sighed, rubbing his burning cheek.

"Besides, I want Rembrandt to get all the money."

Chapter Twenty-four

THE DEAN WAS holding a veritable court in his office. Ashby Tippett had lost no time in spreading the story of Fido's princely donation throughout the medical school, and one by one Nimblewit's colleagues had stopped by to congratulate him. "Nimblewit's Luck," they called his miraculous last-minute reprieve to themselves and one another. "Nimblewit's Luck"—as though Susan's filial love, Crotey's brilliant imagination, and Fido's dog-like devotion had nothing to do with wresting victory from the very jaws of ridicule.

But the dean, though he accepted his Faculty's envious admiration with a rusty blush, now knew that he owed his deliverance to his once-despised instructor; for Susan had not delayed to inform her father that Fido had been only the trusty tool, and Rufus's the great fertile brain wherein was hatched the ingenious plan. And she had refunded him forty dollars.

Strangely enough, it had been this latter act which had impressed Nimblewit the most. It demonstrated a greatness of soul in Rufus Crotey which made the dean regret having taken a legitimate profit on the re-sale of two dozen eggs. It is odd but true that neither Susan, Rufus, nor the dean himself ever felt even a fleeting suspicion that the Nimblewit honour was not safe with Fido. This feeling went far beyond a simple faith in Fido's discretion; it was the instinctive feeling that Fido, asked to reveal any confidential matter, would only shake his great head and reply: "That ain't right;" and the Inquisition itself would be powerless to make him alter his mind or his words. But Nimblewit did have serious doubts about his instructor. For Crotey had been presented with a deadly weapon, and thirty-five years in a medical school had taught Nimblewit to expect that sooner or later it would be pointed at his breast, and Crotey would demand: "Your —— or your reputation," which is in a dean's case his life. The only question in Nimblewit's mind was what would be inserted into the blank.

A rise in salary? Academic promotion? His daughter Susan? The dean leaped in his swivel-chair and swung around to gaze out over High Street with unseeing eyes. What a come-down this would be from the brilliant future he had planned for his daughter: wife of the Medical Director of the Mary Margaret MacSweeny O'Hoe Memorial Hospital and Medical Centre; daughter-in-law of Patrick Aloysius O'Hoe, in whose most casual word was a gilt-edged security.

"Doctor Nimblewit," his secretary was saying insistently, "Mr. O'Hoe is on the phone."

"Yes, yes, thank you, Dorothy." Nimblewit revolved 90 degrees and took up his telephone. "Commissioner?" he said into the mouthpiece. "Dean Nimblewit speaking."

The dean listened. Then he said: "Still very satisfactory." The receiver rattled again. "Yes, I quite realise that, Commissioner," Nimblewit replied. The receiver murmured. The dean replaced the phone, and made a note on his desk pad.

No; he resumed the current of his thoughts; his daughter Susan—never! And again his secretary broke into his reverie. "There is a gentleman to see you," she said, "from Spanner and Company."

The dean made an impatient gesture. "You know I never see book salesmen, Dorothy."

"I know, sir; but Mr. Sidney Spanner isn't a salesman; he's the senior vice-president."

"Well, send him in," said Nimblewit, wondering what the senior vice-president of the largest medical book publishers in the country wanted with him. After an exchange of courtesies with Mr. Sidney Spanner, he found out.

"Doctor Nimblewit," he said, "it has come to our attention that you are engaged in writing a textbook of sex for medical students." The dean quivered like a gaffed salmon. "So I thought I would just run down here and see if you had made any arrangements yet for its publication?"

"No," said Nimblewit in a hoarse voice.

"Splendid! In that case, my company will be honoured to have the privilege of publishing your book, and we shall be happy to offer you the most advantageous terms." Spanner lowered his voice confidentially. "I may tell you that, stimulated by the Kinsey Report, the medical world is on the verge of taking a great interest in sex, and the man who first comes out with a textbook on the subject designed primarily for medical schools will reap a harvest, sir. Mark my words, Doctor Nimblewit, he will reap a harvest."

The dean moistened his lips with his tongue, then asked: "Who informed you I was writing a book of that sort?"

"We have our sources of information," Spanner said genially. "They also tell us that several other medical book publishers are eager to have a textbook on sex for medical students ready for the next academic year. That means, sir, we must have your manuscript, complete with illustrations, in our hands by July first. That gives us precious little time, but the first in the field, doctor—the first in the field reaps the harvest. May I ask the present status of your manuscript?"

"It is unfinished."

"I quite understand. Nevertheless, in view of your reputation, doctor, we are prepared to sign a contract for its publication, and announce immediately in the *Journal of the American Medical Association,* the *Journal of the Association of American Medical Colleges,* and elsewhere, that the book will be available by October fifteenth. For advance orders, you understand, and to forestall other publishers."

The dean could not force himself to admit to Spanner that there would never be a *Text-book of Sex for Medical Students* by Horace Nimblewit, B.A., M.D., etc., etc. He said: "I shall write you of my decision."

Spanner arose, and held out his hand. "I don't want to press you, doctor, but we would appreciate having your decision promptly. We have information that another professor is also writing a sex book. Frankly, we would prefer to publish yours, in view of your reputation; but—well, business is business. I'll leave our contract with you, and shall look forward to receiving it, signed.

It was a mark of Nimblewit's perturbation of spirit that for one wild moment he thought of setting fire to his study, and then bewailing the tragic loss of his unique manuscript. But brick houses don't burn to the ground, Reason reminded him, utterly destroying manuscripts in steel desks. Nor does the Angel Moroni reveal the burial-place of a text-book of sex for medical students transcribed on plates of gold. Yet there must be some way out of his pickle, the dean insisted to himself, besides confessing the truth, or leaving it to be inferred; some way as simple and ingenious as parlaying five dollars to nine hundred and sixty. . . .

"Dorothy!" he called. "Send for Doctor Crotey immediately."

Rufus entered the dean's office in some surprise, which rose to astonishment when Nimblewit closed his office doors, patted him into a chair, offered him a cigarette, and called him "Rufus my boy." All this attention almost made him stammer; it did make him wonder.

After inviting Rufus to dinner at his house that evening, and making it appear that this was the reason for the unusual summons, the dean remarked: "Perhaps you have heard that I am engaged in writing a textbook of sex for medical students?"

Rufus didn't know whether he was supposed to know this officially or not. "Well," he admitted cautiously, "I did hear something to that effect."

"Where?"

"Under the sofa at Doctor Chouse's."

"Ah yes," said the dean. "Rufus my boy, I have the highest opinion of your capacity, the utmost confidence in your discret—*Where* did you say you heard it?"

"Susan told me, sir."

"Ah yes." Nimblewit put a finger inside his collar, tugged, then swivelled round until he was facing the window. "Sidney Spanner, the medical publisher, was just here, trying to persuade me to sign a contract for its publication. A very advantageous contract, I may say. I am very much inclined to sign it, and send them my manuscript in a few weeks."

"Yes, sir."

"However, I have only the one copy of my manuscript," the dean went on. "I am afraid to trust it to the mails or express. But as I say, Rufus, I have the utmost confidence in you. If you would be kind enough to take it to New York personally . . ."

This was the place for Rufus to say he would be glad to; he said it.

"You would keep in mind the danger of losing the manuscript," said Nimblewit, "as for example dropping it over the side of the Newcastle ferry-boat. So many things can happen to a unique manuscript, you know."

"Yes, sir. It really should be first typed in duplicate or triplicate, if you don't mind my suggesting it, sir."

"Rufus," said the dean, "please do not be dense."

Rufus blinked. There was silence in the office while he figured out that Nimblewit wanted him to drop a non-existent manuscript overboard, then take the rap for losing it.

"I expected more than this of your intelligence," the dean remarked to the window.

"Sir."

"Rufus, my book must not be published!" the dean said dramatically. "Er—for personal reasons," he ended weakly.

"You mean, sir, Susan and Mrs. Nimblewit wouldn't like it if you published a book on sex?"

"My wife," said Nimblewit plaintively, "will give me no peace until I do."

"Yes, sir." Rufus was being deliberately unhelpful.

"The fact is," the dean confessed to High Street, "I have only had time to finish part of the book—the first three chapters—but Mrs. Nimblewit thinks . . ."

"I see, sir. Mrs. Nimblewit thinks you have written it all."

"My wife," said the dean in a whisper, "thinks I can't write it at all." Rufus laughed decorously. "I can't," said Nimblewit.

Rufus stopped laughing—and began to admire the dean's ingenuity in finding a way out of his terrible predicament at the small cost of one instructor of anatomy.

"Well, why don't you get yourself a ghost-writer, sir?" he asked out of compassion for the unfortunate dean.

Nimblewit swung so vigorously around in his swivel-chair it revolved through 540 degrees before he came face to face with his instructor. He stared at Rufus as though this simplest of suggestions were also the most sublime.

"A ghost-writer!" he murmured. Then, aloud: "Who, you?"

"Me? Oh no, sir. Mr. Bigginson."

"Mr. Bigginson?"

"Yes, sir; Rembrandt Bigginson. Properly expurgated, his reminiscences would give you everything any medical student ought to know about sex. And no doubt, sir," he went on, "he could even be persuaded to illustrate your book."

Nimblewit gave a long sigh. "No, Rufus," he said at last. "For a moment I had thought—but no; it must be the Newcastle ferry. If Mrs. Nimblewit read Mr. Bigginson's book, she would know at once I had never written it."

"If that is your only objection to the idea, sir——"

"You don't mean my wife could be made to believe I wrote what Rembrandt Bigginson knows?"

"No, sir; but perhaps she wouldn't be able to disbelieve it."

"You don't know Mrs. Nimblewit."

"You don't know Rembrandt. Excuse me, sir, I didn't mean to be smart——"

"You must be smart," said the dean.

"Of course, I'll have to ask Mr. Bigginson about ghost-writing the book, but I think he'll love doing it."

"How much——"

"Oh, you can talk to him about terms, sir, while he's painting your portrait."

Nimblewit swallowed hard. "Yes, yes; while he's painting my portrait."

"Yes, sir," said Rufus, rising to leave.

"Rufus."

"Sir?"

"Perhaps you will bring Mr. Bigginson with you to dinner tonight. Mrs. Nimblewit is fortunately still away, and we can discuss the matter of the ah portrait."

"Yes, sir."

"Dress will be informal," the dean hastily added.

When Rufus returned to his apartment at the end of the day, he told Mr. Bigginson they were invited to dine with the dean that evening. "What, again?" said the artist in dismay.

"Doctor Nimblewit wants to discuss the matter of his portrait with you."

"Bless me! So Susan finally blackmailed him into it, bless her innocent little heart."

"She's innocent, all right. And moreover, it's not blackmail; it's a fair swap."

"If you are speaking about one of my portraits and two thousand dollars, Rufus my boy, in all fairness I cannot call that a fair swap. You mean, Nimblewit wants his split?"

"You misjudge the dean." Rufus thought of Nimblewit's ingenious scheme to toss him to the wolves. "You misjudge him badly. No; all you have to do for him in return is ghost-write a textbook on sex for medical students."

"God bless my soul!" said Mr. Bigginson weakly. Then a wicked gleam lighted up his eyes. "Oh brother! *Ça sera formidable!*"

"Hey listen, Rembrandt," Rufus said anxiously, "it's only for medical students. *Medical* students."

"*Formidable!*"

"Furthermore, you'll have to discover some way of convincing Mrs. Nimblewit that her husband actually wrote it."

"That understands itself," said the artist. (French is the natural language of Love.) "It is necessary only to

207

incorporate here and there a mention of certain small intimacies with which the dean and his wife amused themselves during *la lune de miel*."

"Have you ever seen Mrs. Nimblewit?"

"I have not yet had that pleasure."

"Well, all I can say is, you'd better do well to think up a better method."

"Another method, possibly," said Mr. Bigginson. "A better method, never."

After dinner Nimblewit and Mr. Bigginson disappeared into the dean's private study. Susan and Rufus sat in the living-room together.

"Well, how did you do it this time, Mycroft?" she asked.

"I guess you might call it blackmail," he said carefully. He had old-fashioned ideas about what a young girl should know.

Susan looked at him sharply, but all she said was: "The swineherd always has to pass three tests before he wins the fairy-tale princess. Your first two were relatively easy. Your third and last is to get Daddy's consent to our marriage."

Rufus said gloomily: "I'll bet your father thinks I know too much about him now to want me around."

Chapter Twenty-five

RUFUS WAS HELPING Mr. Bigginson stretch his canvas for Dean Nimblewit's portrait. They were working in a small disused anatomical laboratory on the top floor of the medical building, where a large skylight furnished a perfect north light. Rufus didn't tell the artist what the two grooved stone-topped tables at one end of the room were used for. While he held the canvas taut over the wooden frame with an iron canvas-stretcher,

Rembrandt hammered in tacks along the edge. First a tack in the centre of one side, then one in the middle of the opposite side; a tack in the middle of one end, another in the centre of the other end. From these centres, the artist tacked towards the corners of his canvas, turning the frame between tacks and instructing Rufus where to grip the canvas between the corrugated jaws of his stretcher and lever the fabric tight against the tack Mr. Bigginson had just driven in. At last Rembrandt neatly tucked down the corners of the canvas, and fastened them securely; then lightly tapped thin wedge-shaped stretcher keys into the mortised joints of the wooden stretcher; and finally he thumped the centre of the taut canvas with a satisfied finger. All the while he stretched his canvas, he talked to Rufus around a mouthful of carpet tacks.

"Rufus my boy, until Nimblewit lent me those books by Foilove, Letcher, and Dildo as a guide to the organisation of my own reminiscences, I thought I had passed the age of blushing. But really: to talk of such things in cold blood makes one's blood run hot to one's face, and cold to one's trousers."

"Did you learn anything?" Rufus asked.

Rembrandt was so indignant at this insulting question that he missed a tack, and hammered his left forefinger. *"Merde!"*

"Learn anything from such books!" he spluttered. "My dear boy, you leave me speechless, absolutely speechless. *(Whack!)* Did I, Rembrandt Bigginson, for whom cocottes queued up—whose scientific researches led to the discovery of Bigginson's Dimple—who at the age of thirty spent Armistice Night in Paris in an ambulance without adding to his store of knowledge: his pleasure was another story *(Whack!)*—who once saved Havelock Ellis from pulling out handfuls of beard by a timely gift of the hot dope—who . . . But you leave me speechless, absolutely speechless." *(Whack!)*

"Ouch!" cried Rufus, dropping his canvas-stretcher,

209

which Mr. Bigginson had just walloped. "I'm sorry, Rembrandt."

"Hrrmph, hrrmph," said the artist, driving in half a dozen tacks in silence. "One would think those gentlemen had invented the subject. Bah! I see a bride and groom in their hotel on that first night which has a chapter all to itself in every book Nimblewit lent me. The bride excuses herself, and goes into the bath; carrying her dressing-case, from which in the privacy of her aseptic surroundings she extracts Foilove's book, and hastily re-reads chapter four. Meanwhile, alone in the bedroom, the groom has pulled out of his valise Dildo's book, and hurriedly reviews a similar chapter. *Merde!*"

"Don't stop! Go on!"

"They go to bed. Soon the entire hotel is aroused by the sound of scientific argument as Foilove's disciple struggles with Dildo's pupil. The manager knocks on the bedroom door, wise as all hotel proprietors in the ways of the human heart. He is carrying Letcher's book; he hands it to the bride and groom opened at chapter four; he bows, retires. *Merde!*".

"I can't wait to read the dean's book," said Rufus.

"It will cost you approximately six dollars to do so." In three days Mr. Bigginson had already developed the author's intense dislike of having his book read free. "Of which seven and one-half per cent will go to your dean," he added, "and seven and one-half per cent to his ghost-writer."

Rembrandt Bigginson was a different man when he was painting. Like old Franz Florus, who also caroused as much as he painted, Bigginson was deeply and seriously devoted to his art. Had he lived in Florus's day, he might have been a minor master himself: there are talents which, born into a favourable *Zeitgeist*, flower into near genius. Conversely, one wonders how many admirable seventeenth-century English dramatists or Dutch painters, had they been born three centuries later and their seed received into the stony places of the twentieth century, might have been undistinguished journalists or anonymous commercial artists. As a portrait painter, Bigginson disparagingly called himself a dauber. (When a professional artist uses this derogatory term, his standard of comparison is the brushwork of a Hals or Augustus John, not the work of your talented Aunt Mabel.) No matter how propitious the *Zeitgeist*, he would never have made a third, as painter or portraitist, to the serious and noble Peter Paul Rubens or the courtly and refined Van Dyck. But he might well have been a peer in the circle of Jan Steen, who kept an ale-house until he and his artist companions had drunk up all the stock, when he would pull in his tavern sign, and set to work at his painting; then, the moment he had finished a couple of little pictures (now worth more than a little money), he would sell them for a few pieces of silver, replenish his supply of wine and beer, and put his painting materials back on the shelf as long as there was a drop of drink in the house. And Rembrandt Bigginson might have been a boon companion of Adrian Brouwer, who, being paid for a picture, disappeared completely for nine days, and came shouting back on the tenth: "Heaven be praised, I am rid of all that ballast!"

And along with drunken old Franz Florus, he might have said in that paradox comprehensible perhaps only to the artist: "When I work I am alive; when I give myself up to pleasure, I die;" whereupon Florus, Brouwer, Jan Steen, and Rembrandt Bigginson all gave themselves up to pleasure.

Now Mr. Bigginson, having sketched Dean Nimblewit in charcoal on his white canvas, slung his newly-set palette over his left arm, took a brush in his right hand, and peered at the dean through his painting spectacles. Under the artist's scrutiny, Nimblewit began to smirk self-consciously, which was a waste of effort on his part, for at this stage all he was to Rembrandt was light and shadow, form and colour. Another observer would have seen an elderly man in doctoral robes, a gold-tasselled mortar-board cap topping a face which bore a disconcerting resemblance to a worried hound's, a human skull (it was Ruddock's, though the dean did not know this) cradled in his right hand. An academic St. Francis musing on mortality, conceived by Zurburan but executed by Rowlandson—so this observer, looking at Horace Nimblewit, might have reflected, smiling.

Mr. Bigginson dipped his brush into the tin of poppy oil attached to the edge of his palette, smeared up a brownish mess of paint on the clean wood surface, and laid in the shadows of the dean's face with assured strokes. To so skilled a painter, the laying-in of a portrait was mechanical work; if every subject has a unique personality which it is the artist's task to portray in paint, each has pretty much the same ground shadows under a north light.

"You can talk, if you like, sir," Mr. Bigginson said.

Nimblewit asked the question uppermost in his mind: "How are you progressing with the book?"

"I am now engaged in writing chapter five."

The dean stared at the plump artist with the nimbus of soft greying hair, chubby face, tortoise-shell glasses perched low on a button nose, round belly making a bulge in his paint-encrusted smock—the image of unworldly innocence. If Nimblewit had not read with scandalised awe Rembrandt's manuscript fourth chapter, he would never have believed it possible that Mr. Bigginson was now engaged in a reasoned analysis of the advantages of various positions. It was as though the dean had caught Satan writing *Little Women*, using the barb of his tail as a pen.

"Hok, hok," he said; "my wife——"

"Mon vieux," said Rembrandt, making an exuberant semi-circular swipe with his brush, which gave Nimblewit the jowl of a bloodhound, "I have not forgotten your small problem." He held his brush between his teeth like

a bone as he used his finger to remove an excess of brownish pigment and permit the dean to look more like his own breed. He continued speaking (somewhat indistinctly) with the brush still in his mouth, meanwhile wiping his finger on his smock and selecting a narrower brush. "It is quite simply solved by inserting into appropriate places in my manuscript the details of certain small intimacies known only to you and your wife. That will, of course, convince her that none other than you could have written the book."

"Certain small intimacies?" echoed the dean rustily.

Rembrandt took the brush out of his mouth and thrust it through the hole in his palette, where he held it in place with his thumb. "In the phraseology of Philander Foilove, 'individual refinements of technique which by a process of mutual adjustment one and one's partner learn—' But really, my dear dean, you must spare my blushes by capturing my meaning."

"You mean," Nimblewit said hoarsely, "like the things in Foilove's tenth chapter?"

"My dear chap, not at all! Permit me to escape into metaphor. Foilove's mechanics are but the Fords, the mere tin lizzies of the erotic art. What you must intercalate into my discussion are the custom-made Isotta-Francinis which Mrs. Nimblewit will immediately recognise as having been formerly manufactured expressly for her."

"Something not in a book?" said the dean hopelessly.

Mr. Bigginson sighed. "We must not flatter ourselves; it will be in some book or other. Our ingenuity in such matters is purely relative. As an elderly philosopher, I am sometimes inclined to believe that the only way one can be original in the sex act is to perform it normally."

The dean said: "I trust I may claim to be a normal man."

"*Mon Dieu!*"

Mr. Bigginson painted in silence as he tried to find a different method for convincing Mrs. Nimblewit that her husband could have written a book whose precepts he had plainly never practised—at least on her. Here Rembrandt danced a little jig of triumph, at which the dean was so surprised he dropped his skull.

"Bless me!" said Mr. Bigginson. "You may rest now, Doctor Nimblewit. Bless me!" For it had occurred to him that if Mrs. Nimblewit could be led to believe that her husband had practised on other women, the dean's authorship would pass unchallenged in the midst of a greater hullaballoo.

The artist had informed Nimblewit that he need only sit for his head and hands; that he would use a lay-figure for painting in the background and drapery. So it was that Rufus Crotey, dressed in the academic robes of a doctor of medicine and the gold-tasselled cap of a dean, clutching Ruddock's skull, found himself posing for Mr. Bigginson while the underpainting of the dean's head dried.

"I feel like a sheep in wolf's clothing," he remarked.

"I presume you are using the word in its fabled rather than colloquial meaning," said Rembrandt, mixing green paint for the velvet facing of the doctor's gown. He howled like a wolf watching a pretty girl pass the pool room.

"Not like that, Rembrandt," said Rufus; "like this." He gave the post-World War II version of Mr. Bigginson's pre-World War I call of the wild.

"For heaven's sake!" gasped Susan as she came into the studio. "What are you two doing?"

They howled at her.

"I've heard saner sounds coming from the windows of Quackenbush," she said. "If Doctor Slipstream should hear you——"

"He would join in like a gentleman," said Rembrandt. "Susan, I must ask you to remember that your father and I have been intimate friends these thirty years. You have often heard him speak of dear old Biggie, have you not?"

"Now I know you're crazy."

"Don't be dense, Susan," said Rufus.

She ignored him, and said to Rembrandt: "Whom do you think you're going to fool with that tale? And why?"

"Your mother," said the artist. "And for the sake of domestic concord, which I, having happily escaped as a bachelor, am always glad to encourage in those less fortunate than myself."

"Well, I still haven't the faintest idea what you're up to, but I'll go along. There's something the matter with the mouth," she added, pointing to the portrait.

The artist said huffily: "My dear young lady——"

"It doesn't look at all like Rufus."

After eight working days, Nimblewit's portrait was virtually finished. The dean telegraphed his wife in Louisville (the horses were running at Churchill Downs) to return home to advise the artist during the final sitting. Never one to decline an opportunity to put in her two cents' worth, Mrs. Nimblewit wired she was returning immediately on the 7.8. And so Mr. Bigginson and Dean Nimblewit set the stage for their little comedy. Rufus was instructed to take Susan off somewhere to dinner (since he had started painting and writing, Rembrandt had stopped cooking; he and Rufus had returned to the Greek restaurant; Fido had returned to his fraternity table, and Susan to her own home), and at seven o'clock the dean and Mr. Bigginson settled down in the former's study with a bottle of cognac.

Nimblewit was nervous as an actor on the first night of a play, and he eagerly drank the brandy the artist poured him. Rembrandt, taking his own drink for pleasure rather than priming, quickly rehearsed the dean in his part. It was a splendid rôle. It would amply repay Nimblewit for every indignity he had ever suffered under his wife's tongue; and as the cognac warmed him, he began to wish it were true to life.

On finding that neither her husband nor daughter had met her train at the station, Mrs. Nimblewit arrived home in a taxi and a rotten temper. Mr. Bigginson was peeping out of the study window; he said warningly: "On your mark, sir . . .'" (The dean sloshed a stiff drink into his glass, and gulped it down.) "Get set . . . Go!" And as Mrs. Nimblewit entered the house and called "Poochie dear," the dean and Mr. Bigginson roared out the words of "Down in the Lehigh Valley," the former in English, the latter in French.

The noise drew the incredulous Mrs. Nimblewit to the partially-opened study door, at which she listened and sniffed, her eyes starting from their sockets.

"By God, Biggie," she heard her husband's boozy voice, "I remember the time we taught those words to Charlotte. Ah, that's something I'll never forget."

A drunken chuckle answered him. (Mrs. Nimblewit did not recognise the voice, but she had never heard a more dissolute sound in all her life.) "A fair return for what Charlotte taught you, *mon vieux*," it said. "I'll wager you never thought at the time you would be using that bit of technique in your textbook on sex."

Mrs. Nimblewit quivered. She controlled herself, and pressed her ear closer to the crack in the door. "Ha, ha," her husband said; "the funny thing is, when I told Pussy I was going off to a scientific meeting that time, it was perfectly true: Charlotte and I did do a little scientific research together, ho, ho, ho!"

"You old dog," Rembrandt said. "Hic, you old dog!"

"Let me read you this part of my fifth chapter, Biggie old man," said the dean, reaching for the sheet of manuscript Rembrandt had prepared for him. As he read, Mrs. Nimblewit began to blush, then tremble.

"Horace, you old dog," came the unfamiliar drunken voice. "Hic, you can't fool me; you got that from Fifine at Madame Schultz's."

"I did not," said Nimblewit, consulting his notes. "I remember perfectly well where that came from. While Pussy was away at the Kentucky Derby that time, I met you in New York, and we went to Gertrude's."

"Gertrude never showed it to me," said Rembrandt jealously.

"Oh, it wasn't hic Gertrude. It was her friend from Paris—Nicolette."

"Ah, Nicolette!" said Rembrandt, kissing his fingers with a loud smacking sound. "Then Fifine was the one who . . ." His voice fell to an inaudible level.

"Chapter seven," said Nimblewit. "Hic, chapter seven!"

"You old dog, you! Didn't any of your women ever mean any more to you than subjects for experimentation? Thank God, I'm an artist, Horace. Hic! Women to me mean Love . . . Beauty . . ."

"Ho, ho, ho," said the dean; "you should see my wife. Love! Beauty! Well, I'll say this for the old bat, she has always left me alone——"

"Old bat!" Mrs. Nimblewit screamed, bursting into her husband's study in a towering rage. "Why, you old goat! You lecher! You—you—you——"

"Pussy," said the dean. He tried to rise from his chair, but fell back. "Welcome home, my love. I didn't expect you until later."

"I see you didn't." She pointed a quivering finger at Mr. Bigginson. "Who is this drunken bum?"

Rembrandt struggled to his feet, made her a low bow. "Charmed, madame," he said.

"Pussy, Biggie," said the dean. "My old friend Rembrandt Bigginson, who is painting my portrait."

"That bum? He is Rembrandt Bigginson!"

"Yes, my love. A dear old friend of mine and Geoff's."

"Get out of my house, you old goat!" she yelled at the artist. "And as for you," she said to the dean, "you cheating double-crosser, my lawyer will get in touch with you." She went out of the study, slamming the door hard behind her.

"Hrrmph, hrrmph," said Mr. Bigginson in embarrassment. "I confess I never thought of that, Doctor Nimblewit."

"Ha, ha, ha, the old bat!"

"Come, come, sir; she's gone now."

"Goo' riddance," said Nimblewit. He began to sing in a somewhat slurred voice.

"Mon Dieu," said Mr. Bigginson. He rubbed his head so that his soft hair stood out like a greyish halo, giving him the appearance of an abandoned angel.

"Th'—ol'—batsh," said the dean.

Chapter Twenty-six

WITHOUT UNPACKING HER travelling-bags, Mrs. Nimblewit had turned round and left town on the 10.10 train; and Mr. Bigginson had to put the finishing touches on the dean's portrait without her advice. Following the usual custom in such matters, Nimblewit had called in several of his oldest friends in the university for comment and criticism, and finally the portrait committee for their official approval.

It was a skilful and impressive portrait Rembrandt Bigginson had signed and dated in the lower right corner before turning it over to the chairman of the committee and accepting his cheque for $2,000. The artist was not one of those masters whose portraits revealed the soul of the sitter. He did not strive for, nor unconsciously achieve, a subtle insight into his subject's personality or a profound reading of his character; and, considering the people Mr. Bigginson painted, perhaps that was just as well. The real reason why he continued to make a sufficient living by the difficult art of portrait painting through good times and bad was that he flattered his sitters. All Rembrandt's men were brave; all his women, fair. Perhaps that showed a greater insight than a shirty art-critic would be willing to grant him, for that was precisely how Mr. Bigginson's subjects appeared to themselves. Consequently Nimblewit was neither surprised nor especially flattered that the artist had made him look like the most Olympian of deans, the most Vesalian of anatomists: he took such a portrayal as his just due, and a measure of Mr. Bigginson's skill. Though the dean still resembled a hound on canvas, even Willoughby Chouse was heard to admit it was one of noblest pedigree.

Now that his work was completed, the artist was determined to leave Zebulon at last. The interlude was over. Spring had arrived. Rembrandt Bigginson was seized by the wanderlust, and Vigée-Lebrun, by now bored with her kittens, began to walk restlessly around the apartment, flicking her white-plumed tail, querulously meowing. Rufus understood, without knowing why, that it was useless to ask Rembrandt to remain any longer; but he refused to let him depart as casually as he had come. He gave him a farewell party.

Rembrandt cooked his final dinner. Susan, Rufus, and Fido ate lugubriously, which put Mr. Bigginson out of patience. "Bless me," he complained, "I'm not on my way to the Front; only to Bucks County, Pa."

"It's going to be awfully lonesome without you," Susan said dolefully.

"Stop toying with your food, Susan."

"It'll be funny, living alone again," Rufus said mournfully.

"This won't be the same joint without Rembrandt," Fido rumbled. "I been thinkin', Rembrandt. What say you stay here and we paint a horse-fly on the dean's schnozzola, what say, Rembrandt?"

"No, Fido."

"Whatta *you* say, Suze?"

"Oh, Daddy's in enough trouble as it is."

Rembrandt looked guilty. "For Pete's sake," said Rufus. Now that the dean had his testimonial portrait, and the promise of a ghost-written textbook on sex by July first, he couldn't see why Nimblewit wasn't feeling on top of the world. "What's the matter with the dean now, Suze?"

"He and Mother are squbbling. Mother writes to me and says: 'Tell your father thus-and-so.' Then Daddy tells me: 'Write your Mother and tell her this-and-that.' "

"They ain't speakin'," said Fido wisely. "My mamma and my old man are like that too, Suze. My mamma says: 'Francis, tell that rum-pot to put on his shoes before some-one calls the Board of Health,' and me old man says: 'Francis, tell that old bat if she don't stop naggin' me I'll clout her one.' Aw, that don't mean nothin', Suze."

"Fido is right, Susan," said Rembrandt. "As long as they are communicating with one another through you rather than their lawyers—hrrmph, hrrmph, hrrmph, who is Francis?"

"Da me," said Fido.

They grew more cheerful. Susan and Rufus washed the dishes, then helped Fido or Francis choose his kitten from among Botticelli, a dark red male, Gaddo Gaddi, a tea-with-milk-coloured male, and Marietta Tintoretta, the mahogany-coloured female.

"I like this kitten," Fido said, pointing to tea-with-milk Gaddo Gaddi with a finger larger than the kitten's thigh; "but I like that one's name. Botticelli. I like that. Botticelli."

"That is easily remedied," said Mr. Bigginson; "I'll switch their names for you."

"You can't do that, Rembrandt. It ain't legal to change names. That's like criminals."

"Fido is right," said Susan. "You must leave their names alone, and switch kittens, isn't that so, Fido?"

"Sure," said Fido. He asked the kitten's mother politely: "Is it okay by you I take Botticelli, V.J.?"

"Prrrthpp," said Vigée-Lebrun.

"Gee, thanks, V.J. I'll take good care of him. Hullo, Botticelli," he said to the tea-and-milk kitten. "You got a new papa now."

"May I have one too, Rembrandt?" Rufus asked. "It'll be company for me when you're gone, and I'm kind of used to having a cat in the house now."

"Indeed you may."

"I'll take Marietta Tintoretta."

Fido nudged Rufus. "Ask her, Rufe."

"Madame Vigée-Lebrun, may I have the paw of your daughter, Marietta Tintoretta?"

"Prrrthpp."

Suddenly there was a terrific banging on the outside door. Vigée-Lebrun arched her back, puffed out her tail, and hissed: "FFFFTTTT!" Botticelli, Gaddo Gaddi, and Marietta Tintoretta all arched their backs, puffed out their tails, and went ffffttt. Angelika Kauffmann scurried under the bookcase. Wish O'Hoe flung open the door and staggered into the apartment. Behind him came Ennis the bouncer, an apologetic look on his face.

"I'm sorry, pal," he said to Fido. "I couldn't keep him away peaceable and I didn' wanna have to put the slug on him."

"Hullo, Wish," said Fido. "What's up? Hullo, Ennis."

"I came to tell you good-bye," said Wish, swaying in front of Mr. Bigginson, "and good riddance."

"That is very kind of you, young gentleman," said Rembrandt, quieting Susan and Rufus with a gesture. "I trust you will join me in a stirrup cup?"

"I'll drink anything once," said Wish.

"Fido," said Mr. Bigginson, "ask your large friend if he will join us."

"This is Ennis, Rembrandt," he said. "Ennis, meet Suze and Rufe too."

"Glad to make your acquaintance," said Ennis, shaking hands with a hairy, broken-knuckled paw.

"Hey, Ennis," said Fido, winking rapidly at Rembrandt, Susan, and Rufus in succession, "look in that mirror, huh?" He pointed at the *trompe-l'oeil* of himself looking out from a carved gilt mirror frame.

Ennis looked into the mirror. "One of them kind of trick mirrors, huh? I seen them before at the county fair. Make you look like a gorilla."

"Hey, Ennis, take your hat off," Fido urged. Ennis took off his hat. "Now look in the mirror."

Ennis began to laugh. "Wotta mirror," he said. "Makes me look like you, Fido."

Fido pushed him away. "Lemme see." He stared at the painted wall. "Sure does," he agreed. "Hey, Ennis, how come Sadie let you off?"

"I ast Dave to look after things while I'm gone. Well, I guess I gotta be gettin' back. Doc O'Shawnessey is out there, and he can lick Dave."

"Aw, we're havin' a party for Rembrandt."

"A party? That's different." Ennis shook hands again with Rembrandt, and said: "Many happy returns of the day."

"Thank you, sir," he said. "Will you join me in a festive drink?"

"Don't mind if I do."

"Rufus, the cognac."

"Make mine milk, Rufe," said Fido.

"All right, everybody," Ennis said, waving his tumbler of brandy, "all together." He began to sing by himself:

> "Happy birthday to you,
> Happy birthday to you,
> Happy birthday, dear teacher,
> Happy birthday to you."

"Gee, Rembrandt, I didn' know it was your birthday." And Fido sang:

> "Happy birthday to you,
> Happy birthday to you,
> Happy birthday, dear teacher,
> Happy birthday to you."

"Why, Rembrandt," said Susan, "and you didn't tell us!" She and Rufus sang together:

> "Happy birthday to you,
> Happy birthday to you,
> Happy birthday, dear Rembrandt,
> Happy birthday to you."

"Nuts!" said Wish O'Hoe.

"This young gentleman seems to be the skeleton at the feast," Mr. Bigginson observed.

"You want he should sing for you, Rembrandt?" Fido asked.

"Try and make me!" Wish challenged.

"Aw Wish, you know I couldn't do that. Da Ennis——"

"Sure, pal," said Ennis. He lighted a cigarette, puffed until its tip was glowing red, then suddenly grabbed O'Hoe and held him with one hand while he jerked off Wish's right shoe and sock with the other. Then he shifted his grip to Wish's ankle, and brought his burning cigarette towards the sole of his bare foot. "Sing," he said.

"Happy birthday to you," Wish carolled lustily.

> "Happy birthday to you,
> Happy birthday, dear Rembrandt,
> Happy birthday to you."

"Thank you, young gentleman. I am deeply touched."

Ennis began to sing "For He's a Jolly Good Fellow," and Susan, Fido, and Rufus all joined in. But Ennis held up his hand and stopped his quartet. "You ain't singin'?" he asked Wish politely.

Wish put himself behind Fido, and said: "Nuts to you."

"That ain't right, Wish," Fido rumbled. "You can't come to a guy's party and be a skeleton at the feast." He stepped aside; Ennis lunged; and Wish wobbled away just in time.

"Some party," he jeered. "Standing around singing kid songs."

"You want action?" Mr. Bigginson courteously inquired.

"Yeah."

Rembrandt pulled a pair of dice from his waistcoat pocket.

"That's more like it," said Wish.

"If Susan and you gentlemen will excuse us," said Mr. Bigginson, "I shall be back with you in time for the next chorus."

"Okay, mister," said Ennis. "Fido, you take the bass; I'll take the baritone; Red, you sing the tenor; Beautiful, you just warble along." He led the quartet into Silver Threads Among the Gold in honour of their host, while Rembrandt and Wish O'Hoe got down on their knees in the centre of the fibre rug, and shot craps. The game was complicated by Botticelli, Gaddo Gaddi, and Marietta Tintoretta darting out from under the day bed and trying to pounce on the dice. Mr. Bigginson made eleven passes in a row, then stood up, dusting his knees, just as Silver Threads Among the Gold was concluded.

"Holy Mother of God," said Wish. "Give me a drink."

Rembrandt tucked a large wad of notes away in his pocket. *"Mi-mi-miiiii,"* he intoned; then launched out into Down in the Lehigh Valley in French.

Susan sang Heaven Will Protect the Working Girl. Ennis obliged with Waiting for the Robert E. Lee, with steam-boat obbligato. Fido sang Me Mother Was a Lady; and Wish O'Hoe, mellowed by cognac and Rembrandt's skill with the dice, rendered When Irish Eyes Are Smiling in a McCormack tenor.

Singing is thirsty work; drinking begets singing: a vicious circle. At about the fourth revolution, a woman in the next house phoned the police, and two cops in a squad car drove up and hammered on Rufus's apartment door. When they couldn't make themselves heard above the din of My Name Is Samuel Hall, they broke in with: "What the hell's going on around here?"

"Hi, Jim. Hi, Grover," said Ennis to the cops.

"Hullo, Grover. Hullo, Jim," said Fido.

"Hi, Fido; hi, Ennis," said the cops. "You guys heard any noise around here?"

"Naw," said Fido. "We been here all evening, and we ain't heard a thing. What's up?"

"Some dame phoned and complained about a wild party."

"Dames will do anything for publicity," said Ennis wisely.

"Yeah. How come you're not out at Sadie's, Ennis?" one of the cops asked.

"It's Rembrandt's birthday."

"By God," said the other cop, "banks close on holidays, but I never heard of no cat-house——"

"Hey, there's ladies present," said Fido.

The cops touched their caps to Susan. "Well, sorry to bother you all," said Grover.

"That ain't any bother," said Fido. "We'll start from the beginning."

"Mind if we kind of listen?" Jim asked.

Ennis slapped his thigh. "I never thought I'd sing to no cops," he said. Jim and Grover roared with appreciation. "Okay," said Ennis, "everybody ready? Rembrandt, Fido, Wish, Red, Beautiful?"

" 'Oh, my name is Samuel Hall . . .' "

"By God, that's all right," said a cop at the end. "Do you know The Rosary?"

"I dunno," said Ennis doubtfully. "How does it go?"

The cop sang it.

Rufus's landlord came down into the basement by way of the inside steps. He made his way through the back of the apartment into Rufus's living-room, an irate expression on his face. Ennis, Fido, and the two cops turned round and stared at him. Grinning weakly, the landlord backed out.

Susan sang She Was Only a Motorman's Daughter to a realistic accompaniment of clang-clangs from Ennis and one the cops. As a climax, they imitated a collision between two trolley-cars. In a panic Angelika Kauffmann darted from under the bookcase, squeaking madly, and ran up the inside of the cop's trouser leg. The cop yelled and grabbed for his belt-buckle. Susan screamed.

"Siddown!" Fido bawled, his mind as usual reaching heights of genius in a medical emergency. He gave the cop a push, and the cop sat down on Angelika Kauffmann. When he arose, the mouse dropped limply from his trouser leg.

"Poor Kaufman," said Fido sadly, "he was a white mouse, if I ever seen one."

Vigée-Lebrun and her three kittens came out from under the day bed and sniffed curiously at the body of their playmate. "Let's get the hell out of here," said one of the cops to the other. They left.

Angelika Kauffmann's tragic end had a sobering effect on the party. Mr. Bigginson said he was no ancient Egyptian; he couldn't carouse with any abandon in the presence of a *memento mori*. Rufus excused himself, and gave Kaufman a sailor's funeral. When he returned from the bathroom, he found Ennis trying to buy Gaddo Gaddi. Mr. Bigginson repeated that he never sold a kitten; he said he tried to find them good homes with nice people.

"I reckon that let's me out," said Ennis disconsolately.

"Your home appears to be a little unconventional," said Rembrandt, "but on the other hand, you are nice people."

"You don't think I'd of let him associate with them girls?" Ennis said, shocked. "An innocent little baby like him?"

"Take him with my blessing."

"Thanks, mister."

Fido nudged him. "Hey, Ennis, you gotta ask V.J."

"Who the hell is V.J.?"

"She's his mother," said Fido.

"His mother," Ennis reverently repeated.

"Nuts," said Wish O'Hoe. Fido and Ennis began to converge on him from two directions. "Nuts to guys who don't respect mothers," he said quickly.

Then Mr. Bigginson was left alone with Rufus and Susan. "Hrrmph, hrrmph," said the artist. "A memorable party, Rufus. And now, if you will be kind enough to transfer my impedimenta into the tonneau of the Mercedes, I shall lure Vigée into her basket, and we shall depart."

"At this time of night? I expected you to stay, and leave in the morning."

"My dear Rufus: once Rembrandt Bigginson has signed his work, he never touches it again."

"Oh, Rembrandt," Susan cried, "does that mean we won't ever see you again?"

"God bless my soul! Whatever gave you such an absurd notion, Susan? I shall travel from the wilds of Bucks County or the stews hrrmph stewpots of New Orleans to dance at your wedding."

"What wedding?" Rufus asked. "She says she won't marry me unless the dean gives his consent."

"That's just a wise precaution, Rembrandt," she said. "So when we begin to squabble (you know what a terrible temper he has), I can say: 'If my father hadn't made me marry you, I'd be the wife of Patrick Aloysius O'Hoe Junior now, with wealth, position, and seventeen kids.' Oh, stop eavesdropping, Rufus, and carry Rembrandt's things out to the car."

He carried Mr. Bigginson's two travelling-bags, his folding easel, sketch-box, and palette to the Mercedes. Rembrandt raised the top of the willow basket, Vigée-Lebrun said "Prrrthpp!" and jumped inside.

"Hrrmph, hrrmph," he said, "I don't suppose Patrick Aloysius O'Hoe, Junior, will mind if I kiss you good-bye, Susan?" Then he picked up Vigée-Lebrun's basket and walked briskly out to his car, a short plump figure in spats, his lower chins hidden by his Windsor tie, his black felt hat clapped on his cloud of greying hair. Susan trotted along beside him. The artist placed the willow basket on the front seat, then turned to shake hands with Rufus.

"Rembrandt," said Rufus, squeezing the artist's hand hard, "I wish you'd tell me one thing before you go."

"Anything, my boy; anything. Within the law," he added virtuously.

"Where is Bigginson's Dimple?"

"Don't you dare tell him, Rembrandt!" Susan ordered.

"My dear young lady," said the artist, climbing with dignity into the driver's seat of the Mercedes, "I had no intention of doing so. Rembrandt Bigginson is no spoilsport. *Au revoir, mes enfants.*"

Chapter Twenty-seven

DEAN NIMBLEWIT PASSED the short remainder of the academic year in a mood of mixed, or at least of alternating, triumph and disquiet. He had been too fuddled, fortunately, to understand, or perhaps even to hear, his wife's allusion to lawyers; but he knew he was in the mess of his married life. Mrs. Nimblewit was still away from home, still sending bitter third-person messages to Susan's father, from which the dean concluded that Mr. Bigginson's playlet had been brilliantly successful. This was what made him feel triumphant. He felt disquieted whenever he attempted to guess what his wife was going to do about it; knowing Pussy, he could not believe she would take it without scratching back. Divorce never entered the dean's mind for the ingenuous reason that he knew he had never given his wife any grounds. But he did know she was cooking up some fiendish revenge, and he had sufficient respect for her powers to poison his triumph.

Mrs. Nimblewit was doing just that. Once her first

explosion of wrath was over, she had recognised that divorcing her husband would be no salve for her injuries; it might soil the dean's honour; it could not avenge her own. By his early marital performances, Nimblewit had put it psychologically out of Gloriana's power to take the classic revenge of the wronged wife, even had her age and general stringiness permitted. The best she could think of was to confess to her husband that Susan was not his child; and this admirable riposte had to be abandoned because Mrs. Nimblewit loved her daughter better than her revenge. Her next thought was to eschew all further race-meetings; remain constantly at home (her only solace the private wire to her bookie's); and make her husband's remaining life a perfect hell. This she resolved to do, and again arrived in Zebulon on the 7.8.

Once more she took a taxi home. "Poochie," she called out from the entrance hall in saccharine tones. "Poochie!"

The dean was in his study, editing Mr. Bigginson's fifteenth chapter, which had arrived by mail that day bearing a Provincetown, Mass., postmark. At the sound of his wife's voice, he quivered all over. "I'm in my study," he replied.

Mrs. Nimblewit ran into the study and threw her arms around her husband. She kissed him. "Poochie!" she cried emotionally, "I am home to stay! I shall never leave you again. No, never!" she exclaimed dramatically, kissing him over and over, ymmm, ymmm, ymmm. "I shall never leave you again!"

The dean tore himself from her embrace and staggered back with a hoarse cry. She reached out after him, drooling: "Poochie, Poochie, ymmm, ymmm, ymmm."

Poochie tucked his tail between his legs and fled, yapping frantically. Left alone, Mrs. Nimblewit smiled happily. "Charlotte," she said aloud. "Fifine—Nicolette—Bah!"

Even in his office, the unfortunate dean now wore a haunted expression. When his secretary, appearing in the doorway between their two offices, spoke to him un-expectedly, he jumped. He was given to suddenly snatch-ing out his pocket handkerchief and scrubbing his mouth. He began muttering to himself. "Poor old Nimblewit," said his Faculty, shaking its head, "beginning to break up. Happens every time a dean gets his testimonial portrait painted while he's still alive. Remember old Grudgins? Remember Chincough, eh?"

It was a welcome relief for the dean to immerse him-self in his end-of-term official duties. The most important of these was that final Faculty meeting whose main busi-ness was the voting of medical degrees. This year, Patrick Aloysius O'Hoe, Jr., was of course a candidate. Nimble-wit knew very well what would happen if Wish were un-successful: Boss O'Hoe would telephone the chairman of the Democratic National Committee; the chairman would phone the Biggest Democrat on the university's board of trustees; the Democratic trustee would ring up the chancellor of Zebulon University; and the chancellor would summon the bungling dean of the medical school to his office, where . . . Nimblewit winced; and to fore-stall that extremely unpleasant experience, decided to do some preliminary telephoning himself. He would remind his colleagues discreetly that Democracy itself, in that final Faculty meeting, would be carefully watching every-thing they did.

Like Albert Wanion collecting for the portrait fund, Nimblewit worked down the list of his Faculty until he came to Cedric Osbert Dee. As he waited for Dee to answer his phone, the dean stared out over High Street, mentally counting votes.

Dee lifted the black receiver. At this moment the yellow, red, blue, orange, green, and violet telephones all began to shrill in harmonic unison. He immediately dropped the black phone, and seized the yellow one in his right hand, the red one in his left. "Zebulon Bee-hive Industries, C. O. Dee, president," he shouted; "one moment, please! Zebulon Plumbing and Heating Company, C. O. Dee, president; hold the wire." He grabbed the blue and orange phones, so that he now held two in each hand. "Zebulon Real Estate Associates, C. O. Dee, president, speaking; just a minute. Zebulon Poultry and Dairy Farm, C. O. Dee, gentleman farmer, here." Then he reached for the two remaining phones, holding three in each hand as dexterously as the Sheep in *Alice*. "Zebulon Snack Bar, C. O. Dee, manager, speaking; hold on. C. O. Dee, Incorporated, C. O. Dee himself speaking. What can I do for you?"

He talked and listened to six phones at once. His juggling and replies grew more and more frantic, more and more confused. His face congested; his utterance thickened. "Yes, a two-room beehive with milk bath . . . Six dollars a lot, delivered crated in Pinehurst . . . No, no; not galvanised honey; pasteurised bees . . . A hundred and a quarter half-inch pipe, less ten and ten . . . deduct the cost of the cow from the flush-toilet . . . Debit C. O. Dee with the spilled milk . . . bar bees from snacks . . . gentleman plumber . . . four hundred foot frontage straight from the comb . . . I'll take less . . . ten-and-ten . . . ten-and-ten . . . ten and . . ."

Amid a rainbow of telephones, frothing at the mouth, Cedric Osbert Dee fell to the floor in a fit.

Dean Nimblewit called the Medical Faculty to order that evening at seven-thirty. Rufus sat in his accustomed place on the back row, Johnnie Mazzard beside him. In the short space of one academic year, Rufus had become a man. Moreover he had learned that his Faculty gods, like the Olympians of Lucian, had all too human failings. But as Zeus and his crew of rascals, harlots, and thieves ran the world quite as well for the two thousand years before the death of Pan as their successor in the millennia since; so Nimblewit and his Faculty somehow kept the world of Medicine limping and hobbling along in the gait peculiar to all human institutions. In a sense,

Medicine is like Religion; its priests may be impure, but its worshippers seem to derive considerable bodily and spiritual comfort from their ministrations.

The secretary of the Faculty read the minutes of the preceding meeting in his characteristic croaking drone. The dean said that before coming to the main business of the evening, he had several announcements to make. Several weeks ago he had been in receipt of a communication from Mr. Brabble, the eminent lawyer, expressing the wish of an anonymous client to present the sum of $5,000 to the Department of Bacteriology in appreciation of Professor Dee's great contributions to medical science; the money to be expended at the sole discretion of the head of the department. (This most ingenious loop-hole in the Federal income-tax laws had not, however, been discovered by Mr. Brabble.)

Nimblewit said that unfortunately Doctor Dee was indisposed ("Hell," said a voice from the floor, "he's over in Quackenbush in a strait-jacket!"), but he was sure he would be surprised and pleased to hear of this recognition of his multifarious activities.

"I very much regret to have to inform the Faculty." the dean proceeded to the next announcement, "that this will be Doctor Drumslager's final appearance at one of our meetings. He has resigned from the Medical Faculty of this university as of July first, to become dean of the Medical College of New Jersey."

There was an astounded silence at this dramatic disclosure. Then came a scattering of ambiguous applause, and someone cried ironically: "Speech! Speech!"

Byron Drumslager arose and bowed to his colleagues. "Gentlemen," he said, "I leave you with regret. A famous man once said, 'Some are born to greatness; others achieve greatness; still others have greatness thrust upon them.' It is not for me to say in which of these categories I am to be placed, but this I can tell you in all modesty: greatness has its regrets no less than its pleasures.' "

"So I have found it, Byron," said Pietro Spandone.

232

Drumslager frowned; resumed: "It will probably be several years before Dean Nimblewit can replace me. Fortunately, I have trained young men for this eventuality, so that in leaving you I am not altogether deserting you. Grandsons of Sir Henry Pepercul, I like to consider my young men; for as Sir Henry looked upon me as a son and taught me everything he knew, so I have taught my boys as much as they were capable of understanding. It was in Sir Henry's clinic that I first caught a glimpse of that profound truth which many years in my own clinic have convinced me is the foundation-stone of all Medicine. I leave it with you as a legacy of advice to be a guiding light to your footsteps when I am no longer here to lead you. Gentlemen of the Faculty—*Primary things precede secondary ones.*"

He bowed; sat down. Carnifex arose. "On behalf of the Medical Faculty," he said to Drumslager, "may I say to you, *Parturient montes, nascetur ridiculus mus.*"

Dean Drumslager inclined his head; trust those old boys for the elegant compliment.

"What'd he say, Johnnie?" Rufus whispered to Mazzard.

He shrugged his shoulders. "Me, a grandson of Sir Henry Pepercul," he muttered. "I wonder if he's a baronet?"

"Why?"

"Why, so when Dean Drumslager finally passes on to his reward, I'll be Sir John Mazzard, that's why."

"And now," Nimblewit was saying, "I shall ask the chairman of the committee on degrees to read his report."

As a general thing, all candidates receive their degrees, for medical schools prefer to do their major culling out at the end of the freshman year, and what minor pruning that remains no later than the end of the third year; so that a senior medical student must fall pretty far from grace to fail to receive his degree. Consequently, many students relax their efforts to some extent during their final year, betting (generally correctly) that the disciplinary action of withholding the M.D. degree will be considered too drastic a punishment to fit their petty crimes. But no student in the history of the medical school had ever relaxed as completely as Patrick Aloysius O'Hoe, Jr. Wish had given the committee on degrees its only serious difficulty; and the committee followed the inevitable course in so important a matter of passing the buck to the Faculty as a whole. The dean asked for discussion on the committee report.

Carnifex arose to say that Mr. O'Hoe rarely had condescended to attend surgical clinics, and that his final written examination on the course would disgrace a good butcher——

Drumslager interrupted to say sarcastically that he had it on good authority that O'Hoe was not going to be a butcher. He added that he himself knew no surgery, and had to ask his wife to carve the turkey; yet the Medical College of New Jersey evidently considered him a fit man to govern their affairs. No doubt the Medical Director of the Mary Margaret MacSweeny O'Hoe Memorial Hospital and Medical Centre would also be above menial labour.

This diplomatic remark cost Wish the vote of every surgical specialist on the Faculty.

Then Slipstream arose and, in that gesture now habitual with him, vigorously scratched the air where the tip of his nose had been. "I do not know any surgery myself," he said; and resumed his seat. When the laughter had died down, Nudge glanced at the wall clock and moved that the committee's report be accepted as read. Furbelow seconded.

The chairman of the committee reminded the Faculty that, while all candidates but one had been recommended for degrees, no action, one way or the other, had been taken in the case of Mr. O'Hoe.

Nudge said he understood that perfectly; his motion would dispose of everyone but O'Hoe, at any rate. The motion was then passed by unanimous voice vote, Rufus and the other instructors present keeping a tight silence.

Then Drumslager said: "I move Mr. O'Hoe also be granted his degree."

"Second," said Furbelow.

"Discussion?" said the dean in a non-committal voice. But there was no voice raised to discuss: everything had been said, really, at the end of O'Hoe's freshman year.

"Question, Mr. Dean," Drumslager urged. "Question, question."

"All those in favour, please signify by saying aye."

"Aye," growled half the Faculty.

"Opposed, no."

"No," the other half growled.

The dean consulted the secretary of the Faculty, then said: "All those in favour, please rise." Led by Drumslager and Chouse (allies for once), eighteen professors arose. Tippett counted them carefully.

"Those opposed, now please rise."

Carnifex, his fellow surgeons, and Albert Wanion (his resentment over his exclusion from the O'Hoe bounty expressed by a happily virtuous action) then arose— eighteen professors in all. The secretary counted them, then spoke in a low voice to Nimblewit. The dean stared out into space, not through stone walls into the street this time, but higher, through the roof, as though in search of divine assistance. And this time his Faculty did not laugh as Nimblewit sweated over the tie vote.

There was not a man present but realised the P. A. O'Hoe, Jr., was unfitted for the practice of medicine. Such mass opinion usually results in a student of Wish O'Hoe's calibre being dropped at the end of his first year. Political pressure, not tips on the market or races, had kept Wish in medical school: those of his professors who took his tips knew very well they were not, as Wish himself foolishly thought, bribes. (Francis Bacon, who had also accepted presents from those whose cases he was to judge, was astonished and indignant to hear them termed bribes in the course of his own trial; his judgment may have been at fault; his conscience was clear.)

For four years, the pressure from above had been exerted first on this one of Wish's professors, then on that. Now it was all publicly concentrated on the dean himself. The individual teachers had been unable to resist the pressure of the administration. Now, with one part of their minds they hoped Nimblewit would dare to resist the politicians; with another they hoped he would share the common humiliation, and succumb.

But it never occured to Nimblewit for a single moment to break the tie by casting the vote which would have refused Patrick Aloysius O'Hoe, Jr., his M.D. degree. The dean was sweating because he had to stand up in front of his Faculty and publicly confess that he himself was a mere creature—a larger-size puppet who jumped when the strings were pulled. Characteristically, he sought to place the onus on someone else; he chose Dee. Had Dee only been present, the O'Hoe faction would have had the preponderant vote, and Nimblewit would have been relieved of the hateful necessity of making a public decision. He toyed with the idea, while the minutes slowly passed, of sending Slipstream over to Quackenbush to get the maniac's proxy. He whispered again in Tippett's ear; the secretary shook his head: voting by proxy was forbidden by the Faculty rules.

"Mr. Dean!"

Nimblewit removed his eyes from an unhelpful heaven, and focused them on the associate professor of dermatology and syphilogy. "Doctor Wanion."

"Mr. Dean, I desire to change my vote."

"By God," said Mazzard to Rufus, "Nimblewit luck again!"

"As you know, Mr. Dean," Wanion said, "Mr. O'Hoe passed my courses. His work wasn't distinguished, but it was quite satisfactory. I feel I ought to cast my vote in accordance with my own experience with Mr. O'Hoe as a student in my courses, much as I deplore his attitude and record in surgery and some other courses. I am therefore in favour of granting Mr. O'Hoe his degree."

Wanion saw his full professorship in Nimblewit's grateful eye. "Mr. Secretary," the dean said to Tippett, "will you be good enough to poll the Faculty once more?"

Patrick Aloysius O'Hoe, Jr., was awarded his M.D. by a vote of nineteen to seventeen.

"A motion is now in order," said the dean, following the requisite academic formula, "that the entire senior class be recommended to the General Faculty to receive the Doctor of Medicine degree."

"I so move," said Nudge.

"Second," said Furbelow.

"Allthoseinfavoursignifysayingaye. Opposedno."

"Move we adjourn!" Nudge called out.

"Second!" Furbelow cried, racing for the door and the second show at the Odium Theatre.

Chapter Twenty-eight

WHILE THEIR DEGREES were being conferred upon nascent physicians, lawyers, engineers, scholars, masters, and bachelors; and while a Big Democrat delivered the commencement oration; Patrick Aloysius O'Hoe sat on the platform along with the deans, the chancellor, board of trustees, and other exalted personages. Big Pat wore the gown and hood of an LL.D. (*honoris causa*) of Byrlady University. His great smooth face and hairless dome shone with pride and benevolence, just as though he were the humblest father there; and when Wish received his ribbon-tied diploma from the hands of Dean Nimblewit, the Boss of Mercia jammed his elbow into the trustee beside him, and boomed: "That's my boy!"

At the end of the exercises, the academic procession reformed, and marched away from the outdoor amphitheatre through a double hedge of yoo-hooing friends, relatives, perfect strangers, and innocent bystanders. The procession broke up on the grass before the university library, reassembling into family groups. Mrs. Nimblewit and Susan were waiting for the dean.

"Yoo-hoo, Poochie!" Mrs. Nimblewit called, waving her handkerchief to attract his attention. The dean winced, looked wildly about him, and then, to prevent even more public repetitions of the hated nickname, crept reluctantly to his wife and daughter.

"You looked lovely, darling," said Mrs. Nimblewit. "When you passed out those diplomas—what an air!—like a groom putting a wreath over the head of a Derby winner. I wish now I hadn't missed all those Commencements in the past. Oh well, there will be next year's, and the next, and next."

"What's the matter, Daddy?" Susan said anxiously.

"Nothing, dear. Nothing," he said. "I'm not as young as I once was; these affairs are a strain."

"You must begin to take it easy, Daddy. You musn't work so hard; you must stay at home more——"

"I was thinking of going up to Wood's Hole this summer, as a matter of fact," said the dean, "and working out a little problem in one of their guest laboratories."

"Oh good, Poochie," said Mrs. Nimblewit. "I'm sure I'll love it there. Better a hole with you than Saratoga alone."

The dean's heart sank. For weeks the only place he had felt safe from his wife was the Men's Room of the Faculty Club. Would he be safe in his grave, he wondered; or would this diabolical revenge last even beyond that?

Rufus Crotey, clad in hired cap and gown, joined the dean's party. "Good afternoon, Mrs. Nimblewit; good afternoon, sir," he said politely. "Hi, Suze: ready to go now?"

"Good afternoon, Rufus," said the dean in a despondent voice.

Mrs. Nimblewit sniffed. "Have you congratulated Doctor O'Hoe yet?" she asked Susan.

"No; but I congratulated Daddy."

"Sh!" Rufus warned. "Here they come;" and he went.

Patrick Aloysius O'Hoe and his party bore down on the Nimblewits. Besides Big Pat, there was a short fat woman bedewed and spangled with a province's ransom of diamonds and pearls; the newly-created Doctor O'Hoe; and a plump young woman with a pleasant plain Irish face, a spray of orchids on her shoulder, and as yet only one diamond the size of an ice-cube on the third finger of her left hand.

The great man affably greeted the dean. He presented Nimblewit to the fat Mrs. O'Hoe, who smiled graciously; then to Miss Bridget Flattery, his son's fiancée. Dean and Mrs. Nimblewit did not exchange looks. Mrs. O'Hoe said, gazing fondly at her daughter-in-law-to-be: "Bridget is the niece of Cardinal Flattery." Miss Flattery blushed.

The dean presented his women-folk to the O'Hoes. "Sure," said Big Pat genially, "Miss Susan is that pretty she must have Irish blood."

Miss Nimblewit blushed. The dean and his wife uttered a forced smile. "Well, Dean Nimblewit," said Patrick Aloysius O'Hoe, holding out a soft white hand, "we must be running off now; the chancellor is expecting us. Sure and next year it will be my turn to return the favour when you come out to the Commencement of Byrlady for your LL.D?" He bowed gallantly to Mrs. and Miss Nimblewit, and strode off, his own LL.D.'s gown billowing out behind him.

"Well, what do you know——" Susan began. Then she saw Fido. "Oh Fido, wait up! Fido!" She ran off towards him.

Mrs. Nimblewit turned to her husband. "Irish blood," she said venomously. "It's a blessing I came home in time last autumn to break up that case between my daughter and that shanty Irishman. I don't see how you could so demean yourself, Poochie. Do you want your grandchildren to look like Irish terriers?"

"I—You—I——," mumbled the dean.

"Irish terriers. *Bah!*"

"Hey, Wish, wait up!" Rufus called out. Wish hesitated, and Rufus caught up with him and said formally: "Doctor O'Hoe, there's something I ought to tell you before you leave."

"Yeah?" Wish raised his eyebrows superciliously. In his pocket was the old man's graduation gift, the unbreakable life contract as Medical Director of the Mary Margaret MacSweeny O'Hoe Memorial Hospital and Medical Centre, and he considered he was lowering himself to speak to anyone under a full professor.

"On this Medical Faculty," said Rufus, "instructors have no vote."

"What the hell do I care?" said Wish contemptuously. Then he did a double take. "Why, you dirty double-crosser!" he screeched.

"So long, *sucker.*"

With his mortar-board perched on the top of his head, Fido looked more gigantesque than ever. Susan said: "Congratulations, doctor."

"Aw," he rumbled in embarrassment.

"What are you going to do now?"

"Go down to the Union Restaurant for a steak," he said promptly. "Come on along, Suze."

"I can't; I've got a date with Rufus. But I meant, what are you going to do professionally, Fido? You're through bodyguarding Wish, aren't you?"

"Yeah. I told Mr. O'Hoe I resigned."

"My father told me Doctor Lanthorn wants you in surgery; Doctor Nudge in orthopædics; Doctor Chouse in internal medicine; Doctor Wanion in D & S; Doctor Slipstream in psychiatry——"

"Yeah; that's what I'm gonna do," he interrupted.

240

"What?"

"I'm goin' in psychiatry with Doc Slipstream."

"But, Fido: you told me psychiatrists were dopes!"

"Sure they are. I told Doc Slipstream that when he ast me, and he said I was the biggest dope he ever seen. Hey, Suze," Fido asked anxiously, "you think I'm a dope?"

"You're the sweetest dope in the world, Fido."

He looked relieved. "That's all right, then. Like I told Doc Slipstream, if I'm a dope, I gotta go in psychiatry. That's logic."

Mrs. Nimblewit had concluded her informal remarks to the dean, and had turned her back. Wish O'Hoe caught her eye, and beckoned her to him. "Hey, Mrs. Nimblewit," he said in a confidential voice, "Sam McGinnis, the old man's chauffeur, gave me a red-hot one. The mob has it all doped for Nemissus to take the fifth tomorrow at Jamaica. It's gonna be the coup of the century."

"Nemissus in the fifth at Jamaica," she repeated, her eyes glittering.

"Yeah. We got to be careful not to drive the odds down. Don't place more than five C's with any one bookie."

"I know; I know."

"Give it everything you got."

Mrs. Nimblewit nodded. To an old operator, a wink was as good as a shot of ephedrine to a horse. "I don't know how to thank you, Doctor O'Hoe."

"By keeping it to yourself," said Wish, walking away. "Remember the odds." He grinned to himself as he rejoined the family. Sam McGinnis had mentioned Nemissus, all right, but only to spit contemptuously. Nemissus was a dog, and the dean's wife was about to lose her chemise.

The dean was standing all by himself, so Rufus approached him. Nimblewit started, and said: "Yes,

Pussy?" When he realised it was Rufus, he groaned aloud.

"Don't you feel well, sir?" Rufus asked solicitously. "Is there anything I can do for you?"

"There's nothing anyone can do for me," said the dean, his eyes on his wife chatting with Wish O'Hoe. Rufus thoughtfully followed his gaze.

"Will you want me to stay around the laboratory this summer, sir?" he asked

"Yes," said the dean.

"I'm sorry to hear that, sir."

"Why?"

"I wanted to go on my honeymoon."

"You mean, you intend to get married?" Nimblewit sounded as though Rufus had proposed to enter the cage of a man-eating tiger.

"If you will give your consent, sir."

"My consent?" the dean muttered in perplexity. Then he got it. "For *Susan?*"

"Yes, sir."

"No; certainly not."

"I was thinking," Rufus went on reflectively, as though he hadn't heard Nimblewit's refusal, "you might know some medical school out in California that needed an assistant professor of anatomy." He now felt about the medical school of Zebulon University as he did towards that floozie who had initiated him into the third chapter of Philander Foilove's book: he was grateful to her, but he would be just as happy if he never saw her again. He continued: "And to keep Susan from feeling lonesome so far away from home, I was thinking we might invite Mrs. Nimblewit to live with us—if you can spare her."

The dean's eyes glazed. "California," he muttered. "Three thousand miles . . . Pussy . . . Peace . . ."

Rufus lighted a cigarette.

"Yoo-hoo, Poochie!" Mrs. Nimblewit shouted. Wish had just left her, and she was eager to get back to her private wire, and begin operations. "I have to leave now. I'll see you later." Rushed as she was, she took time to blow him a gluey kiss.

Nimblewit shuddered. "Ah, my boy," he said, "it is always a shock for a father to realise that his little girl has grown up and is about to fly the nest. But it must be; it must be; one must philosophically accept the parents' fate. Take her, Rufus take her out to California."

"Thank you, sir. And consider, sir: you are not losing a daughter; you are gaining a son."

The dean uttered a short sharp cry.

"And I, a mother," Rufus concluded. His candid gaze gave no hint that he was lying; he would as soon have allowed a tarantula to live with him as his future mother-in-law. "If you don't mind, sir, will you tell Susan now that our marriage has your approval?"

"It has my blessing," said the dean devoutly.

Rufus called Susan away from Fido, and said to her: "Your father has something to say to you."

Susan looked solemn at this formal style and their preternaturally grave faces. "Daughter," said the dean, "Rufus has just told me he wants to marry you."

She lowered her eyelashes. "If we have your consent, Daddy."

"You have my blessing," said Nimblewit.

The swineherd had passed his third and final test; Susan regarded the red-haired magician with awe.

The dean continued: "Rufus is a fine young man. He will go far in his profession."

"To California," Rufus said to Susan.

"Far," said Dean Nimblewit, "very, very far . . ."

THE END

243